Author photo: Pauline Lord, London, England

Sandi Hall is a novelist (*The Godmothers*, *Wingwomen of Hera*) and playwright (*Just Passing Through*, *Change of Heart*, *Death Duties*), and has also published short stories. Her life is not solely centred on writing, however. Since the mid-1970s, she has actively promoted the rights of women. Included in that activity has been the formation of and candidacy in the New Zealand Women's Political Party; and organising seminars with titles like How To Be A Feminist Without Going Mad.

For income, she has worked in radio, marketing, and television research. As she likes to travel, she has also been a nanny in Hawaii, taught English in Mexico, and written advertising in Zambia.

She lives in Wellington, New Zealand, with two friends and a cat named Milo.

To my children and grandchildren:
Ryan, Francesca, Elisabeth, Tyler, Natalie and Scott,
and for Dorothy Vogl, Red River Flowing Grasses
and Jane Anger.

RUMOURS OF DREAMS

Sandi Hall

Spinifex Press Pty Ltd
504 Queensberry Street
North Melbourne Vic. 3051
Australia
women@spinifexpress.com.au
http://www.spinifexpress.com.au/~women

Edited by Barbara Burton
Typeset by Alena Jencik of Grand Graphix Pty Ltd
Printed by Australian Print Group.

National Library of Australia
Cataloguing-in-Publication data:

Hall, Sandi.
Rumours of dreams.

ISBN 1 875559 75 2.

I. Title.

A823.3

Women best understand each other's language.
– St Teresa of Avila, Interior Castle

As a woman I have no country ... as a woman, my country is the whole world.
– Virginia Woolf

Even Christ needed someone to believe in him.
– Winnifred Holtby, South Riding

RUMOURS OF DREAMS:

NOW AND THEN

RUMOURS OF DREAMS:

NOW

I awake knowing I have had the strangest dream, but all that remains of it is a sense of sunlight whiter and dryer than here, and hills that were brown with dying grass.

There was a woman too, someone familiar but also someone I cannot identify with my wakeful mind. Freudians and Jungians alike would say it is a nascent memory of my mother, or of being in the womb, and New Agers would say it is my spirit guide or higher self. If only I could believe in such easy and comforting philosophies, but my life refutes their tenets, and I have been plagued with questions to myself for as long as the skein of my memory measures on its spindle.

Rose jumps onto my feet and makes her way up my leg onto my bottom, then walks my spine like some miniature, four-handed masseuse, exotic with knowledge and knowing just where to press. At my shoulder, she peers under my hair to see if my eyes are open, as she intends they should be. Her old-bronze eyes are stippled with flecks of black, black as her small wet nose, and from such closeness, I see right inside the glistening oysterish landscape of her ears.

She purrs her approval of my opened eyes and walks back down my body to knead my calf, an encouragement to me to leave the bed and move to the kitchen. There, she will accolade by means of hip sinuosity and tail curvaceousness my abilities as a food provider, almost the highest rung on her laddery list of attributes desirable in large warm beasts like me.

I am not sure which rung has primacy; warmth or love ...

I do know that when I danced with her at the beginning of her pregnancy, her love for me flowed into mine

3

for her, and made an audible click in my psyche. When all of her kittens proved to be female, an unusual enough happening in itself, instinct told me that their chromosomes firmed and remained Xs at that moment; but rationality, so hard to avoid with its lean muscular appeal, said it couldn't possibly be so.

Even if I should wish to, I would not know who to consult about such phenomena; to qualify in the field, such a person would first of all have to think dancing with cats a perfectly natural thing to do. And second, to believe that Rose really loves me, no anthropomorphising here. The kind of blood-and-mind love that comes only from an entwined ancestry in which our screaming limbs burned together in the wicker cages of fury. Rose remembers, as I do, how centuries before, when the molten flow of persecution snaked through Spain and France, we escaped northwards to the lands of ice, where we ate milk shards from yellow bowls and learned to draw the chariot of the moon.

My name is now Stella Mante and Rose and I now live on this northern island of Aotearoa, an island of hills with trees at their feet, surrounded by an apple-green sea. According to the new government of this country, as a foreigner, an alien who has not lived within its control, and who has no recognised numbers, I should not be living in this four-tiered house, each level a single room (with a curl of stairs) and open to the sea. According to the new government, I should be living in a holding house in Manukau City, where old buildings are meek under the stern shadows of new ones, and dignity is not the order of the day. But fortunately, we have a friend, Sabe, who chooses to live in Auckland, its mother city, and who with ease has taken on two more duties, as paperworker and sentinel. Through her kind efficiency, Rose and I are safe.

I get up and stand naked in the warm sunlight pouring through the long window by my bed. I stretch hard, coming into my body. On the horizon are thrusts of black kite-shaped sails, just a handspan from the blocky trudging boats of the fishing fleet. Rose sits half turned away, and begins to busy herself about her person. Her right leg could give lessons to flagpoles. But her left ear swivels and flutters and I know she is only marking time until a change in my energy tells her that I am going to the kitchen, in the right direction at last.

I have only recently come to this island with its story-book hills between which the kaleidoscopic eyes of the sea peep — eyes which are sometimes slits of wrinkled silver, sometimes rounds of cobalt, sometimes scrutinies of jade. I came here in an ancient coach whose lines still proclaimed its royal lineage, even though the dust of decades had dulled its scarlet paint and wheels of black. I came with my boxes and my bags of carpet, my small but perfect library, my stones of glory, my vases and pails and my three essential spectrum finders, each for use at specific lights and times.

I have come because I am looking for a woman I knew long ago. Her first name is Mary, that most common of female names in the world according to Christianity, which itself has spread its viraginous tentacles into half the minds of humanity. I have no idea what other names she uses, or how she earns her keep, or why this is the island she now walks. But I do know that she is here, the signs are unmistakable: unusual weather patterns are often the beginning, followed by a heightened prominence in the world's media of a place not often considered newsworthy. Then, over a period of months, sometimes turning to a year or so, the country's people will become less tolerant of restrictions, often restive under taxation rules. It is in these times that new voices are heard through the land, that women cry out against traditions which hold them inexorably in an iron-maiden clasp, and that young men dream of dragons, of favours, and the sweet bliss of unacknowledged admiration.

I must find her, for she holds the secret truth that could free millions, that would change the world. Long ago, we both lived in a land of fish and goats and the small-flowered almond tree. There, our lives merged inextricably before the pungent blood of woman-being streaked my thighs. My attention to life had been focused early and I was alert like the slipping vixen with a lair full of cubs.

Onto one small plate I place some Thai rice that has been steeped in chickenstock, rice which is black before it gets into hot water, then swells to become the purple of Pekinese tongues. In the rice I hide squares of ham, then lay this meal at Rose's feet. On another plate, I put slices of mango and the last of the cylindrical, sweet green grapes left by the man in the pirate shirt who, with his seashell wife, was my outrider and escort from Manukau City to this headland. I add wholegrain toast skimmed with honey, pour a glass of the thick tangerine juice that has become my especial delight, then take my breakfast out to the bower, which is old and trellised and heavy with the fragrant lilac weight of wisteria.

The bower also smells of wood-rot, and the faint wet scent of the emerald moss on its floor, these aromas melded, with the wisteria's fragrance, into an exhilarating perfume by the bouquet of the sea. The view from the bower, of foreground hills and an alluring expanse of ocean (this morning striving for an Illyrian shade of mauve) is only bettered by that from the top floor of the house.

My search for the woman named Mary has been a long one, more than several centuries. I do not know if I am immortal, or whether it will be the finding of Mary which starts Age shaving my tree of life again. Certainly its blade was halted in that radiant moment when, with

Santer in ecstasy beside me, I felt myself move into alignment with the magnetic tides of Earth; its currents have born me effortlessly ever since.

Along those times, I have run with many, including Grace, who rescued me from the winter rains of England, giving me sanctuary in that green place of forests and intaglio'd stone. Grace was tall and moved gently, but these things I noticed only later, and with my forefront sensibilities. At that first moment, fevered though I was, what I saw was an invisible radiance, dark and vital as claret wine is when held against the light. And in the air, an echo of sound as if moments before, a sword had been drawn along castle stone. Her brown eyes regarded me gravely and behind her was deepest night, not a timbered wall where, in panels of oil, dolphins leapt beyond the rocks on which the Syrens sang. So again I knew I was where I should be, and that she was my next step.

Rose arrives at my feet and stares up at my plate, nose investigating the air on which the aromas of my breakfast cling.

'Perhaps it was Grace in my dream?' I ask her, but she returns a contemptuous glance. After a moment, I nod in agreement. 'You're right, she's not so intangible. So who then?'

Rose crouches by my ankles and we both gaze out to sea. The whiff of the dream-woman strengthens and with it a clearer feel of her sunlight self and the shape of those hills on whose backs the grass was dying. Then I know: Damascus and the white head of Hermon lie to the north, the great cleft of Jericho nearby; and in the east is the boat in the sky, left by the force of the water, so like the force of woman, swirling and offering no resistance until it is dammed or damned.

The woman in my dream was Szuzanna, who had captured my half-dead childself in her arms, nourished

7

and claimed me, and given me the wisdom and strength necessary to stay alive.

Who my parents were not even my dreams can tell me. Szuzanna said I was about three when she heard the bray of the goats in the far pen and saw me trying to suck a nanny's small dark teat. Even now the tang of their black shit is comforting to me, and I find elegance and beauty in their slim ankles and silken triangular chins.

'Szuzanna,' I say aloud.

Rose gives an acknowledging mew as she suddenly springs forward to leap at but miss one of the narrow-winged moths which come to feed from the clustered pistils of the yellow hibiscus. She sits down suddenly, rethinks her timing, then thoughtfully licks her paw. Exhilaration rises briefly, wrenching my gut and leaving me light-headed. Szuzanna! Time stretched in the present becomes a little of the future, but most of all the past.

Mary can't be far.

I feel again the circle of Santer's arms, his head lying on my belly, the smell of him strong with nuts and sweat and meat. He is as thin as dry cornstalks, his elbows sharp against my flesh. In the cage of his ribs under my hands I can feel the beating of his confused heart, expanded as it is with fear and longing. He is a man moulded by lies and bigotry, who has drawn love from stones and wears his beliefs around him like a fading, tattered cloak.

Clouds have thickened across the morning blue. The milky stretch of the sea has taken on the umbra of a bruise. I look for Rose, but she is nowhere to be seen. A summer shower breaks. Rain drips copiously through the wisteria and suddenly my feet are cold. Thinking of Mary, of the question I know she can answer, and of what is possible in a truth-leaked world, I pick up my plate and go through the wet, fat-dropped morning to my watchtower house.

RUMOURS OF DREAMS:

THEN

JERUSALEM

When I first saw him, the fact of him there in my special place filled me with fury. It was my place, and there he was, squatting in it, one hand pulling back the reeds a little, the other balancing his weight. I knew, in a rush of anger, that he was watching the watergoose and its tiny, stripy babies, just as I had planned to watch them myself.

I ran down, making a lot of noise. He looked up, his face screwed up with disapproval. I knew he was going to tell me to be quiet: I would have myself. When he saw I was a girl, not the boy he'd been expecting, he let go of the reeds and stood up. 'This is my place,' I told him hotly. 'Go away.' I glared at him.

'No one owns the river land,' he replied calmly. He was a smallish boy, and his clothes were clean, but he had bare, dusty feet.

'I know that, but this is my place,' I insisted belligerently. 'I'll show you.' I knelt by the second last mound of tussock, slid my arm through its edges and drew out my box. 'See? I keep special things here. This is my place.'

He accepted this evidence immediately, looking at the box. Then, 'I would like to watch the watergoose,' he said after a moment. 'If I go out of here, then come back and ask your permission, may I?'

This offer acknowledged my sovereignty and gave me power, which made me feel generous. 'Yes, that would be all right,' I told him graciously.

The watergoose and its babies are entrancing, their

grey bodies striped with a darker grey that has an edge of pink. The goslings shake their tiny heads, little black eyes alert. Their orange beaks snap at the dancing flies that jig just above the water. The watergoose paddles slowly, plucking an insect from the water without interrupting her guardianship of the goslings. She murmurs to them if they go too far from her, and they quickly return.

We say nothing for a long time. The watergoose makes a low, trilling call and the goslings slip under her open wings. The river sends up a smell that is cool and fresh but edged with the dankness of rotting. The watergoose slides into the reeds; under its half-spread wings, the downy goslings cluster and cheep. With her brood settled about her, the watergoose draws down her neck into a shape of repose. The reeds seem purposely to arch over them, the brown water to support them. They look utterly content.

'How do they know what to do?' the boy says in a quiet voice. His hair is curly, short, and very dark brown.

'Animals always know,' I retort, 'and if they don't, they die.' He muses on this as we stared at the river. The light of morning hesitates, then strengthens into the light of noon, hot and glassy. It strikes the water, is painful to my eyes. Against its melty glare, the watergoose is a dark solidity in the gloaming of the reeds. The boy sighs. He sits back on the bank, hunching his arms around sallow, dust-creased knees. The river breeze has died, the scents on the air now mainly of dust and hard old grass.

'What is your father like?' asks the boy, laying his chin between the rounds of his knees. His chin is broad, curving away on either side of a central, shallow cleft.

'I don't have one,' I tell him shortly. 'Or a mother,' I added, anticipating his next remark.

'You don't have any parents at all? Where do you live?'

'I live with Szuzanna, at the Garden Road Inn. It's her inn, her and her brothers, and I live with them.'

He turns his head to look sideways at me. His eyes are warm brown, like ripened dates. 'My father died last year,' he says.

'What about your mother?'

'She's all right.'

He stands up. His left hand is almost in front of my eyes and I see his bitten nails, skin frayed down past the fingertip, dust making the outlines clear. 'Come back if you'd like to,' I say quickly.

He studies my face, then smiles and nods. In a few paces, he is gone from my sight and I am pleased. I liked being alone, not having to concentrate on another person, and so able to allow my senses to open their spread. I lifted the lid from the box, took out my weave of ribbons and my strongest ring bone. Now I am at the centre of the world.

Later, as I help Szuzanna prepare the evening meal, I tell her about the boy, and that his father is dead. She asks what the boy's name was, but I do not know. The arrival of people at the inn puts an end to her speculations on his identity. I finish putting out bowls of olives and bread, of dates, squat orange persimmons, grapes, and juicy, purple-skinned figs. For some reason, the figs remind me of the boy, and in my private mind, I see the shape of his chin against the rounds of his knees. It is then I decide to call him after that clefted shape: santer, our word for chin.

Actually, he tells me his name is Joshua, but no one except his foster-father and teachers uses it. His mother calls him Shuki. When I tell him what I have called him in my mind, he laughs and so it becomes approved as my name for him, the beginning of the bond between us. Before the river dries, which it does every year, he comes to the riverbank several more times.

13

I tell him of Szuzanna and of the inn she runs with the help of Malachi and David, her brother twins. And me. I help make the food, feed the hens and milk the goats. I also kill the scorpions when they get too big, grind almonds for halvah, and help decant the wine. I bring food to the inn's guests; Szuzanna has taught me to calculate, so that I can take their money, and also go to the market streets with Malachi.

Szuzanna says it only took a few days for me to adopt her as my mother; but in my private mind I remember it was the warm milk I first stayed for, and for it I bore the leash of clothing and the cuddling restraint of her arms. Love was not a word or feeling that I knew.

Santer and his mother had come to live in Jerusalem recently, he told me, following the death of his father. They now live in the household of Joseph, a wealthy man who is in the Council. Joseph treats him as a son, Santer says, sending him to study and giving him duties related to his work. Santer likes living there, but he is anxious about his mother, who, he tells me, seems worried and upset.

The following year, shortly after the rains of winter, I met Santer's mother. He didn't often speak of her, and when I asked questions about her — for I was very interested in mothers — he would answer lightly, evasively, an inexplicable look in his eyes. Under my persistence, he finally told me his mother was different, which I took to mean crazy, like Michah the washerwoman's child, whose head seems loose on his neck, spittle sliding from his slack mouth. I was astonished to see a flush darken Santer's cheekbones, he who was usually so calm.

'She is not crazy,' he blurted out, 'she's just — well, different, she says different things, that's all.'

'What kind of different things?' I asked, truly interested.

14

But he slapped his hands to his side, helplessly. 'Just different,' he said again, furiously. I knew he wanted me to change the subject, so I did, because we were friends. Although Szuzanna treats me as a daughter, in my private mind I do think of other possible mothers. I have wondered whether it was possible for Santer's mother to be my mother, even though I know it couldn't be so. But while I had the thought, I felt warm and excited, and had a glimpse of a different me.

On the day I met Santer's mother, Malachi and I were in Lower Market street, which I loved. It was all shout and bustle, tables piled with melons and eggs, cheese and dates, protected from the sun by the looping curves of tents. Donkeys and flies, the screams of camels. White light, pink and orange fruit, bracelets of silver and armlets of bronze. Great swathes of cloth and piles of baskets, oiled new saddles gleaming in the shade. Malachi and I were making our way to the chickens, Szuzanna not trusting him to exercise good judgement in the purchase of new hens. 'Make sure he buys the young ones, Mary, have a look at the combs yourself. And I've told him you are to choose the sheeting; he wouldn't know a decent piece if it was wrapped around his head!'

As we went past the Slave Stone, I saw Santer near its platform, talking to Parchios, the trader in slaves from Macedonia. He was a frequent guest at the inn. I waved eagerly to Santer, but he didn't see me. The hens and the roosters were in a small, hot tent at the end of the street, on the very periphery of the market. They were clustered around a leaking trough, some drinking, others broody in the dust, beaks open in the heat. As I haggled with the chicken dealer, I was thinking how to leave Malachi and visit a little with Santer. Before our purchasing was completed, I had thought of a way.

We walked back up the street, and I saw Santer was still with Parchios. I pulled at Malachi's sleeve. 'Szuzanna

15

wants some women's potions, Malachi. I should go there now.'

He gave me a long-frowned look, a doubtful humming rising in his chest. The shop that sold the potions was only for women, which embarrassed him.

'What about this, Malachi, you go to the wine stall, and when I've finished, I'll come there and wait outside for you.'

He nodded, pleased with this solution, and looked for a wine stall, the hens quiet in a bag in his left hand, a bolt of sheeting on his shoulder. I ran back down the bustling street, dodging two chanting Pharisees, one of whom threw me a look of sharp reproof. Santer was still with Parchios, who had five slaves standing behind him. None looked very happy. Two were females about my own age. I could feel their eyes on me as I approached. Another trader was shouting from the Slave Stone, two black-skinned men behind him. I stood where Santer could see me and he acknowledged me with a little lift of his hand as he continued his conversation.

' — but preferably quite young, are his instructions. He says the older ones have little work left in them, and he has to carry the expense of winding sheets and stones to weigh down the top of the graves.'

Parchios was sunburnt and nimble, his fingers seeming to dip into Santer's palm, the coins there rise of their own volition to fall into the money pouch at his waist.

'The sands of the Negev be nothing as compared to the blessings on the head of Joseph,' he shouted merrily. 'I will return in the seventh month, before the winter rains, with the finest young slave, you can render him my promise on that!' He untied the neck-reins of two of the male slaves, whose shackled hands showed the horny blunting of hard work. 'These two will serve Joseph for many years, either in his fine garden or in the bath building, and lucky they are to be going to such a fine master,' he roared both to them and to Santer.

As we passed the remaining slaves, one of the females gave me a hard look; the other was crying. I wondered for a moment whether I had been born to a slave, someone who had lost me during work at the olive groves, or on a journey, perhaps. This was a new thought to me: usually my imaginary mothers are laughing, wealthy, beautiful, and always young.

'What are you doing here?' Santer asks as I come to him. His smile is wide, his eyes warm. He is wearing a pale green toga with figured edges which has a large bronze shoulder clasp. His sandals are supple and polished, his feet clean within them. He looks much older than when we last met, though he is not tall. I know he is nearing his thirteenth birthday. If Szuzanna is right and I was three when she found me, then I am eleven, but small for my age. Santer gestures to the slaves, indicating the direction we are to go, and we walk off, their neck-reins slack in his hands.

'Marketing with Malachi, Szuzanna couldn't come. Santer, may I go with you, see where you live? Is it far? May I, may I?'

He grins and rapidly touches his fingers and thumb together to indicate I am gabbling, but agrees, and soon we walk under the King's Gate. Joseph's home backs onto the lower south east wall of the Upper City. Santer hands the neck-reins of the slaves over to a dour man he calls Acton, and invites me into the house to have a drink of water. I rinse my feet in the shallow dish by the door before I enter.

The house is shadowed and cool. Santer takes me down a long hallway in which, on shelves and pedestals, in alcoves and mounted on the walls, scores of intriguing objects are displayed. There are platters of gold, others of china wrought with wonderful curves and intersecting lines. There are tall, jewelled cups, of copper and gold,

17

embossed with enigmatic marks. Shallow bowls of deep rust-orange have black figures around their sides. There are rings and armlets and neck collars, jewelled and plain, and scribings on paper beside them. One part of the display is devoted to clothes of leather, and instruments of war: there are old breastplates, crescent swords, wristlets, a dagger with a handle of plaited bronze, its blade twisting like a snake. There is a pair of thick, cracked shoes, their buckle-bands old and snapped. These have an acrid redolence, more than of old leather: it was the sweat of the man who had worn them, the smell of battle and fear.

As we walk, Santer murmurs the names of the lands where many of these objects originated: Thrace, Gaul and Mesopotamia, Mytilene, and the spice lands of Indie far to the east. His words are incantations around me, the long hallway my first philosopher's stone. I felt something new within me come alive.

Santer ushers me into a small room near the kitchen, where a slave brings us cups of water and a plate of nut-cakes, flat and crunchy and sweet. In the wonder of all the things I've seen, I have forgotten Santer's mother and when quick, light footsteps announced someone's arrival, I did not think of her. I had just finished a nutcake and was rinsing my fingers. I looked to the doorway as a woman entered. She is slender, and at first I think she is quite young, not much older than me. She is short and very thin, with a narrow brown face and large, dark, anxious eyes. She is also very beautiful, her cheekbones and her mouth, and a slight, dusky cleft in her chin.

'Shuki? Shuki! I wondered where you were.'

Her voice is low, breathy and hesitant. Her body seems to radiate tension. She wears the long full robes of a Jewish woman, and the double ribboned-coverings around her head. Santer gets up, but makes no move toward her.

'Joseph asked me to speak with Parchios, mother,' he says quietly. 'I have just returned. This is my friend Mary, who I've told you about. She lives at the inn on the Garden Road.'

His hand made a small movement to me. I stood up hastily, trying not to wipe my hands on the fabric against my thigh. I stepped forward and made my motions of respect. Closer, I see she is older than she at first seemed, perhaps twenty-five or six. The skin is stretched tightly across her narrow cheekbones, her lips are wide and well-curved, her teeth very white against their dark plum colour. She stares at me intensely, doubt mingling with something I cannot describe in her look.

'Mary as I am Mary, but not as I,' she says suddenly, and then, nodding emphatically, 'There will be room in the boat for you.'

She turned from me to step closer to Santer, touching his breast with the tips of her fingers. I felt erased somehow, as if I had winked out of existence as she turned from me. 'Do not leave me, Shuki,' she whispered, 'I pray you, do not leave me.'

'Have you eaten today, mother?' Santer asked, taking the hand that touched him and looking at her solicitously. He is almost taller than she is, and in their profiles, they are clearly mother and son. He turns her back to the door. 'I have completed the business Joseph asked me to do, and so will be here now, at my studies.' His voice is calm, soothing. 'Eat now, and rest. I will see you later, in the garden, when I have finished. We will talk together then.'

She went out of the door with him, the white fabric of her shawls slipping a little from her head, revealing thick waving black hair, dark and without a shine. I hear their voices again, but cannot distinguish the words; then the rapid patter of her feet, going away. Santer returned, wearing the look I had noticed come on him before as we talked about his mother.

'What did she mean, there will be room in the boat for me?' I blurt out as soon as he enters. 'What boat?'

He shook his head. 'I don't know,' he says brusquely. 'I told you what she's like. I don't know what she means.'

I realise it is time for me to leave. We say little to one another as he walks me back to the market street. It is only when I am sitting in the cart among the netted bags of almonds, the new hens cackling their distress at my back, that I think of Santer's mother as his mother. She is much younger than Szuzanna, that I could clearly see. How old was she when she gave birth to Santer, I wonder, and what would it be like if it happened to me?

Szuzanna is terse when Malachi at last guides the cart around to the back of the inn and begins to unload it. It is after sundown, though the west still glows with long streaks of purple and flame. From the kitchen comes the glorious smell of fresh semneh, and saliva suddenly spurts inside the pockets of my cheeks. I carry the new sheeting into the kitchen, which is too hot after the fresh, early evening air. On the table, several roasted chickens are piled on great wooden platters, and there is a shallow basket full of new lemons.

'You must learn how to hurry Malachi along,' Szuzanna scolded behind me. 'I've been expecting you for a good two hours. Why have you been so long?'

Automatically, I screwed up my nose and said, 'Wine tent.'

Szuzanna clacked her tongue and said with exasperation, 'I should have told him I thought trader Nathaniel would be back today.'

'And is he?' I ask quickly.

I like trader Nathaniel, who brings his slaves here to rest them before taking them down into Jerusalém, and often has thick gold rings to show me, with unusual symbols on them, or cloak-pins and bracelets fashioned in curious ways. Nathaniel does not mind me asking him questions; in fact, he seems to like to tell of the places he has travelled, what the buildings are like, the food, the trees and birds. Nathaniel always inspects the goat pens where his slaves rest, making sure the straw is fresh and that there is plenty of water and cleansing cloths for them to use. The food platters he orders for them are always plentiful.

'Yes. Wash your hands and face, quickly now. Let me see — .' She took me by the shoulder and turned me, looking at my back and my front. 'No, you'll have to put on clean clothing, this is too dusty. But hurry. There are seven other guests apart from him.'

In the room I share with Szuzanna, I knelt on the floor by my pallet and pulled my clothes over my head. The water in the bowl was beautifully cool to my face. I squatted by the bowl and rinsed my body before attending to my feet. When I'd dressed and shaken my curling hair vigorously, I took the bowl to the window and tipped the water out onto the lemon tree below. Over it, I could see the goat pens, where Malachi and David were standing, watching as Nathaniel brought his slaves in. One was a man carrying a small bundle which looked like a baby. I looked for its mother, but the slaves in this group were all men.

Trader Nathaniel was sitting outside with the other guests when I took his meal to him. Lamps of olive oil smoked and danced, blooming everything with a ruddy, flickering light. 'Is there a baby with your slaves, Trader? Has it got a mother?' Nathaniel, who was looking at me with a pleased smile, plucked at his eyebrows at this question. 'The babe, ay, the babe. I fear for its life, but its father will not let it go.'

'Where is its mother? It looks very small.'

'She was killed when they tried to get away, child. I tried to get the father to leave the baby with one of the

21

old women of his village, but he would not be parted from it.' Nathaniel shook his head and rubbed his nose. 'I fear for the little one. Most buyers will not look favourably on purchasing an unproductive mouth.'

I stood at his side in total, shocked disbelief. I had not thought of slaves as people who didn't want to be slaves. I had always thought they were born to be slaves, somewhere in other places, and that people like Nathaniel had to go and harvest them, just as I pick the ripe olives and beans. It had not occurred to me that there would be fighting, or people being killed. Or even that they had babies. I saw again the face of the female slave by the Slave Stone, tears making visible tracks in the dust on her reddish brown face. My body suddenly felt cold. She was about my age.

Nathaniel broke open the bread I had brought, and smeared it liberally with semneh. He crammed the whole into his mouth with an appreciative sound. At that moment, he looked like a monster to me, with tiny beads of oil trapped in the hairs of his moustache and beard. His teeth were as dangerous as any viper's fang. I ran to the kitchen, where Szuzanna had just set the pyramidal copper water jugs to boil. 'One of the slaves has a baby, Szuzu,' I cried to her, and my urgent panic gave me her full attention immediately.

'A baby?' She was taken aback.

'Yes, I saw it, it's very small, I don't think it even walks yet. Szuzanna, are slaves people like you and me? Don't they want to be slaves?'

Sadness shadowed her face. She made little protesting sounds in her throat as she drew me to her, stroking back the hair clinging to my forehead. She clucked her tongue a little. An awful fear rose in me and misery flooded my eyes.

'They are people, yes, it is true. They are people. And they do not like to be slaves, but what can they do?'

'They can run away,' I cried fiercely, 'they can hide, not let the big things get them.' I did not hear my words, my mind filled with a loom of rocks and a searching snarl beyond them.

'I think they try as hard as they can,' said Szuzanna quietly, and suddenly I heard Nathaniel saying 'killed trying to get away.' The horror of it burst over me. I began to sob loudly. Szuzanna held me close. Vomit rose in my throat and began to choke me. Szuzanna stroked my back and tried to calm me, but it was many minutes before she was successful. Then, 'Let's go and see the baby, shall we? Let's take some fresh milk and bread with us, yes?'

'Yes,' I agreed, and cast my eye around the kitchen wildly, 'and some semneh too, and halvah and dates and, and — eggs,' I cried. I wanted to take baskets and baskets of food to the baby out there.

'Shall we just take the milk and bread first, and see how the baby is? We can come back for anything else.'

Her voice was gentle as she wrapped a fresh loaf in a cloth and gave it to me, and nestled a gourd of milk in her arm. She took up a lamp in one hand, holding my hand with the other. As we went across to the goat pens, I had a brilliant idea. I tugged hard at her hand, and whispered to her. She bent down to give me her ear.

'Let's take them out of there, let them run away!'

Szuzanna knelt to look directly at me. Her eyes were glossy and sad, her generous mouth too. 'They cannot speak our language, sweetheart. They do not know where they are, and they have no money. They would be lost quickly, and as quickly caught again, perhaps even punished.'

She stroked my hair.

'Nathaniel is a good trader, he takes care of his slaves,' she said placatingly. 'They will go to places where they will be well treated, I am sure.'

I did not believe it would be better for the slaves to stay in the goat pen, but I could not find the words to say this to her. Rage and frustration fought within me. I cried again, gulping for breath, my fists clutched and beating helplessly against Szuzanna's protecting, understanding arm. It was harder for her to quiet me this time, but she reminded me of the baby and told me my tears might frighten it. I shuddered into silence.

Clutching the bread, I went with her to the twisted staves of the goat pen. Szuzanna put down the gourd, held the lamp high and gave an interrogatory cry. She found a safe place to wedge the lamp, then picked me up, holding me in its glow. 'Tell them you want to see the baby,' she said.

I folded my arms around the bread and rocked it like a baby, then beckoned to the shadowy mass of slaves.

'Please,' I entreated, 'please.' Once again I began to cry. There was silence, then movement. I heard rapid whispering.

'Please, please,' I called to the shadows again, tears streaming down my face. A man edged into the indistinct circle of light the lamp cast. He came slowly, shuffling toward us unwillingly, plainly urged on by the men behind him. He held the baby up on his shoulder, its bare legs and feet dangling under his arm. He came closer and closer until he at last stood in front of me, with only the palings between us. The down of the baby's hair was the same colour as his, yellow brown, a little lighter than straw. I offered him the bread. He took it with his free hand and threw it behind him, where it fell among the other men. I didn't know what to do next, so I just held my arms out to the baby. The man gave a loud sob, then put the baby in my arms. Szuzanna gave a little grunt of satisfaction and lowered me to the ground. Seconds later, I realised the baby was dead.

The weight of the baby stayed around my heart long

after we found a place to bury it. Szuzanna urged Nathaniel to put off the final trek into Jerusalem so that the child could be buried, and its father present. Nathaniel could not evade my eyes, hurrying with his consent.

Nothing that Szuzanna could say eased my distress. I knew Nathaniel had killed the baby, together with the man who would buy the baby's father. In my private mind, I saw Nathaniel and another man tossing the baby between them, its head lolling on its inadequate neck. Malachi dug a grave in the olive grove; he stayed while the tiny body was put into the ground. I saw David watching in the distance, briefly halting his work. Long after Nathaniel had taken the slaves away, I could see the face of the baby's father, folded in on itself and closed with grief.

For a few weeks, I spoke of slaves constantly, asking questions until the disgusting truths of it were clear. As time went by, I spoke less and less of them, laughed and even sang. But in my private mind I was neither consoled or resigned to an acceptance of their condition and, in the purity of my rage, vowed that when I was an adult I would somehow put an end to slavery, even if I had to do it on my own.

The spring sorocco was scouring plain and hill with its hot, sand-filled fists before I saw Santer again. He arrived at the inn quite early one morning, accompanied by an older man and two slaves leading some donkeys. I had just finished milking the goats and was carrying milk from the pens to the settling pans in the cheese shed. 'It's Joshua!' I cried to Szuzanna, who had the ovens already smoking, and the bread ready to set.

'Who?' she asked, craning her neck to peer through the window.

'Joshua! Santer! My friend from the river.'

'Ah, that Joshua,' she said as I ran to the front of the inn to welcome him. The two slaves were by the donkeys, and Santer and the older man had almost reached the door.

I greeted them cordially but formally, for this was business, and escorted them to the table under the grapevines, then brought the morning food of bread, olives, goat cheese and fruit. I was very pleased to see Santer; the awareness of our friendship gave me the courage to do what I did next. I filled a second platter with identical morning food and took it over to the two slaves squatting by the donkeys. I heard the older man with Santer shout at me and looked back. He had risen, but Santer had him by the arm. The slaves had thrust the platter behind them, watching the older man with wary eyes.

'The food is yours,' I said loudly, nodding and smiling vigorously, knowing now they probably spoke a different language.

Santer met me as I returned to the inn. 'Whatever god they worship will hear about you tonight,' he smiled, and seemed to be pleased.

'This must be a wealthy business, to give food free to slaves,' said the older man waspishly. His nose seemed to diminish the breadth of his cheeks.

'All bellies feel the same hunger,' I retorted, hearing the note of challenge in my voice. Santer laughed aloud and drew me away from the table.

'It's good to see you. You haven't been to the city for a long time.'

'Or you to the river,' I reply.

'No.' He looks thoughtful. 'I think those days are past.'

'Where are you going today?'

'Capernaum,' he tells me with obvious pleasure. He has been chosen to go, with the older man who is in Joseph's employ, to execute some business for Joseph, lodging copies of civic decisions as well as purchasing some Roman goods that had not yet been made available in Jerusalem. For Joseph is to marry Santer's mother in five weeks time and wants all the latest delicacies of Roman fashion on display. It is to be a small celebration, says Santer, but one that would do honour to Joseph's name.

I am pleased for Santer. 'Now he'll be a proper father! How do you feel, do you like Joseph? Are you glad he is marrying your mother?'

'Yes. He's a substantial man. They have known one another since they were young. And I am being tutored, which I like very much.'

'Mary?' Szuzanna's voice is cross.

'Stop on the way back?' I ask quickly as I turn to go. 'Coming, Szuzanna!'

'Wait,' he says, a hand diving in his robe. 'I'll pay the reckoning, how much is it?' Szuzanna appears at the door of the inn, then goes in again when she sees that Santer and I are doing business.

'How much?' Santer asks again.

I look over at the slaves, who are watching us and eating grapes. One lifts his hand to me. 'Two, for four breakfasts,' I say to Santer turning back to him. I thought it was not fair to charge him full price for both the extra breakfasts, since I hadn't consulted him before I brought out the food. I decide to split the cost between us.

He grins and fished out the coins. 'How much is it for two people,' he asks lightly. His clear brown eyes are warm with amusement, which draws from me an answering smile. The coins clink in my palm. We are nearly at the door, the older man scowling at our approach. I laugh and toss the coins in my hand as I veer to enter the inn.

'Surely you can work that out for yourself,' I call back to him.

The last time I saw Santer before Szuzanna got ill was at his bar mitzvah feast. He came to the inn early one morning, just as Szuzanna and I were beginning to make the bread. He formally invited me, through Szuzanna, to be a guest at the celebration feast following his ceremony. She took a long time to answer him, kneading the dough and shaping it into loaves as she asked him questions about the gathering. There were to be five other girls as well as me, and six other boys, Santer making the significant thirteenth person. Szuzanna observed that the gathering was to take place on the day after our next market day, which meant that 'it would not be a wasted trip.' Santer explained that provision had been made for myself and two of the other girls to stay overnight in Joseph's house, with an older woman sleeping in our quarters to guarantee our night safety.

Szuzanna squeezed orange juice into a tall cup and gave it to Santer, telling me to get the bread and olives, halvah and figs. He was explaining who the other guests would be, most of them sons and daughters of families known to Joseph, and connected either through business, or the Council. Szuzanna was watching him closely, unusual for her. I was astonished when she said abruptly that she wanted Santer to grant her a bar mitzvah boon, his first act as a newly-made man. That Szuzanna should ask anything of anyone was almost shocking to me; she had always approved of my independence, even when it ran counter to her own idea. 'Know what you want and how to get it, and you'll sleep well each night,' she often said, adding, 'do for yourself means no disappointment.' Santer was delighted by her request, asking what service he could be to her. I could hear a rumble as he spoke, his voice suddenly deepening on the last syllable of the last word. He looked embarrassed, which made me laugh. After a moment, both he and Szuzanna joined in.

'More proof of my coming manhood!' he declares. 'Tell me what I can do for you in that desirable time, Szuzanna.'

'To regard Mary as a member of your family,' she says with a quick, slightly challenging smile. If I had been shocked before, I am now silenced utterly. I could only stare at her, wondering.

Santer laughs and agrees instantly. 'She shall be my sister from this moment,' he announces with a flourish. He tears off a corner of the bread in his hand and puts it into my mouth. 'We shall share the same bread,' he intones with mock solemnity, his eyes sparkling at Szuzanna with a glint of mischief. 'Shall I now call you mother?' She flicks his shoulder with a long finger and scolds him lightly, but she was very pleased.

Less than a year later, she was dead and I was living in Joseph's house.

She began to fail about two months after Santer's bar mitzvah. My eyes saw, but could scarcely comprehend the changes that took place in her. Her hair leached from glossy black to the frowsy grey of old donkey hair. Her body that was rounded as a full fruit was now withering beneath her skin. At the end, huge black sores appeared on her shoulders and between her shrunken buttocks, and her full breasts became mere envelopes of brown. She had Malachi carry a message to Santer, telling him she would soon die, and that she expected Santer to take care of his 'sister' when she did.

She died on a green evening, with a little breeze stirring the grape leaves, in which the bee-eaters were squabbling over their nightly roosts. The pain had left her earlier in the day and her face became smooth. A flicker of her smile returned to her eyes as she looked at me, then around this little room which had sheltered her sleep for more than thirty years, then to the sky outside the open window. I thought for one wild moment that she was getting better. All day, David and Malachi had come in and gone out, in and out, their so-identical eyes heavy with tears, Malachi's sorrow rising in that deep humming from within his chest.

I was holding her hand when, with a long sigh, her spirit left her flesh. And though I've now seen it many more times it is as astonishing always as that first time, that pied piper moment between life and death when time spreads like quicksilver on the horizon's pool and all souls at that brink raise their lustrous arms and dive.

Santer came to her funeral, and discussed my departure with Malachi and David, and with Hannah, their large-bodied capable cousin who came from Magdala, their home village. The departure seemed impossible for me. Impossible to think of being anywhere but here, impossible to abandon the place where the warmth of Szuzanna's robust spirit was there for me in every corner. When I thought of leaving, something slipped inside my private mind, and I felt held over a terrible crevasse of dark. Between the two hard nubs that were my emerging breasts, the skin was painful, and below them was an ache that pulsed and throbbed and clawed.

Santer arrived on the day he said he would, driving a small and to my eyes flimsy looking cart drawn by a liver-brown donkey. David had left for the fields much earlier, but Malachi, who had kept giving me massive hugs over the past days, was waiting for him.

'She is not to go if she does not wish it,' he says to Santer immediately. Santer looks from him to me, questioning.

'No — no, only if she wants it — I thought you did?'

At the sight of him, I finally did. Santer is closer than Malachi, second only to Szuzanna. She had arranged this for me, and I had put my trust in her a very short time after she held my infant body between her hands and coaxed me away from the nanny's teat. I climb into the fragile-looking cart, not able to look at Malachi after his last humming hug. Neither could I look at the inn. I look ahead, and with my eyes stinging, stand up beside Santer to watch for the saffron walls of Jerusalem to rise before us, portico to my new home.

That Joseph should honour Santer's bar mitzvah boon was something that I did not question at the time, having no understanding of the perceived function of daughters. My arrival was quiet, kept to the household, and I learned later that due to my presence at the bar mitzvah, many thought I had arrived at Joseph's house with Santer and his mother. I was a little apprehensive of meeting Joseph, although Santer assured me he was nobody to fear. But I knew Joseph was not like Malachi, or David, or Nathaniel, or any of the men I had some knowledge of. He was a man of learning, of words, a man who had around him many things which were used only to appreciate mystery and beauty. He was almost a father to Santer, and would now be almost a father to me.

Joseph was not at home when we arrived. I met him in the late afternoon, in the large southward facing room that was particularly his. There were several scrolls on the marble-topped table, cross-legged chairs and three lounges, shelves with small exquisite bowls on them, and between the windows on the long south wall, a pedestal with a large golden lion on it. The whole

31

room had a presence that added to my nervousness, so far removed from my experience that I felt anxious and alert, as if there was the scent of enemies on the air. Joseph had asked that I come alone.

In my interview with him, for that is what it was, he questioned me closely. He was pleased to discover I knew calculation as well as having a practical knowledge of food preparation and housekeeping.

'What else have you a knowledge of?' he asked, his voice neutral, but his eyes assessing me with an objective interest.

'Goats, sir. I can milk them, make goat cheese, and once helped deliver a pair of kids.'

'Admirable,' he commented, his eyebrows raised. 'However, not a skill you will need to practice here.'

'No,' I said, diminished.

He was sitting on a long stool which had rolled, grooved ends and feet shaped like steps. Through the shuttered windows came, very faintly, the angry scream of a camel, and a slip of bells.

'How old are you, Mary?'

'Nearly twelve, sir.'

His eyebrows raised. 'As much as that? You are small for your age.'

I could think of no reply to that, so said nothing. I studied him in quick little glances: he looked very different from Malachi or David. He was as tall as they, perhaps slightly taller, but half as thick-bodied. He wore a long, elegant robe and intricately fashioned sandals. His toenails shone smoothly, the colour of almond shells. I watched his eyes, in which screens seemed to slide. His lips were dark red, and full, framed by his beard.

'Are you strong, Mary, or are you often ill?'

'I do not remember ever being ill,' I told him.

He kept looking at me. 'Good,' he said eventually. He motioned me to come to him and, when I was beside him, took my right hand in his. His face, where it wasn't covered by black, glistening hair, had smooth brown skin, almost plump. His eyes were large, with strongly curved black brows and thick lids, one heavy fold protecting them. I wanted to like him, to be liked by him. My temples were pounding and my eyes beginning to smart.

'My wife's son has chosen you to be his sister,' he said, his voice mellow now, and quieter. 'I have agreed that you shall live here in our family.'

'Yes, sir.'

'Having so recently lost your own mother,' he continued, 'you will probably look to Joshua's mother for comfort.' My heart-pain at the thought of Szuzanna closed my throat; even if I had wanted to, I could not have said that Szuzanna was not my mother.

'It is necessary therefore, that you know she is carrying a child, and is not strong,' continued Joseph. 'She needs a great deal of rest. Try to help her, if you can, to make her days pleasant. If you have any problems of your own, that you cannot solve by yourself, or with Joshua, came to me, not to her. Will you do that?' His hand gave mine a little shake. I quickly looked upward to his eyes, nodding my head, and looked down again. 'Good,' he said again. Then, seeming to choose his words with care, 'And if — if my wife should become — distressed, be unable to calm herself, or to rest properly, you will come and find me, please, or Joshua, if I am not at home. Do you understand?'

'Yes,' I finally croaked, and drew my hand away.

The thought of being a mainstay to Santer's mother was both overwhelming and alarming. At first I was in awe of her because she was that marvellous thing, a real mother. I'd had many fantasies about real mothers, which included laughter and dancing, closeness, hugs and kisses, talking and doing things together — similar to my life with Szuzanna, but much much more. That was as close as my eager mind could come. But Mary seemed constantly to be nervous: loud voices and sudden noises alarmed her excessively. She shrank from shadows on walls, and always gave a little start when she discovered people behind her. The sudden whirr of pigeon wings invariably drew a little gasp from her, even though it occurred more frequently than the canting calls of prayer. Only in her own rooms did she fully relax, and there she had a gentleness, almost an innocence, that was very endearing. Awe died. Its phoenix was a curious mixture, a sort of impatient tenderness.

I did not realise fully, until I had been in Joseph's house for several weeks exactly what the exchange in homes had cost me. Gone was my freedom, the easy informality of my days, and the assumption, never verbalised, of my ability, strength, and indispensability. At the inn, I knew absolutely that if I did not do my tasks, they would remain undone until an acerbic voice reminded me of my duties. Here, I had no real duties to speak of, and no freedom to run to the river (which in this season was only a faint discolouration of dirt under the tussock grass) or either market street. It was expected that I would stay within the precincts of the house, forcing me to devise various strategies when I absolutely had to get out.

As well, I hated living with slaves. The dead baby and its father returned vividly to my mind; I frequently looked into the faces of slave men to see if I could recognise him. I found anger rising in me to hear Joseph give orders in a voice of complete authority, and to hear a slave's submissive response. Joseph had told me that Salome, who was in charge of the women's quarters would get me anything I asked for, but I asked for nothing, and took pride in it.

The garden became my refuge in those first weeks. Though not large, it had been subtly planned so that it seemed bigger than it was. There were many little nooks in it that seemed made for privacy, and birds were active there, and big furry bees. The head gardener, a man called Boaz, was at first wary of me, watching me without speaking, and ignoring most of my questions to him. But when he saw that I did not run through the plants or snap their heads off with my restless fingers, and could spend hours without speaking, watching him dig, prune and plant, he began to speak. His talk was all of plants, which he preferred to human beings, saying they were much better company, and smelled far better. His duties covered both the home garden, and the large one among the city gardens outside the northern wall.

We were almost exactly the same height so I could look directly into his eye. His face was very dark, with a large-pored nose, and creases running deeply down his cheeks. He had thick-fingered hands and a little gold ring in his ear.

'Why do you have a ring in your ear?' It was just after dawn, the sky milky with new light, its clarity echoed in the shivering globes of dew that clustered on frond and leaf.

'Why do birds sing? I need six holes dug, just here, this far apart.' He measured three inches with his finger and thumb. I stopped chattering and bent to the earth.

Once, in the garden, I was an unwitting spy on Joseph and Mary. I had fallen into a heat-doze while lying under a small orange tree, watching bees go into the succulent flower cups. Their voices woke me; I lay there, drowsy and only half listening to their talk.

'— because something is going to happen. I shall die very soon'.

'No, no, you will not die, little wife. The something you feel is the birth of our child approaching. You will not die. I shall make sure of that! Your women tell me your health is good, but that you need to rest. Lots of rest, that's the answer, don't worry! All will be well, I am certain.'

They sat on one of the stone benches and she gave a little sigh. His arm went round her, and she laid her head on his chest. The scent of orange blossom was heady, but I was now not interested in the orange blossom. Perhaps only I saw her tears, for she did not weep aloud. There weren't many, but they hung on her face the way the last drops of rain do on reeds and fronds, testament to her inner, private storms.

When Joseph was away on his frequent business trips, Santer made me acquainted with Jerusalem's magnificence: the Temple of Herod, thirty years in the building, and still not finished, gleaming and proud in its gold and bronze, its vast sacrificial slaughter-yards, from which a special channel ran just to carry away the blood; the Tomb of Absalom with its shining columns of white marble, and its sad inscriptions; and the lovely pool of Siloam, a gentle plash of water into water, always green and cool. My favourite place, and one that I managed to visit by myself once in a while was the Mount of Olives.

The lush olive trees with their twisting, rough trunks and silvery green leaves, made me feel good inside, calm and clear. Once, we followed a load of olives round the outer eastern wall and across to Gethsemane, where the giant oil presses were. I loved the smell of the freshly crushed olives, pungent and smoky and laden with the rich scent of the yellow oil.

But I had very little to fill my days, and my times with Santer were the only wholly enjoyable ones. I now understood more clearly why Mary was so eager for his company on that day of our first meeting. He and I talked a little after every noon meal, but we always met in the late evening, in the garden, standing at the wall and looking across the valley, over the small orange squares of light that fastened the shape of the houses to the dark fabric of the night.

It was during one of these talks that I found the answer to my boredom. Santer was telling me of his lessons, which not only included studying the Laws, but also learning to read, and so to write.

It was as though a light had turned on in my private mind. 'I want to do that!' I exclaim, 'I want to learn to read, and to write, do you think I could have a tutor?'

'It's not thought necessary to teach girls such things,' replies Santer cautiously.

'But you told me yourself that in Rome — and in Greece — that women as well as men learn to read and write,' I protest.

'Mmm. But this is Jerusalem,' he says.

Anger fills my head and despair strengthens me. 'I might as well be dead as do nothing all day,' I cry stormily. 'I should go back to the inn. At least I can milk the goats!'

'Don't be foolish,' he says sharply, putting an arm around me and squeezing my shoulders hard before letting his arm drop. 'That's silly talk, it won't get you anywhere. Let me see what Joseph thinks. I might be able to get him to say yes.'

This brought another summons from Joseph, to come to him in the Gallery, which was the long hallway I had walked through on my first visit. He was not alone. His back was turned toward me as he stood at the tall working bench where he examined, labelled and repaired his artefacts. A second man, about the same age as Joseph, was with him, wearing the clothes of a Greek. Joseph had a large old bag in front of him on the workbench, its neck stretched to its width, its stuffing of grass and strips of cloth spilling over its edges. He was carefully freeing a covered object from this wrapping.

The stranger looked up at me inquisitively, but Joseph paid no attention to my arrival. The object was now free of the bag. Joseph put it on the bench, deftly taking the final coverings from it. When the last wrapping came free, a creamy curve of ivory was revealed, carved and pierced and rimmed with silver. I could not restrain an appreciative gasp, and my hand went involuntarily out to it.

Joseph gave me a curious look.

'Do you know what this is?' he asked me.

'It's ivory, Trader Nathaniel had some once. He said it grows on an animal that is as high as a camel's head, but fatter.'

The stranger laughed. 'A good description!'

'Where did you say it was from?' Joseph asked him.

'Indie,' the man replied. 'I believe they use such things as this to pay homage to their goddesses — and their kings,' he added hastily, for if it were a holy object, Joseph would not have it, however attractive its price.

'My fortune then, that Herod is dead,' Joseph said to him lightly. It was the first time I had seen him smile, or felt his body's spirit. It leapt out, swift like a blade and was sheathed again as quickly.

The stranger's eyes gleamed. 'It is to your liking?'

'Perhaps,' Joseph replied, looking at the ivory critically. 'It's quite a pretty thing. What price do you ask?'

They set to exchanging prices, their voices equable. Each new offer was accompanied by a reason, either extolling the object's grace, or casting doubts on its rarity. But I could tell that when the deal was completed, it was Joseph who had most fully had his way. He did not speak to me at that time, taking the stranger off to his private room, telling me over his shoulder that he would talk with me later. But I do believe that he was impressed that I knew of the ivory, for when we did speak, it was not to argue as to whether I would have lessons, but to arrange a portion of each day in which to take them as soon as Joseph had found a suitable tutor. And, in the meantime, he suggested Santer write out the letters of the alphabet for me to learn, and practice copying until I could do that with a fair hand.

It was rare for Mary to leave the house, and although she was now Joseph's wife, her belly large with the coming child, still she seemed to prefer her son's company above all others. Often I saw anguish in her eyes as she watched Joseph, but when she looked at Santer, her eyes were always full of light. I had yet to see her merry, or hear a laugh rise from her throat, but when Santer was with her, talking or silent, she became tranquil, her appealing mouth relaxed, eyes serene.

My first real talk with her happened when my menstruum came upon me. Szuzanna had told me of it almost a year before she died, but I had forgotten it until I felt a sticky wetness, and discovered blood on my inner thighs. The sight of it alarmed me; I searched my body for a cut, wondering why there was no pain. Then I discovered it was coming from inside me. I sat in the cleansing room, worried and wondering what I had done to myself, then remembered at last Szuzanna's words about the blood coming from inside me, how I was not to be afraid, that it was the sacred blood from which babies were born, and when it began it flow, it meant that I was a woman. I was filled with a longing for Szuzanna that made my body feel tight and swollen under my breasts. I wept bitterly for her, and with those tears came to understand that in every way which mattered, Szuzanna had been my mother.

Hiccupping with misery, I realised I had to find someone to help me, and that I had no recourse to Santer, even if he had been there: Szuzanna had warned me that men must not be connected to the menstruum in any way, though she couldn't give me a convincing reason why this should be. That left only Mary.

I went down the walkway to Mary's private rooms, for once heedless of the garden and the late afternoon glory beyond the wall. I was inarticulate when she opened the door, but one look at my face told her I was distressed, and she brought me inside. She led me through the ante chamber into her sleeping room.

I was surprised by its sparseness. In this great house, where ornaments filled every niche and friezes scarfed the walls, her room had nothing decorative in it but a small vase of pink almond flowers and a branch of lighted sacred candles. She wore a dull pink robe which had dark green borders, and had put her mantle off her hair. In the soft light of the room, she looked as she had when we first met, a girl scarcely separated in age from me, and I spoke to her as if she was such a girl.

'My menstruum has come, I think. I've never had it before, but there is blood on me. I don't know what to do.' I didn't know how to handle my body and was afraid to sit down. I was also afraid that my blood would splash down onto her floor. She gave a low exclamation and went to a small chest by her bed, from which she took several white folded cloths, and the bands in which to hold them. These looked forbidding in her narrow hands, and one cloth caught a little on the single ring she wore, a chased circle with no jewel on it, on the middle finger of her right hand.

'Do you know about these?' she asked, holding the pile forward.

I nodded, remembering Szuzanna's instructions, and tears were close again. Mary put the cloths in my hands and pointed to an archway in the back wall. 'There is the cleansing room. Use anything in it you need.'

Her cleansing room was large with beautifully patterned tiles on its floor, and jugs of water sat beside bowls of differing sizes. There was also a small bath, which was very much a luxury, and several drying cloths of the new, thick-piled sort that Joseph said came from a land far to the north, in Persia. I put water in the largest bowl, took off my clothing, and washed myself. I fitted the menstruum cloth between my legs and put on the bands. The cloth was very white and soft, the soap I had used spreading a sweet scent on the air.

I looked at the bowl of water, now distinctly bloody. Szuzanna had told me I must be very careful where I emptied the water, for it was almost as offensive as the blood itself. I could not understand how the blood could be offensive, since it was the blood from which babies were born, and wondered if men had a menstruum, and if it was their blood they were afraid of, and whether it was very different from my own, more like the blood that ran down the channel in the Temple of Herod. Right in front of me was a channel, ready to take the water away; and if I did not spill it down that cleft, what would I do with it? Then, as I looked at the pinky water, pride rose in me, strong as wine: that was my very own blood in the water, blood from which children could rise, the most powerful blood in the world.

I wanted to take the bowl to the atrium and place it on the wide chest there for all to see. The image was so vivid that I involuntarily laughed aloud. And then, wonder of wonders, I felt Szuzanna's presence around me, so strongly that I swivelled on my haunches to look around the little room. Mary called out, asking if I had everything I needed. I looked down at the bowl, then grasped its fat edge.

'I don't care what they say,' I whispered to Szuzanna, and slowly tipped the water down the channel, trailing my fingers in it as it went. 'There is nothing bad about my powerful blood!'

Later, I discovered that the channel took the water under the walkway and into the garden, and that water with women's blood in it was treated as faecal matter and discarded in exactly the same way as it was. But since that day, I have refused to think that my monthly blood was anything like faecal matter: later, I claimed my blood as sacred, because of its centrality to life, and still take special delight in sending each month some remnant of my precious blood out into the world.

When I returned to Mary, an extraordinary sunlight was on her walls, an intense apricot streaming through the room's high, west windows. In its glow, the candle flames were pale. Mary was sitting on the room's single chair, a tunic I recognised as Santer's in her lap. She was stitching closed a long, fraying elbow rent. I wanted to tell her how I felt, as I would have told Szuzanna, but she wasn't warm like Szuzanna and I didn't know how to begin.

She looked up. 'Did you have all you needed?' Her voice was kind.

I nodded.

'Keep the cloths I gave you,' she continued as she sewed. 'Salome will bring you more, and a chest, and a soaking jar. You must always rinse the cloths immediately, and put them in to soak right away. It's very hard to remove the blood once it has dried, you see, and that makes the fabric very rough. Salome will also bring a drying rack, for your room.' There was not another chair in her room, so I sat on the edge of her sleeping pallet and watched her sew. I wanted to talk about my menstruum, to discuss, as I would have with Szuzanna, what it meant that I was now a woman.

'I am proud of my blood,' I said after a peaceful silence. 'I am proud that I can have children with it.'

She lifted her head, her face darkening as if something had come between her and the window. 'Blood on the bed, blood on the child,' she muttered quickly. She dropped her sewing, her hands went up to her mouth.

'Pardon?' I said, thinking I had misheard her.

'A child of blood,' she whispered, groping in her lap. Her eyes searched the corners of the room. She gripped Santer's tunic tightly in both hands.

'What do you mean?' I asked her, bewildered.

She stared at me, her eyes wide and full of distress. Then she seemed to see my face properly and looked confused. She blinked rapidly and gave several little gasps accompanied by rhythmic little nods.

'That's right, that's right,' she said in a rapid whisper. 'Make certain you wash the cloths immediately. Old blood makes an ugly black stain. Use lemon juice, and ointment for your hands. Wash the blood away, wash all the blood away.'

Her child was born a few days later, a small dark boy they called James. I heard Mary cry sharply for Salome as I copied my letters one morning, and the child was born in the late afternoon. In answer to my queries, Salome, worry plain on her broad face, said that Mary was fearfully weak. Though Joseph seemed pleased with his new son, Santer too was clearly worried. He stayed home from his studies, because his mother called for him frequently, and he told me he didn't think she would recover properly for weeks. I said I would like to see her, to pay my respects to her, and he suggested early morning, after she'd rested. I picked a spray of the starry vine flowers of jasmine and took them to Mary's room. Salome held the door, at first saying that I should not come in, that Mary was not herself.

'I'll just put these by her bed, and leave, that's all,' I promised, with some insistence. Her small, oval eyes flicked from side to side, reluctance shining from their black depths. 'Please,' I entreated, and she finally gave way.

Mary lay in her bed, its covers unruffled. There was no sign of the infant, and later, Salome told me he had been given to a wet nurse, as Mary was unable to suckle him. Mary did not speak to me, but watched me, her eyes huge and unreadable. I arranged the spray on the chest beside the candles. I could feel her eyes on me. When I'd finished, I went to her and knelt beside the bed.

'How are you, Mary?' I asked in a low voice. 'Are you feeling better?'

'I did NOT,' she said very loudly, and again, 'I did NOT.' Her mouth worked a little and then, before I could understand what was happening, she spat full in my face. 'Unclean,' she hissed at me, and struggled up on one elbow. Salome sprang forward, drew me away from the bed.

'I told you she was not herself,' she cried softly, very upset, as she gave me a clean cloth. 'The birthing was too much for her, she is not herself. She did not know what she was doing. Please do not tell the master — she did not know it was you.'

I wiped my face, repulsion, anger, and surprise itching my veins. On the bed, Mary now lay with her eyes closed, her face pale with purple scimitars under each eye. She looked so ill that my heart opened to her and compassion came. Salome's words snapped open an image in my mind, of this house with several shadow houses built around and through it, invisible halls where decisions I only glimpsed were made and important conversations were secretly held. Mary seemed like a wraith, powerless and of no consequence; my own body felt loud with health and vigour.

'I should have listened to you, Salome,' I said, handing back the towel. 'You told me she wasn't herself and I didn't listen.' I went to the door, with one backward glance to Mary. She scarcely made a mound under the bed sheetings. Pity again took hold of me: she seemed barely there. 'I am sorry to have upset her. And don't worry I won't speak of this, I'll come back another time.'

For several weeks, Mary quivered between life and death, the house now quiet and grave; when she began to recover, Santer was radiant with relief, his laughter echoing down the halls.

Shortly afterwards, the solution to my tutoring was found: I was to go to a household in Bethany, which had recently employed a young Roman tutor named Decius. The owner of the household had three children, two daughters Martha and Mary and a son, Lazarus. After the death of his wife, the householder, who was a prosperous farmer, had set the older daughter, Martha, to be the keeper of his house, since she was thirteen and already a woman. Lazarus was eight and it was to provide him with a formal education that Decius had been hired, for a bodily affliction meant the boy was unable to travel from his home. Since Martha, the young housekeeper, was to receive tutoring that she may better understand the business of household management, the addition of a third pupil was an excellent way to share the cost of Decius's fees.

'In fact, there will be a fourth pupil, from another family known to that household,' Joseph informed me. 'I am told his name is James.'

So began my education, in the house of Lazarus and Martha where I lived for three days of the week. I was escorted there by Santer when he was available, and Acton if he was not. I arrived at breakfast time and left in mid-afternoon of the third day.

Lazarus was shockingly thin, with a yellowish skin, large brown eyes set shallowly above hollow cheeks, and a mouth stretched to hide his pain. His mind was quick and sardonic: shortly after we met, he told me his bones had been boiled by a fever when he was five and, consequently, were almost too soft to use. He could not walk about, or even sit upright, for very long. I liked him right from the start.

It was hard not to like Martha, who was a plump and comfortable person, and already a good cook. I shared her sleeping room and very soon looked forward to the platter of pastries that she brought in with her each night, to have on hand 'in case we feel hungry in the night.' We ate most of them before we slept, and Martha ate whatever was left over as she performed her morning ablutions. She wanted to know about the size of Joseph's household, which she had assumed I was taking lessons to enhance my management of, as she was doing. 'No, I want to learn because it is interesting,' I told her. 'This is a delicious one, Martha — how do you make the pastry so flaky and crunchy, and keep the currants inside it soft?'

Martha's cheeks glowed with pleasure, and she looked down with modest pride. 'I'll show you tomorrow, after lessons, if you want to. I'm going to make some more then.'

After the third lesson, we were joined, to Martha's patent annoyance, by their sister Mary, a very passionate girl one year younger than me. Though we were almost the same age, she seemed much younger than me, and Martha's objection to her presence (that Mary had no reason for learning as she, Martha, did) was rebutted very easily by Mary, who turned to me.

'How old are you?' she demanded peremptorily.

'Twelve.'

'What do you do in your father's home?'

I looked at Martha and gave a little shrug. 'Nothing. We have slaves.' I admitted. Mary flounced back to Martha. 'So there,' she proclaimed. 'I'm not being left out.'

An appeal to their father brought his agreement, and Mary stayed.

Mary either loved a thing, or hated it: indifference was beyond her. She loved birds, flowing water, crisp nutcakes, the smell of new shoes, the sound of a flute; she hated, with equal vehemence and passionate outburst, chipped crockery, animals and their pens, blood and knives, and any odorous smell. I had the feeling that if Lazarus had not been her brother, she could not have borne the sight of him. I liked her vitality and her sense of humour, both qualities which Martha lacked, but couldn't resist teasing her. James proved to be a soft-eyed boy of average intelligence, with a slender, deep-naped neck and dampish white hands. He was as soft as his eyes and cried very easily and was exceptionally boring. I discovered those soft eyes could not see anything a good distance away, and much of what he saw only a few steps away was very blurred. But not even this knowledge could lift the boredom I inevitably felt after a short time in his sole company. Of all of us, he was the quickest with the rote lessons, and the first to become fluent at Latin and Greek. Of them all, Lazarus was the one with whom I formed the closest friendship.

I had not expected to be tutored with Santer, for Santer went to the synagogue with other youths his age, and was taught by the rabbis. His was specialist learning, particularly for youths who would succeed to the San-hedrin, perhaps as soferim who would write the new interpretations of the halakhoth, or become a rabbon, who studied and interpreted the torah shebe-al pe, and much later, perhaps a rabbi, who taught the lessons of the great, five sectioned book, the Pentateuch.

But I had not expected Santer's learning to be so very different from my own, and was very surprised to learn he was not being taught any other languages at all. He was almost envious of my expanding knowledge of Latin, and increasing fluency in Greek. But it was when I told him of Alexander, who had conquered all of

Greece, Egypt, and the lands of Persia before he was thirty, and Santer had not yet heard of him, that we decided something more must be done. From then on, much of our time together became a reiterating and discussing of my studies, in which Pompey, Brutus, and the Caesars strode, and Herod the Great's thirty years of peace were discussed more than the terrible killings of his final years. I brought Homer to him (whose Penelope seemed no mystery to me, just a woman content in her own home, like Szuzanna was), and Cicero, whom Decius seemed almost to revere as a god. With almost Mary-like fervour, Decius told us of Cicero's prosecution of Gaius Verres, a rapacious governor of an island called Sicily. Gaius Verres had decimated Syracuse, one of its cities, 'so that so little was left, it would not supply a dowry for the meanest wedding,' Decius declared. Cicero prosecuted Gaius Verres for extortion by a superb presentation of his prosecting case in a way that was new to the Roman bar. He had included the smallest details — 'so extraordinarily precise in his preparation, so eloquent in his oratory, that the defence abandoned its case before Cicero was even half-way through!' Decius told us triumphantly. Lazarus made me smile by wondering aloud — though not loud enough to reach our tutor's ears — whether Cicero or any of his friends had owned property on the island of Sicily.

I asked Santer whether he would be studying languages and history at a later time, but he told me, rather wistfully, that at the synagogue, the Pentateuch was regarded as Sifra, the Book of all books, and that to study and understand its words alone was the work of more than one lifetime. I couldn't understand how anything written down by people could take so long to learn, but he said it wasn't just learning the words, it was also understanding their meaning and, that down the centuries, many scholars had expressed insights, all of which had to be considered for they each interpreted the Old Words in subtly different ways.

I offered to teach Santer what I was learning if he would teach me what he was learning. At first, he seemed reluctant to agree with this. But I kept my lips sealed, just looking at him when he asked me questions, and his curiosity finally forced him to agree. For the most part, I found what he told me to be of less interest than the things I was being taught. It was interesting to hear of the Old Words, but they were all about laws and rules — do this this way, not that — and seemed to be about such a small group of people, none of whom ever seemed curious about the rest of the world. They had very little charisma compared to Ovid, I told Santer, whose poetry of course sent Mary into raptures.

Santer laughed and asked me to tell him about Ovid, so I described Ovid's life a little, how he had been groomed for a public life and had given it up for his poetry, and had become a widely lauded poet, acclaimed for his wit and elegance. 'And then he decided to go into public life, which was not a good decision, because he offended Augustus by having quite a few references to sex in his work, and Caesar Augustus was offended by them.'

'Why?' asks Santer. 'From the others you've told me of, I thought that was an integral part of Roman poetry.'

'Decius says Caesar Augustus thinks such references are damaging to the image of Rome. He sent Ovid into exile six years ago.' I half-whisper this, for I was sympathetic to Ovid, an attitude which I knew would certainly be unacceptable to Rome and Joseph was entertaining some Roman officials in the long room of the house.

Santer catches my glance and laughs. 'I wonder what Joseph would think of Ovid,' he says his face alight. 'Should we mention him and see?'

But I was not interested in playing that game. 'But

49

Santer, the poet I really want you to read is Plubius Vergilis Maro! He writes so marvellously!' I couldn't describe fully how Vergil's work affected me, or how I had fantasised about him as a father.

I could only say, and badly, a little of how he made me feel: 'We have begun the Eclogues, and they all speak so often of goats — so vividly, he must know them very well, like me! That gives me such a belief in him — I feel there is truth in all his lines! He's funny as well, and very political, it's like a secret, or a puzzle. In the Third Eclogue, there are three lines:

> Two central figures: Conon and — who was the other,
> Who marked out with his rod the whole round for mankind,
> What times the reaper keeps, and what the stooping ploughman?

'Those lines are about real people, Santer, two men of Greece who studied the stars over two hundred years ago! Their names were Conon and Archimedes, but Decius says that Vergil could not use Archimedes's name because poetically, it has too many syllables! Too many syllables! It's so annoying, how everything seems to be held by rules — why can't poetry just move properly, without us worrying — like water, going where it will and always beautiful no matter what it's doing!'

'But not quite, if it's twenty feet below ground, and you dying of thirst,' counters Santer.

'Cynic,' I retort, and carry on.

Before teaching us about specific poets, Decius had given us insight into poetry itself: 'a language once spoken by the gods,' he told us during that first lesson. This had shocked Martha very much, but Lazarus had warned him, sardonically, that Decius would need the full pantheon of Greek and Roman gods to keep his position if their father thought Decius was teaching them pagan lore. Decius had apologised hastily, but it was no serious threat: we had all come to respect him and like him, and Martha, in being able to fuss over his comfort, was exercising her housekeeperly wings.

Our current study was Vergil's Fourth Eclogue, in which a time of splendour, peace and beauty was heralded by the birth of a special child. This excited Santer, so I recited what I had memorised of the Fourth:

> A new begetting now descends from heaven's height
> O chaste Lucina, look with blessing on the boy
> Whose birth will end the iron race at last and raise
> A golden through the world: now your Apollo rules.

This seems to stun Santer. He questions me closely about Vergil, and has me recite the lines again. He then tells me of prophecies that his studies are bringing forward, that there would be born a child who was to lead our people to supremacy and with this action, bring peace and prosperity to the world.

'It's quite extraordinary, isn't it, that even there, where beliefs are so different, there was talk of such a child.' His voice is slow, his eyes looking at something above my head.

'Decius says it was only Vergil's way of saying to Anthony and Octavia that he hoped their marriage would bear a son, and stop the wars.'

'Even so, it's interesting that it's the same belief,' he counters.

'It's silly though, isn't it,' I reply. 'A baby couldn't stop the wars, but the adults could stop them immediately, if they wanted to.'

'Perhaps,' he says noncommittally. 'Would you write that Vergil down, so I can learn it myself?'

We are under the great palm, for the night is windy and dark, without a moon. Above us, the long tongues of palm fronds clack and whisper, and below the wall, a snarl of dogs tell of their fight.

'You've changed your thinking, haven't you?' I ask

51

him. 'You don't seem to mind now, when I ask you about your lessons. You did at first, admit it.'

'I did. There is so much that is forbidden, you see — .' He breaks off, squinting up into the tossing leaves. The torches flare up and down, and the touch of the wind is now cold. I stood up.

'Yes, but what changed you? I'm going in, it's cold.'

He stands up. 'I felt better about it when I discovered that one of the earliest unwritten laws was that a woman can be among the seven called to the Torah. That made a difference, because at first, I was afraid I was breaking a holy law.'

I shiver, and he puts an arm around me. His body is warm and I snuggle into his side. We go quickly to the house, and to the sleeping quarters. Acton waits by the visitor's mirror to extinguish the lamps. I nod to him as I always do, and he returns a tiny movement of his head. Santer gives me a brief hug. 'I won't see you in the morning; Joseph and I are going out very early,' he says, his voice low. From where we stand, his mother's room was near.

'Why?'

He shakes his head. 'I'm not sure. I'll tell you about it when we get back.'

'Does your mother know you're going?'

'Yes, I told her earlier this evening, and Joseph did as well.'

'I'll stay with her for a while in the morning.'

'Thank you. Sleep well.'

His sandals made hardly any sound as he went down the corridor to his own rooms. I tiptoed past Mary's quarters. She was now completely recovered from the strange illness which had come over her when she gave birth to James, but I very definitely did not want to wake her.

It was two days before I saw Santer again, and learned

what had taken Joseph and him away from the house so early. Augustus, Emperor of Rome, had died, and all the council of Jerusalem was meeting, to try and probe the most likely consequences to us of his death. Santer, as a student and Joseph's foster son, was allowed to listen to the debatings, but not to take part. Rumours flew everywhere that the passing of Augustus was the death cry of the empire of Rome.

Over the following days I listened avidly to everything anyone could tell me, from Decius to Lazarus's father, and Boaz as we gardened, and all the talk I could garner from stolen market street trips, because after Santer had left me that last evening, his words had come back into my head, that the Old Words said a woman could be called to the Torah. I imagined first that I was such a woman, that I had been studying eagerly with that goal, and that I was studying in the women's quarters, not far from Santer. I imagined dreamily, sleep caressing me softly, softly, that we two could work together deciphering and revealing old mysteries, and drowsily wondered what those old entry requirements were, whether it was the testimony of one's teacher that counted, or an entry fee paid by the student, or whether it was simply a matter of the testimony of the blood.

Sleep was ripped from me at the consequences of this thought: who could say what the testimony of my blood would reveal? Who could say, in fact, who I was and where my allegiances properly should lie? Who even could say that I was a child of Israel? I could just as easily be a child of Syria, perhaps, or even Egypt, fallen from some camel saddlebag-hold on the precarious journey north to Damascus, or south from Lydia. It was many hours before I slept. My pallet became unbearable in my tossings and I got up, put my sheeting around me and went back to the garden.

Without the torches, the night was dark blue, with a

strong mild wind. I felt inconsequential, thin as a fallen petal. The tossing bushes brushed my legs, their scents diluted, made vaguer by the cooler airs of night. I wanted to cry but ordered myself not to, nipping the skin of my inside upper arm with my nails, the soft-cheeked babyskin below my armpit. The nips cauterised my attention, focusing it through the mothy fronds of sorrow. Whoever I am, I am here, I exist, I thought defiantly. And if I have no testimony for my blood, then I shall make my own. If I can offer no proof, then nor can another.

'I shall be who I say I am,' I vowed to the whispering dark. 'I shall be who I wish to be.' There were few colours on the night, and no stars. In Salome's chamber the baby James sent up a mewling cry.

ALEXANDRIA

Through escorting me to Bethany, Santer had come to know and be friends with Lazarus, Martha and Mary and sometimes, when the public debates were heated, he'd stay to discuss them with us.

His attendance at the council's debatings was directly responsible for giving the three of them and me some understanding of the tangled skeins of power that ran around and through our ordinary days. I held my blood secret locked in my private mind and found that its reservation meant that I held myself a little distance from unreservedly accepting any point of view.

It did seem discourteous, to say the least, that all those years ago, Herod had taken the holy vestments under his protection, but had he done this in order to stop the fighting, or to reinforce his power with a religious power? It was true too, that he had placed a great bronze eagle high over the gates of the Temple, when effigies of living things were specifically forbidden; but did not the Torah itself contain reverent allusions to eagles? It had also to be considered that the Romans consistently allowed the practice of customs sacred and traditional to Jews, even to accepting aspects of the Jewish rules on war.

But they were undoubtedly our rulers, I kept reminding myself, and to me, that made us, as far as I could think it through, almost slaves. We were free to a certain length, but wholly according to their jurisdictions, which could — and undoubtedly would — change whenever

Rome wished.

Santer told us what he'd heard only when Decius was gone; mostly, we gathered in Lazarus's room, which had his scrolls and papers on almost every available surface. 'So many points are being discussed,' exclaims Santer in a low voice, his eyes brilliant. 'Yesterday, they spoke of a man who, several years ago, said that it was wrong to swear an oath of allegiance to an emperor — or any human being, for it defies our belief in the absolute sovereignty of God, which is in the Covenant. Over half the voices in the debate said that was true, and we should raise it again.'

'Who was he?' asks Lazarus, all interest. A small abacus, black wooden beads on copper wires, was in his lap, his fingers white against the burnished strands. The sun came into the room at an angle, so that it is filled with light without being harsh to the eyes, and throws leafy patterns on the floor.

'What happened to him?' I ask simultaneously, taking another large olive and popping it in my mouth. Lazarus smiles at me, and Santer nods eagerly. Martha had already gone back to her household duties, but Mary is there, lying on the floor, her head propped on one arm, eyes fixed on Santer's face to show he had her undivided attention.

'To answer you both — his name was Judas and he was from the hill country in the north, that is Galilee. He and his friends started a new philosophy based on that belief. They called it the Fourth Way.'

'Oh — Galilee,' exclaims Mary. 'Decius says that Galilee has produced more agitators from its hills than anywhere else in the world.'

'Has he been everywhere in the world?' Lazarus's tone is dry.

'No, but — .'

'I remember him saying that,' I say to Lazarus. 'He

said it was because Galilee is a crossroads, so that the people who live there — or many of them — can more frequently speak with people from other countries, who have ideas that are different from ours.'

'Yes,' adds Mary, 'and he said that makes the Galileans think more, and think for themselves,' she finished triumphantly.

'You'd have to, if you were like him, saying what you think, out loud to everybody.' 'So what did happen to him?' I asked again, munching another olive.

'That was eight, nine years ago. He hasn't been heard of for the past five,' answers Santer, watching me lick my fingers.

'You can't speak against the Romans and have them ignore you,' says Lazarus, sliding the abacus beads back and forth. 'If you weren't a fool, you'd know someone would want to kill you. That's the trouble with having anti-Roman ideas.'

Santer picks up the last olive, smoothing its oily skin between his fingers as he gazes at the swaying patterns on the floor. 'Imagine that,' he muses, his gaze vacant. 'To know something, to feel it and believe it. Something of your own, not stuff other people have told you about. To say it out loud, no matter what other people think.'

His fingers stop moving; he stares at the floor. I look at the olive. Lazarus looks at Santer consideringly. Mary lays her head down against her arm. 'Determined,' says Santer suddenly. 'That man must have been very determined.'

'Very,' I murmur and stand up. 'You have to be, to get what you want.' And I pluck the olive from his fingers and quickly put it in my mouth. Lazarus roars.

Now that Augustus was dead, Santer explained, the hope was that the new administrators would return the holy vestments, and who to have the responsibility for them was proving a question difficult to resolve. But all speculation was fruitless, for the vestments were not returned; worse, they were taken to be kept in the Antonia military fortress. While this was adjacent to the Temple, it was not in it, and the Old Words forbade the taking of the vestments outside the Temple. A further sorely-felt point was that there was no way to be certain in these new circumstances that only Jews would handle the robes, and for non-Jews to handle them was sacrilege.

For a time, it seemed to me as though something violent was going to happen: the air seemed to press on my body, so I had to draw my breath in heaves. Both market streets seemed empty of people, and there seemed to be more soldiers lounging everywhere. The beggars had disappeared. For several days, Joseph would not let Santer or Acton take me to Bethany, sending over a note which explained that he felt it too dangerous a time for travel.

But nothing did happen, except some quibbling about who was to be Procurator, and an increase in the levies which must be paid to Rome. Santer told us of the fiery speeches in the Council because of that.

When the seething and scaremongering had died down and things were almost routine again, Joseph announced that the whole family was to go to Caesarea Maritima, where he had rented a villa for the summer months. I was very excited and could scarcely contain my desire to be gone. I eagerly did as I was bid, as if the speed with which I performed my task would get us more quickly on the road. My days were almost wholly spent with Mary, Salome, and James, who now was almost eight months old, sorting into vast piles the clothes and linens we would have to take.

My most intimate days with Mary were those preceding our departure for Caesarea. She too was clearly pleased to be going, a tiny smile around her beautiful mouth. It was joy for her to think of Santer present all through the day. She and Salome passed the baby between them as they examined linens, selecting what we should need, from the journey's first stop to our eventual return. It was to be an excitingly long trip, almost sixty miles just to get there, which would take us at least a week to complete. Food, water, and protection were required, for we were to travel through those hills where lived men who made the robbing of travellers their livelihood. So our eventual number was twenty-four, which included half a dozen slaves to attend to the work of the journey, and a dozen armed defenders, whose skill at fighting was the single prerequisite for their journey.

'How long before we start, do you think?' I asked Mary one afternoon, but as I had asked this countless times already, she just smiled a little and shook her head. The piles of linen rose beside us, white undulating pillars almost as high as my waist. Baby James was sitting in a pen made from these, wearing a nursery cloth and a little white robe. The soles of his feet were wrinkled, which I thought amusing, and had been joking with Mary that James was probably walking round the house when we weren't looking, to get his feet wrinkled like that.

'He'll be on those feet soon enough,' said Salome, her broad brown face complacent as she glanced down at James. 'Then we'll wish he was back on his bottom again!' She flicked her braided hair back off her shoulder.

'Shuki was almost walking by the time he was this age,' observed Mary, sitting down next to the linen pen, a glass of lemon water in her hand. Little beads of moisture clustered on her upper lip, and the hair at her temples was damp. Some muscles tightened along Salome's jaw, a spasm of annoyance that was gone before I was certain what I'd seen.

'Yes, he certainly sounds as if he was a superior child,' came her bland reply. But her eyes looked fondly at James, holding a warmth I remembered from Szuzanna. 'He was,' reiterated Mary with quiet insistence. 'He could talk properly before he was two. He is special, Salome, very special.'

'All babies are special,' was Salome's calm rejoinder.

'Yes, but Joshua — you'd know what I mean if you had been there.' She glanced up at Salome, eyes smiling. 'I wish you had been, Salome, it would have been a lot easier.'

'Didn't you have anyone to help you?' I asked.

'No one like Salome. She's as special in her own way as Joshua,' replied Mary still smiling. Salome finally met her eyes, a reluctant smile easing her face.

'I'm sure those around you did well for you,' Salome disclaimed.

'Doing things. It's not the doing of them that makes the difference,' Mary replied, dabbing at her temples with a little square of cloth. 'They all disliked me.' Her soft voice was less hesitant than usual.

'Why did they dislike you?' I asked.

Mary looked swiftly over to me, then Salome. I think, for a moment, she had forgotten I was there. A small frown appeared between her eyebrows. She looked worried and bit at her lower lip. 'It's not very pleasant. They thought I was shameless ... even unchaste — .' She shuddered and briefly closed her eyes.

'What?' I was utterly astonished. I could not have been more dumbfounded if the baby had suddenly sprouted a beard.

'But it wasn't like that,' she said quickly mingling her words with a long indrawn breath, and then a sigh. 'I tried to tell them, but they wouldn't believe me, no matter what I said. But in the end, it didn't matter because Joseph married me, and Joshua was safe.' This hurried speech confused me because I had not remembered that her first husband was also called Joseph; but just as I opened my mouth to ask a question, Joseph shouted for her from the corridor, and she hurried off. The conversation stayed in my mind, with images of a younger, more frightened Mary, surrounded by angry words. The compassion I so often felt for her returned and I resolved to ask Santer about her words when I next had the chance.

Our journey began the following day. The excitement of it drove everything else from my mind. Ours was a cavalcade that included camels and horses, two carriages with canopies, two other carriages with staples and household necessities, some pack donkeys and a small herd of goats, for fresh milking as we went. Joseph and Santer rode horses, as did our guards. The six slaves who came with us sat high on camel-back, surrounded by panniers of dates and olives, and loaves of bread wrapped in damp cloth. We would stay at inns, where they offered, but under tent cover where they did not. Our route took us past my old home, Szuzanna's inn, where some travellers sat under the grapevine in the late morning sun. As we passed, Hannah came out, her hands full with the familiar platters. Then I could scarcely see the place for the tears thickening my sight. Santer appeared beside the linen carriage I was riding in, an inquiring expression on his face. I gave him a watery smile. He stayed with me until the inn was long out of sight.

We passed through country where fields of wheat stood, with their stems shining gilt, and groves of olives and grapes spread their squares of varying green. To our right, as though forsaken by stronger mountains, lay exhausted hills of whitish brown, darker in their dry clefts.

The road was busy. Several long caravans worked their way southward, some of them with hosts of neck-collared slaves, calling from me all my old feelings of impotence and rage. Twice I watched fascinated as, sun glinting on their spears, a Roman phalanx marched by with orderly briskness. Each encounter brought our guards to high alert, riding back and forth to make sure none of our complement got entangled in the downward flow. At the most northerly part of our journey, Joseph stopped on a hilltop and bade us all look northwards, where far away we could see a shape, a single tall peak which was, he told us, Mount Tabor. It looked insubstantial, delicate, a misty shade of purple against the far pale sky.

We came to Caesarea shortly after noon on the eighth day of travel. The port itself was announced by a temple built atop a small hill just outside its precincts. Two colossal statues stood at the entrance to the temple, one of which was Caesar Augustus, the other a strong-faced woman with deep-set eyes, sturdy sandalled feet and capable hands. She held a scroll in her right hand, her left just touching the curls of the child at her side. She was the personification of Rome, Joseph told us, which in a way, the whole port was as well, its construction ordered decades ago by Herod when Caesar had gifted him the land following a victory of war.

I became familiar with the statues later, at this moment barely glancing at them, for my eyes were totally transfixed by the sea. It shone with the most extraordinary light, light which shimmered and spread and quivered. I was mesmerised. It seemed perfectly natural that there were two enormous towers serving as an entrance to this magnificence, and that six more statues stood in greeting to that restless beauty. When we at last came to the villa we were to live in, I was delighted to find that it was very close to the shore, and that my room looked straight out onto the undulating watery plain.

Caesarea was a busy port which also held the Mint, and was the seat of governmental affairs. I understood Joseph's decision completely when it became apparent that many of his business colleagues were also spending the summer there.

Our time there was utterly memorable for me. Both Santer and I were released from all but the most routine duties (to be present at mealtimes was included) and encouraged to swim in the warm waters of the Sea.

I was afraid at first, but soon learned how to dive into the waves, and quickly came to trust my body and its buoyancy. Soon I took for granted the pleasure of plunging into the clear warm rollers several times a day. Later, and because of my enthusiasm, Salome brought the baby to the water's edge, where he clearly delighted in the touch of the rushing tide on his feet. Salome held up her skirts and took his fat little body into the water, seeming to have as much pleasure as James did. Mary's face was softer these days, without the anxiety which usually pulled at her cheeks and veiled her eyes.

Early in our stay, Joseph took both Santer and I to a theatre, to see a touring company from Antioch performing two plays by an ancient Greek writer named Aristophanes. I was delighted by this whole event: by the theatre, its foyer decorated with marble bas-reliefs of the Muses and a curtained stage; by this evidence of adult fun, which I had had no idea of; and by the miracle of the play itself. The play we saw was The Nephelai, and though I did not understand its story very well, I was so utterly dedicated to the theatre from that first evening, that Joseph took us back to see the second play, Ecclesiazusae. This I understood very well — and took such pleasure in it that I went to two other of its performances, both in the afternoon, on my own. With both of the plays, my mind was illuminated by new avenues of thought, but with Ecclesiazusae in particular, I found a relevance to me, a connection with the rebellious part of me that shouted 'NO'. Aristophanes, through that play, showed me women being in the world in ways that were completely contrary to the rules of Judaea.

It was a marvel to me. I talked of it constantly, until both Santer and Joseph told me I was boring; so I stopped my chatter but not my thinking, and shortly afterward, I made my first attempt at writing. I wanted to thank Aristophanes, and thought of making a performance piece, a play, that was designed as a letter to him; the play would include a variety of adventures the letter would undergo before it was finally delivered to him in the Elysian Fields. Each of the adventures was to illuminate a point in Aristophanes's play. The fact that he was dead did not daunt me, for I believed in the connection of life and death and had no difficulty in imagining the action continuing beyond the arras of time.

Behind the villa was a wide terrace which held a long table, and here we ate most of our evening meals, shashlik and kebab, and the filled kebbeh that were Santer's favourite. There were always several kinds of small, dark fish in spiced oil, and semneh and zhug were plentiful in large shallow dishes, as well as platters of bread. After these came several kinds of pastries as well as green and honey wine and bowls of grapes, oranges and other fruit.

This meal particularly pleased Joseph, his face often broad with pleasure. 'Now this is excellent,' he would declare, looking about the table. 'Life by the sea seems to suit us all very well! A pity it is that we cannot live here all the year!'

'Yes!' agreed Santer at once, his face eager. 'There are so many interesting people here, from so many different places. I've been down to the ships, and talked with the sailors. I could hardly keep my mouth closed with their stories — of Constantinople, a whole city as magnificent as our temple, on a river broad as this sea. And another had been on a ship that went as far north as a ship can go and told me the ground there is ice-covered for almost half the year, and the forests full of wolves, giant black beasts called bears, and something called a stag — a four-footed beast like very tall goat, but red, and with horns like trees!'

'What did the sailors look like? Were they very different from us?' I wanted to know. 'Some of them. You could certainly tell the strangers,' laughed Santer. 'One of them had hair as yellow as lemons, another one like copper, and both had eyes of bright blue, like the sky. Very odd. They had bare chests and wore cloth tightly wrapped around each leg, and their arms were covered with pictures and writing.'

'How did you converse with them?' Joseph asked. 'Did they speak Aramaic, or did someone interpret for you?'

'They spoke Aramaic, enough for me to understand. Some spoke Greek,' he added, flashing a smile at me, 'so that helped.'

'What are they doing here, so far from their homes?' asked Mary.

'They are sailors, mother, come to trade,' replied Santer, and went on: 'Their swords —they are so different from Roman swords! Great thick arcs of steel, very intimidating. When I first went near their boats, they waved them in my face! Scary!'

'Why would they threaten you?' cried Mary, at once distressed.

'Because their cargo is valuable,' answered Joseph, then lightly turned the conversation back to animals and far away places. I realised he did that deliberately, so that Mary's face should not lose its fragile tenancy of happiness. This insight began a feeling of respect for him. The next morning, as Santer and I swam in the dawn-flushed water, I recalled the conversation I had had with Mary before we left Jerusalem, and wanted to ask him about it. But I found it hard to say the words directly, so thought it best to ask him about her family.

'Have you met your grandparents, Santer? What are they like?'

He ducks under a swell, and surfaces, blowing. 'They're all right. My grandfather is dead. My grandmother is — my mother is a lot like her. She lives with my uncle, since my grandfather died. My uncle has a small farm near Mount Carmel.'

'Was your mother betrothed to your father by marriage custom, when she was little?' He shakes his head and disappears beneath the swells again. The sun is just above the horizon and the whole of the sea's body was pearly with light. A pale gold pathway leads to the sun, still hazy in the gauze of dawn. Santer surfaces again, but some way off, his way of telling me he doesn't want to continue our talk. But I went over and over it in my private mind, and remembered another thing that Santer had told me when we talked about his mother marrying again, which was that, as children, she and Joseph had known one another in her parents' village. I wondered if Joseph had known Mary's first husband, and whether he knew what it was that made her so frightened of so many things.

An opportunity to ask Joseph directly came three days later. Santer had gone out quite early to go fishing with some youths his own age, and was still not back, even though it was well past midday. Mary was trying not to be anxious at his absence, and had gone to rest after our noonday meal. I was bored, having swum and done some writing all morning, and was looking forward to Santer's return to fill my afternoon. So when Joseph asked if I would like to accompany him on a visit to a scribe, I eagerly agreed.

When he came out of the scribe's office, he surveyed the street, squinting a little in the bright sun. He was wearing Greek-style clothes, which most people wore here in the summer, a shortened robe with slashed arms that made it suitable for driving, white with indigo trim. His sandals had decorated ankle medallions, and a thong across each major toe. I recognised for the first time that he was a handsome man.

'The horse needs a good run,' he said as he returned to the carriage. 'Don't you, Asheron?' he said to it, stroking its nose. Asheron blew threw hairy nostrils and lipped Joseph's sleeve. Joseph looked at me, eyebrows raised.

'There's a hippodrome just beyond the city, where I could let him stretch his legs. Would you like to come? I can easily take you back to the house if you'd rather not.'

'I should like it very much,' I said swiftly.

He nodded, rubbed Asheron's nose again, and jumped up into the carriage. Soon we were bowling along, weaving between other carriages and dodging around knots of pedestrians. Our way took us through the arch and up past the temple, its statues dazzling white in the sun. Below spread the immense Sea, today dark blue and dotted with boats. I wondered which one held Santer.

We turned up into the main road to the north. Joseph held the horse to a high trot as we went round tight corners on a road that also carried soldiers, and a strolling circus with jugglers practising their art, colours arching like rainbows in their hands. There were other carriages, people on horseback, and more than one herd of sheep, complete with shepherds, going towards the slaughter square. Joseph seemed to enjoy dodging all this traffic, and constantly spoke to the horse, praising its dexterity, its glossy beauty, and its lightfoot surety.

'You seem to know all the roads,' I observed as we turned off to the left down a track crisscrossed with wheelmarks. 'Have you driven here before?'

'Many times!' he agreed.

'Were you born near here? Does your family live near-by?'

'If they did, we would certainly visit them,' he said dryly, neatly avoiding a small boy who suddenly ran onto the track.

'How stupid of me,' I said, feeling hot and embarrassed.

He just nodded. I kept silent, not knowing how to proceed, but after he had made one or two general — and amusing — comments about other travellers on the road, I began to feel easier, and soon our conversation flowed again. We turned off the track, went through a wide gateway, and were in the hippodrome, where several other horses were being exercised. Joseph pulled up and had a word with the man at the entrance, gave him a coin, and we were off again, this time at Asheron's chosen speed. Halfway round the second lap, I dared to ask Joseph where he had been born.

'Arimathea,' he said with a reflective smile. 'How nearly I was Greek! Except that my mother and father were Jewish, of course,' he added wryly.

He told me how he had come to be born on that tiny island in the Thracian archipelago. His father had been the personal scribe and steward to a Greek sea-merchant, who paid him a very good salary. He had been betrothed to Joseph's mother while they ware young. When her parents died of the pestilence, her brother brought Joseph's mother to where his father was living, and they were married at once. When he had amassed enough wealth, Joseph's father left the Greek's employ to return to Jerusalem.

'The merchant was generous,' said Joseph, 'insisting my parent go on one of his vessels bound for Tyre, and charging only half the usual amount! My mother did not know she was pregnant when they embarked, but was so violently ill during the voyage that when a storm drove the vessel to take refuge in Arimathea's lagoon, she prayed that the ship might stay there until she was well again. The repairs to the ship took some time, during which my mother discovered she was pregnant. She refused to travel until after I was born. We didn't leave there until I was six months old.' He looked pleased, as if recalling some happy memory, and told of how his father managed to find scribing employment on the island, which stood him in very good stead when he returned to Jerusalem. His words disturbed me, so much so that my plan of asking him about Mary as a child went completely out of my head. I began to think about my own parents as a couple, to wonder if they had been from another country, dying as their boat was driven to shore by a sudden storm. I wondered if my father had perhaps been a scribe, or even a sea merchant, like the Greek.

'Well?' asked Joseph, eyebrow arched in query. 'No comments on my unusual entry into life?'

'It's just that I was wondering about my own father,' I said by way of apology. 'What about him?'

'Who he was, whether he was born on some island, like you were.'

Joseph's face went blank. Then he frowned and guided Asheron to the outer perimeter of the track, where he drew the horse to a halt. He looked at me intently. 'You do not know who your father was? Did not your mother tell you?'

'I do not know who she was, either.'

His eyes searched my face intently. 'But the woman at the inn, the one from Magdala? Joshua said she was your mother.'

'Did he? But he knew she was not, I told him so the first day that we met.'

The frown became a scowl, his eyes full of disapproval. 'Perhaps he did not say so in so many words,' he admitted. 'It was a natural assumption for me to make. I had no reason to believe otherwise.' He rested his forearms on his thighs, his eyes riveted on mine. 'Tell me how you came to be at the inn.'

I was aware of something large at the back of his question, which I answered as succinctly as I could, feeling very uncomfortable, and as if I had done something very wrong. When I'd finished, he held his gaze on me for several long moments before saying: 'So. If you do not know your parents, how do you know you are Jewish?'

'I have wondered that!' I exclaimed, astounded that he had at once come to a point that had taken me years to consider. 'Do I look Jewish?'

He gave a mirthless bark of laughter. 'It's not always that easy to tell. We all look like brothers in this part of the world.' He questioned me thoroughly then, but I knew nothing more than I had told him, and didn't think he wanted to know of my love of goats, or the dark crevasse from which Szuzanna had saved me.

'What about clothes?' he asked. 'She could have learned something from those.'

'I had none,' I told him, thinking of the filthy scrap of violet cord that Szuzanna said had been tangled in my hair, but whether by accident or intent, none could say. Joseph picked up the reins again, taking us around the rest of the track and out to the east road. A mile or so later, he turned Asheron back to Caesarea. Neither of us spoke for quite a time, my own thoughts being occupied with the possibility that I could have been born in Egypt, where, Decius had told us, triangular buildings of stone had been built so tall that the priests were able to climb to the top and converse with their gods. Who could, perhaps, even be my gods.

I quite liked the idea of having lots of gods about, it

seemed more protecting, and friendly.

'I want you to promise me something,' Joseph said suddenly, interrupting this pleasing reverie. 'I don't want you to tell Mary of this. Let her continue to think that you are the daughter of the woman at the inn. Will you do that?'

'Why?' I said at once.

He blew out his breath in a quick little sigh. 'Because I think it will upset her, and I don't want her to be upset.'

I thought of him turning the conversation, so she would stop thinking about swords being brandished at Santer. 'It's very hard for me not to tell the truth,' I began, and then, 'Oh!' We had breasted a small rise, to see the city below, and beyond it, the Sea, glimmering milkily under a high hazy sky. The city glowed in its creamy stone. I could see all the way to the harbour's end, past the statues where several large fishing boats were anchored, black at this distance on that sheening stretch.

'Do you not think a small diversion from the truth is permissible if it stops another person being distressed?' Joseph asked.

I thought of Szuzanna's lies to me before she was obviously ill. 'Perhaps I do. Did someone hurt Mary when she was a little girl?'

He gave me a quick look. 'Why do you ask that? What has she said?'

'Nothing that I can understand, but I think something must have made her the way she is, frightened so easily. I don't think babies are born like that.'

'No,' he said, half under his breath.

'What was she like when you first met her?'

'Oh — shy,' he said brusquely. 'I didn't know her very well.'

His face had closed. He looked at me coldly and repeated again his wish that I refrain from telling Mary that Szuzanna was not my mother. His approach to me stiffened my pride, and rather than answer him, I merely bent my head then turned away from him to watch the mellowing of the afternoon light on the Sea.

Later that evening, as we had our last swim, Santer and I talk of the day. He is full of enthusiasm for fishing: 'I tell you, Mary, it's marvellous! Just you and the fishers and the water, and the boat! The sea so deep you cannot see the bottom, the water clear, but it's just so deep. And the sky — it's very fine!'

'And did you catch any fish?'

'Two hundred and nine, in two nettings!'

'Perhaps you could become a fisherman,' I say provocatively, 'I'm sure Joseph would set you up with a boat.'

'No chance,' he sighs, 'Joseph is too rich.' I chuckle, but say nothing.

'It would be very worthwhile work,' he says defensively.

'It would,' I agree heartily. We tread water, gazing westward at the glowing light. A pair of gulls wheel, turning inward from the Sea. After a time, Santer shakes his head, saying 'Huh.' I look a question at him. 'Just that — I suppose it could get a little — uh — .' His voice trailed away.

'Uh — boring?' I say sweetly.

He makes a great leap in the water and came down on my head, pushing me under and away from him. 'Goatgirl,' he throws at me when I surface.

'Figboy!' I retort, and streak for the shore.

We dried ourselves and sat on the minuscule pier, watching the twilight deepen. The sea was lavender and a flickering pewter, with charcoal shadows against the shore. In the east, the huge star of evening shone with a steady light.

'I wonder what I will do when I am an adult,' I say, struck for the first time by the thought of planning my future.

'You will marry someone rich, Joseph will see to that,

and not work at all,' replies Santer idly, rubbing at his hair.

'No,' I say at once, 'I don't think Joseph will find me a husband, not after today. Anyway, I don't want to marry.'

'Why not?'

'Because if you are a wife, you have to do what your husband tells you, no matter how stupid or drunk or wrong he is. And if he changes his mind, he throws you off like a bad shoe. No, I shall be like Szuzanna, and do what I want to do.'

There was a little silence after I'd said this. The twilight has now reached that stage where it seemed almost that you could scoop it up and lave it on your face. Then I begin to talk about the possibility of not being Jewish. The evening star was on the shoulder of the sky before we had taken this topic as far as we could. Santer was quite taken with the idea that I might be related to Cleopatra, who preferred to die rather than (as I now phrased it) be Augustus's slave. But Santer knows that if we begin to talk of slaves, the sun will likely rise on our discussion, so he stands up. We go back to the villa, with one bird giving several sharp cries as its sleep is disturbed by our passage below.

'Going fishing again tomorrow?'

'Yes. Very early, before dawn.'

'I wish I could come.'

But he is silent, not even sketching out a wild proposal for my inclusion. And I know then he doesn't want me to come, that this was something he is on his own, with new friends. I look at him, and he turns quickly to look at me. His teeth flash white in his dark face as he smiles.

'Well, you can't,' he says cordially, and whatever sting I might have felt in being barred from this activity is blunted by the affection in his voice.

It was out on the sea in those cool, nebulous dawns that I first opened my mind to accepting my mother's truth.

At first, I shivered at the thought and thrust it away; but when I least expected it, when I was in thrall to the silky breathing water, so completely owned by its opal translucence, no sound at all but the lilting of the ripples as they accepted the nets, our bodies blocky and dark against all that milk and pearl, in it would slide, that question, with all its flaming force: what if I am the Child?

When the winds from the Sea became cool even in the sun, Joseph arranged for us to leave Caesarea. He purposely timed our departure to coincide with the departure of the army for its winter station in Jerusalem, saying, 'There will be fewer dogs on the roads they have just travelled.'

I was divided about leaving; I felt as if the villa at Caesarea was really my home, far more so than Joseph's home in the City. But I was excited at the thought of seeing Lazarus and Martha again, and resuming my studies with Decius, for I had begun to think very seriously of my future. I had tried to discuss this with Santer, but he would not be serious, saying only that I would marry, as every proper woman does. His suggestions, apart from marrying, were ridiculous, and included becoming a Roman centurion (so I could legitimately give orders), a shepherd (so I could have my freedom of the hills), or an artefacts trader, like Joseph (so I could satisfy my curiosity about everything). I could not see any future very clearly, but knew that a return to my studies would clarify my mind.

We travelled more quickly on the return journey, the tall finger of Jericho's tower coming into sight on the morning of the seventh day; we were back in the formal comfort of Joseph's home before evening had thrown its purple shadows over Jerusalem's warm, beige walls.

It was very much warmer here than in Caesarea, the garden still full of the mingled scents of a dozen or more luxuriant blooms. Running from it to my room, I came upon myself unexpectedly in the visitor's mirror, positioned at a juncture to allow guests to order their hair before returning indoors. My first thought was 'Who is that woman?', and then I recognised myself. I could see I was taller now, my black hair thick and curling beside a long-cheeked face which had a pointed chin. My eyes were dark and startled under bold-stroked brows. My breasts were obvious beneath the pleated folds of my tunic, and my bare, brown shoulders were rounder than those of a young girl. I ran to my room, looking at my hands, and down at my sandalled feet. Then I wanted to see as much of myself as possible, so I took off my clothes and examined my body with a small hand mirror, the miniature riots of curls that now shaded armpit and thigh, and the hipbones which pulled my belly into a delicate curve between them. I held my hands under my breasts, examining their ruddy brown nipples which, as I watched, puckered and changed their shape. I thought about a baby sucking at the nipples, and a tickling sensation ran from my breasts to my intimate folds. This startled me. I thought of the suckling again, but nothing happened. I decided I liked my body except for my knees, which were knobbly-ugly, and my broad feet with their outspread toes. My toenails were ragged and I thought with dismay of Joseph's nails, smoothly polished and cut.

I lifted the mirror to my face. My neck was not too thick. I looked at my ears, bending them forward a little, the first time I had ever examined their amusing, wayward curves. My nose was shortish, with a little curve in it, and high-cut nostrils. I looked at my mouth for a long time and decided I didn't much like it: it seemed to lack the generous beauty of Mary's mouth, and to be too wide. But at least the upper lip was shapely; the lower one was just ordinary. I put the mirror down and thought about my body. I was not like Szuzanna, whose body had been large and soft, or Mary, who was short and very slender. 'But my body seems quite all right,' I told myself, pleased. 'And there's nothing terribly wrong with my face.'

By the time we had been back in Jerusalem for two weeks, Santer had resumed his studies, but I had not. I was getting very impatient to do so. With this in mind, I asked Joseph one morning if I could speak with him about it sometime during the coming day. I knew he had a full morning at the Council, and with the resumption of his work, his old, rather brusque manner had returned, but I was not affected by it now. I went to his private rooms after my breakfast, to catch him before he left the house. He was just finishing eating, and was wiping his lips. He frowned as he looked at me, then handed the cloth to a slave, rubbed his cheeks briskly, and lightly patted his hands together.

'I have Council this morning and again in the late afternoon, then a debate this evening,' he said briskly, 'but I'll return to eat at noon, and we will talk then.' After he'd gone, I went to the garden, but Boaz was not there, so I sought out Mary who, with Salome, was bathing fat-bodied little James. He was sitting in a large bowl, smacking the water with one hand and gasping as droplets flew up in his face. He was pleased to see me, his two teeth adding humour to his wide wet smile. I talked and cooed with him while Salome hovered over him fondly, and Mary watched, her face relaxed.

Salome took James from the water, holding him on her knee as she wrapped him in a large towel. I turned to Mary and in the lightest, most casual voice possible, asked what kind of studying she had done when she was a girl. In spite of my easy tones, her face shadowed as always when her girlhood was mentioned, and something I could only call pain took the light from her eyes.

'We did not do that sort of thing,' she replied, her voice low. 'We worked in the house, or if the time was scarce, in the groves, helping to pick.'

'What about your friends, did they study?' I kept my voice casual, but I could see I had lost her.

'No-o-o. Excuse me, I have to go to — ,' and she got up, still holding one of James's little garments, and hurriedly left the room.

I drew up my knees and put my arms around them, staring at James, not actually seeing him, seeing a young thin girl in a house where nothing was soft. At the edges of my hearing, behind the baby's merry gabble, I could hear a snarl.

'I did,' declared Salome suddenly, making me jump.

'Did what?' I asked stupidly.

'Study, as a girl. I wasn't always a nurse slave, living in this Mah-deserted city!' Her voice was fierce. 'Until I was captured and forced to come here, I was the favoured daughter of Enlib, my father, who had lands as far as the horizon, and so many horses their hooves made thunder for over a mile. And my name is not Salome, it's Zeralia, most-loved one, and I was born to marry a prince — .' Pride and anger flashed from her eyes. Her voice croaked, and choked off. James's chubby fingers pulled at her neckline, she held him close, her arms shaking, her eyes tightly closed. From their corners, tears slid. Hoarse sobs broke from her throat, troubling James, who also began to cry. Compassion flooded me. I moved to sit beside her, put my arm around her shoulders. I tried to take James, but she clutched at him and shook her head. 'No, please. It's good to hold him, he comforts me'. So I squatted near her, just being with her. After a little, when she was calmer and James was happy again, crawling off and on her lap, she began to talk with me.

She told me of her home, 'a huge tent, bigger, much bigger than those we used when we went to Caesarea, and woven with many colours, scarlet, black, yellow and blue.' Her father had been wealthy, owning a large band of horses which eventually became the target of foreign raiders. Then, in a night of terror, the guards around their tents were slain by soft-footed assassins, and she plucked from her sleep by a fierce-armed man who had ripped her garments open to expose her breasts, shouted something triumphant to other marauders, raped her, then tied her hands and added her to the line of rope-bound people tethered to each horse. Her sister, Anya, older by two years, was one of these. The other prisoners shuffled and pushed together so that they could speak.

'Anya said both mother and father had been killed, run through with swords by the first marauders, who knew father was the leader,' she told me. Her voice trembled, and she had to stop for several minutes. The marauders began their journey with their prisoners that night. After three days of travel, pulled behind the horses, given food only at the beginning and end of the day, the slave-raider's cavalcade had split. She had not seen her sister since. When she was sold to Joseph, he told her her name was Salome. I was silenced by her story, but my face shouted my sympathy. She looked at me with shy glances, hesitant about her open heart. Everything I could think to say to her sounded so small, but I stammered out a little of my early days. Between us grew a wordless empathy. When James was bored with playing, beginning to fret, she wrapped him and cuddled him, giving him a hard crust to chew. The air around grew gentle.

'What were you studying?' I wanted to know. I kept my voice quiet as James was falling asleep.

'About Inanna, our goddess, who looks after the most cherished cord of existence, love.' She told me that in her country, the Divine Being was a mother-goddess, and that women were cherished and respected because of their direct link with Her, through the bringing of new life into Life. She looked down at James, who was now deeply asleep, and I saw how she was connected to him, how he had given her back, in one tiny way, the daily practice of her beliefs and so a precious link back to them.

She told me of their great moon-priestess, Enheduanna, who was also a poet. Enheduanna had lived two thousand years ago, and was probably the first poet in the world.

'Would you like to hear one of Enheduanna's poems?' she asked me shyly. 'You have them?' I cried, incredulous.

'I had memorised some of them, I was lucky.'

Her voice was round, like the pigeon's coo, as she spoke:

> Lady of all the essences, full light,
> good woman clothed in radiance
> whom heaven and earth love,
> temple friend of An,
> you wear great ornaments,
> you desire the tiara of the high priestess
> whose hand holds the seven essences.
>
> O my lady, guardian of all the great essences,
> you have picked them up and hung them
> on your hand.
> You have gathered the holy essences and worn them
> tightly on your breasts.

She recited them first in a language I could not understand, one full with curling sounds and throaty stops, like fingernails tapping sporadically on little drums. Then, line by line, she translated the words, her eyes closed and her bronze skin seeming polished with pleasure. At the end of her words, she opened her eyes triumphantly and I felt the poem as a gift. I touched her hand to thank her; she smiled back at me, but I saw a small tear slip from the corner of her eye. James was still asleep in her arms and I, full of sorrow and respect for her, could think of no way to comfort her. She sighed a little, and laid her cheek against James's head. The silence spun around us, warm and alive, full of strength. Around us or from us seemed to come a blossoming scent, or perhaps it was drifting in from the garden through the windows high above.

When she went to put James down, and attend to her other duties, I went with her, helping where I could. I called her by her name, Zeralia, and her eyes gleamed under quickly lowered lids. We were friends from that time on, as much as we could be in the courses of our differing lives. When she had to go to the laundry room, where the other women were, I went to my room and set down a little of what I had experienced; how fulfilling, somehow, it felt to know of a woman who had been writing poetry as long ago as two thousand years.

Joseph was scribing something on a long scroll when I came into his room. He offered me a cup of lemon water, and gestured to one of the cross-legged stools at right angles to his desk. I was feeling very grown-up, and happy, after my time with Zeralia. 'When will I be going back to my studies?' I asked, taking a mouthful of water and meeting his eyes. The time by the Sea had burnished his skin to a rich umber; his beard curled vigorously, his mouth was firm and red within its glossy black frame of hair.

'Your studies. Yes,' he said, looking back at me with a small frown. He carefully placed his stylus on its brackets and came round his desk toward me. He had resumed his robe, white and finely spun; it draped in perfect folds from the oval, lapis-stoned shoulder clasp to his supple, sandalled feet.

'I admit I am in a quandary about you, Mary,' he said finally. 'I am finding it very difficult to see what is to become of you. It was one thing when I thought you were the daughter of a respectable inn-keeper, whose home was once Magdala. That's perfectly respectable blood, and the inn self-owned, so I could present a dowry price legitimately.' I heard his words with a kind of creeping horror, my body turning cold. 'But you are not such a girl at all,' he continued, 'and there is no point in thinking I could arrange an advantageous marriage without some inquiry. I can't. I am sure you understand that. Every man likes to know what he is to get.'

My muscles were stiff; those around my mouth hurt my jaw. 'But I have no wish for marriage,' I replied curtly.

He bent his head, pursed his lips, nodded slowly. 'That's as well, and very sensible. But if it is not to be marriage, then what is the point of further learning? You already have more than is needed to run a household. Where would more benefit you? There are few avenues for an unwed girl. You will forgive me for being so blunt.' My eyes felt dry in their sockets, and my fingers thin as twigs. He leaned back onto his desk, folding his arms; his gaze was clear and objective. 'Perhaps you have some ideas?' His voice was pleasant, inviting, curious. 'I must say immediately that I am not trying to say you must leave this house. Do not think that. This is your home, for as long as you wish it to be. But it will inevitably occur sometime in the near future that you will want to marry, for you are a woman already. Your beauty has already caught one eye, and expect I shall hear a discreet inquiry. How will I be able to answer it? It requires a great deal of thought.'

I sat upright in my humiliation and looked at him coldly. 'If I could resume my studies, I could work to become a teacher, like Decius.'

'A teacher?' His eyebrows lifted in surprise. His voice was very calm, as if I was ill. 'Women are not teachers, Mary, they are not suitable for it. I thought you knew that. Who would hire you? What good would such learning do?'

I could sit no longer and got up. My body was seized

with a fit of trembling, so that my teeth chattered in my head. 'In another country, I could and I will,' I cried, incoherently. 'Somewhere will want me, I will go there.' To my horror, I began to cry, huge wracking gulps, tears flinging down my cheeks, my chest thudding with pain. He came over to me, taking an orarium from his pocket-fold and handing it to me. His hand patted my arm.

'Come, stop this. I am sorry to have distressed you so much. I did not mean to do so. Forgive me if my words were blunt, but I know you are a strong-headed girl and do not dodge the truth.' I sniffled miserably. 'Look, what I shall do is allow you to return to your studies until I have worked out a proper plan. That's the best thing, I think.' He gave my shoulder a little squeeze. 'Does that make you feel better?' I felt anything but better, I felt useless and worthless, but I still had no control of my voice, so just nodded and held the orarium, now a sodden rag, to my watering nose.

I draggled out of his room and back to my own, where the paper I had been writing on still lay on my pallet. I thought of Zeralia and her terrors and despised myself for being a coward. I blew my nose and clenched my teeth, staring round my room stonily. I most find a way to get control of my life, I thought. But what, how? I thought of the inn, and of the life I might have had if Szuzanna had lived. I could go back there, I thought, and have my freedom. Malachi would welcome me.

But within minutes, my thoughts racing, I had devised another plan. I would discover from Decius where women could be teachers, in what city; I would return to the inn, earn money for travelling, and then make my way there. It would undoubtedly be Greece or Rome.

I even worked out that I would go there via Caesarea, where I would easily find passage on one of the many ships that I had seen in its harbour.

With that plan clear in my mind, I felt happier,

stronger. In the garden that evening, waiting for Santer to join me after his time with Mary, I felt a little glow of warmth inside me that the chill of the night could not touch. But I had not even begun to outline them fully before Santer destroyed them.

'What are you thinking of?' he cries sharply. 'You cannot travel alone, you're a woman. What do you think would happen if you walked through the robber hills we've just come through? Or went up to the captain of a boat and asked to have a passage to anywhere? What do you think they would think of you, a woman alone with no companions?' 'What should he think of me?' I demanded hotly. 'Why should I not go on a boat if I choose?' But despair lay behind my words for, blindingly, I know he is right. Not once in my plotting had I considered who I was, myself as others see me.

'You know very well why not,' he says shortly, leaning on the parapet.

'I *will* live the life I want to,' I storm at him through clenched teeth. 'I will *not* marry someone I've never met, three hundred years older than me, like your mother had to do, just because I am living in this place. It's different in other places, and I want to go there!'

'Be quiet,' he commands me. 'I want to think.'

His words make my heart leap up and all my protestations die away. There is no sound but the querulous mutter of the palm fronds, dry and bitter in a snaking wind. My nose is very cold. I hold its tip between my thumb and forefinger, to warm it, my other hand tucked under my armpit. After a few minutes, Santer smacks the parapet with an open hand, the sound extra loud in the still, cold night.

'Look,' he begins, turning to me, then laughs to see me holding my nose. He pulls me to him, puts my back against his chest and wraps his arms around me, speaking in my ear. His voice is low and vibrant, full of conspiratorial excitement. 'I am not happy either, and I am almost as captive as you,' he says swiftly. 'Joseph is a good man, but I do not like his plans for me and there is little I can do to change them. If I carry on this path, it will become harder and harder to break free — years in the synagogue don't precisely prepare you for a range of occupations. I passionately want knowledge, but not only one kind, only one point of view, and I don't want to spend my whole life in study. I want a much wider life. I tell you, Mary, some of the things I have in my head — '. He draws in his breath, and his arms tighten around me. I feel understood, and accompanied, and warmed by a thudding joy. 'But Joseph won't open other doors for me,' he continued. 'He says he knows my mother has visions of me being a high priest, and he has vowed to her he will pave my way there.' He sighs and is silent for a while.

Then with a little shake of his head, he continues: 'So your plan to leave connects with thoughts of my own, and we shall go together.' I squeal, and hug his arm. 'But we have to plan carefully. Where to go, how much money we shall need. I've got some, and perhaps we could both work at the inn, although it seems likely that Joseph will search for me, and is sure to think of looking there. But we will go, and travelling together, brother and sister, you will be safe. And my mother is safe here, and the baby still small.'

'How will you tell her you are going?'

Another sigh. 'I'll have to think about how.' He shakes me a little. 'We must think of where to go, where is best for us. Joseph has maps. I'm sure Decius has some. Ask him about his journey here, how he came. But I think it is silly to go now that it is coming into winter. I think we should wait until spring, leave just before Passover, when there will be many people on the road. What do you think? Can you wait that long?'

'If Joseph hasn't made any decisions about me I can,'
I cry softly. 'Oh Santer, what would I do without you?'

'Get your head lopped off or worse,' he replies, taking
his arms from around me and standing away from the
wall. 'Not a good look, goatgirl! Come on, let Acton get
to the lamps. I'm for the kitchen though, I'm hungry.
What about you?'

The midnight snack soothed my stomach as readily
as Santer's words had sent the little scorpions of dark
thought scuttling away from the front of my mind. I lay
on my pallet and thought of Zeralia, of the terrors she
had survived and the slavery she bore now, made easier
by her love for baby James. And Enheduanna rose in my
mind, clearly as if she was standing in the room with
me, a small, well-breasted woman holding a smoking
bowl and a little bronze bell. Her words came back to
me, in Zeralia's voice: *you have gathered the holy
essences and worn them tightly on your breast*. I saw the
essences as truths, fragrant and modest like herbs, held
in Inanna's heart and bound with the green thong of
constancy. I thought again that the words of Enheduanna had travelled over two thousand years, through
distances and people I could scarcely imagine, carried
through terror and rape and despicable hardship by Zeralia to my eager ear. I shivered in the darkness, pierced
by an immense thought. I knew that in Rome, women
were poets, and Enheduanna had been a poet two thousand years before. Could I be a poet? And I thought that
I could. I will leave Jerusalem, I vowed to myself in my
private mind, find a place to study, and become a poet,
writing the truths of the world. I held the thought, it
glimmered in my mind like a rope of light. Warmth
crept up from my feet, to my stomach, across my breasts.
I turned on my back and slept.

Less than a week later, a household oversight gave both Santer and I the opportunity to travel together, and be able to speak openly with one another. While we were in Caesarea, our household linens should have been taken to the vast dyeworks at Magdala, Joseph having decided he wanted all the new linen for the house to be dyed the new burnt-orange shade that had come into fashion. Our linens were presently indigo and madder. This new orange, the colour of ripe persimmons, would complement them well. But the order had not been given and if the journey was not made immediately, the dyeworks would close for the winter, and the work have to wait until they reopened in the spring.

This task fell to Santer and me, to take the linens in a single carriage, which Acton would drive. Santer was to ride horseback, scouting the road and hillsides as we went, for the road to Magdala was north, into the wild hills of Galilee. At the last moment, due to the force of Mary's anxiety, a fourth member was added to our expedition, a small, dark-faced man named Hiram, laconic and with slightly bowed legs. We set out in a cold dawn and made very good time, much faster than the Caesarea trip, with no babies to consider, or household troops, or slaves on loping camel-back. And the linens, many as they were, scarcely filled the cart.

As the day warmed, the road filled with traffic, long-gowned and short: mendicants and aristocrats, and several Roman cohorts. The road paralleled Jordan's flow; frequently, great flocks of sheep and goats were to be seen scrambling down deep-cut paths to the gorge below. We also went (to me) inspiringly close to Mount Tabor. The inn we stayed at that evening was dominated by its great presence, bringing me thoughts of the great pyramids of Egypt built to speak to the gods. My dreams that night were full of crests and purple slopes, unseen voices, and high roomed houses full of crystal and mist. As we neared Tiberias, a city in the throes of construction which, rumour said, was being built on an ancient burial ground, the shifting clouds of afternoon seemed to spotlight the palace of Herod Antipas on the hill at the city's back. Its Greek sculptures were so lifelike that at first I thought them real people, which set me to thinking about the reasons behind the graven image ban.

Magdala lay five miles north of the new city, its dyeworks sited along the banks of a small tributary river that ran into smooth, pale Lake Gennesaret. This lake was also called the Sea of Chinnereth and, if Antipas had his way, our garrulous landlord told us, it would become Lake Tiberias. I thought of Szuzanna spending her child years here, perhaps playing in the waters of the lake as I had played in the waters of the Sea.

The dyeworks were fascinating, great vats of colour flanked by thin catwalks along which sure-footed youths ran, turning the linen with long-poled rakes. The smell came to meet us well before we reached the works, so acrid that it stunned the nose, and thus soon became unnoticeable. The day was bright and the dyeboys seemed like black silhouettes dancing in front of my eyes. Santer stayed with the cart and horses, while Hiram and Acton and I carried the linens down the little path to the works, crossing a small bridge that spanned the river from which the works drew their water. Leah, the administrator, introduced herself and her husband. He bore all the signs of having once been one of the dyework's nimble youths: he was small, with a merry face, but the skin of his hands and arms was black. Black feet peeped out from beneath his robe, against which his brown sandals seemed a pattern rather than a pair of shoes. He ducked his head in greeting a couple of times, and went off with some of our linen piled high on his arms.

Leah listened to my request, while Hiram and Acton brought the rest of the linens, and her head nodded emphatically all the time I spoke, jowls swelling and reducing with every nod. She burst into speech almost before I stopped speaking. 'But of course madam, I know exactly what you want — isn't it our very own colour, and one that we are proud of?' She glanced at the array of swatches displayed all across the back wall.

'It goes so well with indigo, don't you think? And safflower — and scarlet too, I think myself, though the purists hold up their hands. But what do they know of the ordering of a household, is what I ask madam, and the answer as you very well may know, is nothing, nothing at all!' She fingered the linens knowledgeably and drew a length of them through her hand. 'Very fine quality, very good texture, madam, they will dye beautifully. And how long will you be in Magdala? Excellent! We do the best quality work madam, and as I am sure you know, that cannot be rushed.'

She then began to talk prices, and I went into spirited conversation with her, haggling so well that both of us were very pleased with ourselves when the bargaining was done. In the week that the dyeing of the linens took, Santer and I explored the little town, finding the house where Szuzanna's people had once lived but none of her family remained there, they having moved to the larger city of Capernaum to the north. One afternoon, we drove north until we could see the shapes of that Roman outpost city on the north-east tip of the lake. But mostly, we spent long afternoons by the lakeside, sitting in the cool autumn sun discussing our future and trying to decide where to go.

Athens was possible, and greatly appealed to me; Santer had been thinking of Rome, but that was now out of the question, because a new senatorial decree had just deported four thousand adult Jewish and Egyptian freedmen to Sardinia. 'Tiberius despises us,' says Santer flatly, 'he says we don't conform. Why doesn't he say what he means —he wants us to deny our religion, to take on Roman belief! So much for their vow of respect — it ends in sending us to a completely foreign country to kill bandits!'

'It's slavery, really,' I say as I have said so often. I look out over the water, a delicate blue in almost imperceptible swells under the high cool dome of afternoon. No boats interrupt the horizon, but a lone bird is wheeling north, an incisive shape against the sky. On the air comes the fragrant scent of cedars, and intermittently, the vaguer scent of drying flowers. I think of my anger when Joseph had so coldly outlined my life: like fury in a cage. Even the memory of it clutches at my stomach.

'Is there anywhere we can go that would put us beyond the rules of Rome?' He begins to throw flat pebbles across the tips of the wavelets. 'East is the only direction, the spice lands of Indie. Rome doesn't have a hold there.'

'The land of ivory, from the monsters called elephant!' I sit up, very excited by this.

'But I don't know if we could study there,' he continues, 'and the route is, I think, quite dangerous.'

'Perhaps we could go there later,' I offer, reluctant to dismiss entirely a visit to this fantastical land.

He throws back his head in outright laughter. 'Of course we could!' he agreed, his eyes sparkling at me. He pulls my big toe. 'You are truly a goatgirl — you'd trot anywhere on those scrambly feet, I think!'

'I would, yes,' is my rejoinder. I prop my head on one hand, and with the other, begin scratching patterns and roadways in the dirt. 'I think I've always been curious about other places, wanted to know what they were like.'

'Mmm,' he says, 'and you've infected me!' Propped on his elbows, he leans back and looks out to the lake, calm and pale as if held in a bowl. Far to our right, a squat black boat edges forward. 'I think we should go to Alexandria, you know,' he says consideringly.

'Alexandria!' the name burst like a great light in my mind, for Decius had often spoken of this famous city of learning, which seemed to have given birth to many truths. Then the light died. 'But Alexandria too is now part of Rome, and the library burned after Augustus refused to withdraw that decree,' I wail.

'Mmm. But it's still a great centre of learning, the university is still open. And there is a second library, someone at the synagogue said, which hasn't been burned. It's been added to over the years, so it's almost as good as the first one.' He pushes himself up and hooks his arms around his knees, ticking off on his fingers the reasons Alexandria should be our goal. 'We know it's a city of learning, and we also know that it has welcomed people from other countries, including ours, for over three hundred years. There's a big Jewish community there. It's still considered the study centre of the world, which is the main reason people go there. And even though there are Romans there, the military power of the city has been removed to Canopus, Augustus saw to that. So there's no danger of military action, and the Roman rule probably won't be too harsh. And finally, the main language is Greek, which we have already learned to speak.' He looks at me, clearly waited for an accolade. 'We can stagger along in it,' I say. 'I don't know how we'll be when speaking with a real Greek!' The light in my mind began to dazzle again. 'Do you really think we could? It would be marvellous, I think.'

'I don't see why not,' he says stoutly. 'We know how to get there. All we have to do is plan it carefully, and have enough money to go.'

'How much would we need to get there? How would we go, how long would it take? I'd love to go — do you think it would be expensive? It's not that far; would we go by land, or on the sea?'

Santer smiles broadly and rapidly clapped his fingers and thumb together as he did to show me I was gabbling. 'I don't know yet, goatgirl. If we agree on Alexandria, let's make a list of the information we need, and what our expenses would be.'

'We agree on Alexandria!' I tell him happily. 'For the moment, it's enough just to think about it!' I fall silent, closing my eyes and turning my face to the sun. Alexandria! How lovely its name is, curving like the waves of the Sea. When I open my eyes, it was to see a tiny movement. Out of the sheltering of rock at our backs, a bright green lizard has come, rush and stop, rush and stop, testing the air for danger with its slithering tongue. Santer follows my gaze. We stayed very still. The lizard comes on until it is full in the sun, not six inches from me. The underside of its jaw is almost the same pale blue colour as the lake; its eyes are shiny, like bits of black mirror. It is poised for long moments, then slowly relaxes. After several minutes, I reach forward, millimetre by millimetre to touch it. In the snip of the second before it darts off, I feel the indescribable softness of its living, textured skin.

'Typical,' comments Santer, getting to his feet. 'Admit it, you *had* to touch it, didn't you? Just looking wasn't enough.'

I rise to this bait as he expects me to. 'I wouldn't know how it felt if I had not!' We argue all the way back to the inn about the getting of experience, and where the dividing line is between participating and interference. Later, we ate our evening meal on the grass outside the inn, after which Hiram went inside to buy beer. At the horizon, the sky was deep with a clear green. Duets of gulls wheeled in the darkening sky. Suddenly Santer asks me whether I thought involving his mother in our departure might not be a good idea. 'What I've been thinking is that I shall wait until Joseph is away over the night, and tell her, give her time to get over the first shock of it, and then keep talking with her until she accepts why I must go. What do you think?'

'I've been trying not to think of your mother,' I tell him, 'because when I do, it's all worry. She — her days spin around you, do you know that?'

'Mmm. She's much better since she had James, though.'

'More relaxed, yes. But there is no doubt you are at the centre of her life, even so.'

'I've always been able to talk with her. I think she will understand, if I can just put the whole thing clearly.'

'You don't think, if you tell your mother and she accepts it, that we could go openly, tell Joseph as well? It would be so much easier if we could.'

He grimaces. 'Perhaps. But it's likely that he would organise me into studying the Old Words there as well, and appoint someone to guardian me, whose house I would have to live in.' He gives me a hard stare, adding, 'He might disagree with you coming. He wouldn't see the point.'

'That settles that, then,' I declare roundly. 'Will you tell your mother I am going with you?'

He reflects for a long moment. 'Not at first. It's not relevant. But afterwards. Does it matter?'

'No.' I think about Mary, and our rather nebulous connection. 'She probably won't even realise I am gone, until someone tells her. I don't think she will miss me.'

'Perhaps not,' he says as we begin to gather up the remnants of our meal. 'But she definitely accepts that you are part of my life, now and in the future. She told me so.'

'Did she?' I am quite taken aback. 'When? What did she say?'

He shrugged. 'Not one specific thing. Just constantly referring to you. Like the first day you met her, remember? She said there would be room in the boat for you, whatever that means. In Caesarea, she told me not to worry if I got lost, because you would know the way.'

'What does she mean?'

'I don't know. She gets upset if I ask her to explain too much — she thinks everything she talks about is as clear to me as it is to her, and if I don't seem to understand her fully, she gets very anxious. Well. You've seen her.'

As I lay wrapped in my blanket in the woman's sleeping room at the inn, Santer's words and those he'd told me of Mary's kept replaying in my private mind. I felt closer to Mary because of it, warmth for her flowing from me at the thought of her silent acceptance of me in their lives. I wished I could do something for her, to ease her nervousness, or make her smile. Trying to decide how to effect either or both of these drifted me off to sleep.

The linens were ready on the sixth day. Leah recounted in full their journey through her transforming waters, and tenderly tucked stretches of old sheet around the stacks of the fresh, bright orange cloth. 'The sun must not touch them until after their first washing,' she told me sternly, 'and in that first wash, be sure to add a generous handful of salt.'

I thanked her as Acton climbed into the cart and took up the reins. Hiram and Santer trotted ahead. A space between the two stacks of linen at the rear of the cart formed an inviting niche, in which I promptly sat. The sun was bright in a pale blue sky, the waters of Lake Gennesaret assuming a melting smoothness, becoming the same pale non-colour as the sky where they mingled and hazed on the far shore. It was very still. All the sounds were loud. I could hear, as if they were close at hand, the pithy, shouted comments of the men in a blunt-nosed fishing boat near the middle of the lake. Gulls floated and screamed, their long wing feathers spread out and glistening whitely, heads bent watchfully for food in the waves.

We left the lakeside, the road winding up into the wooded hills. Tree and bush threw sharp shadows on the road. The oleander flower had long disappeared, but the sun still brought out the aromatic scent of cedar. There were sycamores, with their quivering leaves, and occasionally, a stand of palms. Moving between the patches of light and shadow induced a somnolent mood in me, deepened by the rhythmic hoof-thuds and the rocking motion of the cart. I thought of Alexandria, imagining the great library Decius had described, gleaming white and overlooking a cobalt sea. I could see the sunlit room where I would study and hear the sound of shepherd's flutes. When a dark figure leapt onto the cart, killing Acton by half-severing his head from his neck, I looked at him stupidly, wondering who he was. He snatched the reins from Acton's still-clutching hands, pushed his body from the cart, and urged the horses off the road onto a track that led away to the right. We were well into the track before I regained my senses and pushed myself up out of the linen. The murderer spun round, short sword raised, but seeing who and what I was, he dropped his arm and grinned. That grin frightened me more than anything which had gone before. My heart jolted, my throat closed with fear. I flung myself over the back of the cart. The man shouted and leapt after me. I flew along the track and out into the roadway, screaming Santer's name.

A little hill rose before me, with no sign of either Hiram or Santer. I heard the man chuckle, his feet slapping the ground thickly. My skin crawled with terror as I felt his fingers touch me. I twisted away, my voice a high thin scream. He grabbed my arm and pulled me to a stop, the odour of his body streaming over me. Then all was a confusion of swords and horses, froth from their mouths whipping onto my shoulder, and blood spattering in the dust.

I crouch in the roadside grasses, shivering. 'Did he harm you?' Santer's voice is hoarse. Hiram stands above us, sword in his hand.

'No — no time,' I manage, teeth chattering. 'Is he dead?'

'Very,' says Santer, and the word sounded like a swordthrust. He lifts me to my feet and put his arm around me. Hiram gives his horse's reins to Santer, then goes off to get the linen cart. I could not help the tears coming as we go back to Acton's body, with its near-severed head, and its still, warm feet. Hiram comes with the cart and pulls a sheet from the stack, throwing it over the body.

'Alone, I think,' he says to Santer.

We talk a little about what we should do. I want to take Acton with us, to bury him properly, but both Hiram and Santer point out how difficult this will make our journey, if only because of the smell.

'The best we can do is to wrap him in a sheet and make a grave below the trees,' says Santer.

Hiram nods. 'Deep,' he says, adding 'wolves,' so that I understand.

So I spread one of the new linen sheets out on the ground, and they bring Acton's body to it. Then I stay with Acton and weep for him, pulling the sheet tightly around him. I talk with him, regretting I had not talked with him much while he lived, and weep again.

Santer and Hiram took turns digging the grave, using the spade which hung on the side of the cart. By the time Acton was buried, twilight was thickening beneath the trees. It was lighter on the road, but not much lighter, and we set off very quickly, the cart creaking and swaying as I slapped the reins against the horses' rumps.

'How far to the nearest inn, by your reckoning, Hiram?' asks Santer. They were riding one on each side of me. Hiram shakes his head. 'Far,' he replies succinctly. 'Three, four hours.'

'That's what I thought,' returns Santer, then to me, 'What do you say to a camp?'

'I don't care, as long as I'm not alone in it,' I say. 'Can we make a fire?'

'No,' says Hiram in answer to Santer's look.

'See what you can do,' Santer urges him. Hiram gave a short nod and canters off, returning quite soon with the news that not far ahead, a group of travellers have made a camp in a wide clearing not far from the road. There are many of them, and he has asked if we could join them, explaining we are only three. They asked to see the rest of our group first. Our youthfulness, the linens, and the recounting of Acton's death reassures them, and soon our horses are blowing and sneezing with theirs, and places made for us by the fire. I thought I probably couldn't eat, but there is hot lentil soup, and later I manage a peach.

We slept by the fire, Hiram and Santer taking turns with other men at keeping watch. I was glad to feel the warmth of sleepers on either side of me, and one older woman's reassuring snore. But when I closed my eyes, the figure leapt again, the blade struck, and blood flung out in a high bright arc. So I watched the stars, flicks of water-dazzle in the dark, and felt the dew on my face. And thought of Acton, killed for a cartload of linen. I wondered where he had lived as a child, and how he had been captured, whether that was when he was a child or a man. I wondered if his mother still lived, and hoped someday he would come home, and whether there was a baby with the stamp of Acton on its tiny face.

And I thought of my own near-death, for I had no doubt that the murderer would also have killed me. Eventually. I shivered and gagged, and for a while held my arms crossed tightly on my chest. Think of something else, I said to myself. Think of what you can do to make yourself more safe. I wondered how I could defend myself so that, in a similar situation, I at least had a chance? I remembered a little dagger that hangs in Joseph's gallery, small enough for me, with a handle of twisted cords of bronze and a double-edged blade that moves like a snake. I could almost feel it nestled between my breasts.

It seemed stupid to me that if I was so at risk, I wasn't given a sword or dagger to defend myself, and lessons in its use, that the course of action I was to follow was simply to stay inside. I would not be caught out again, I vowed, and with the thought, Szuzanna's words again slid into my mind. 'Do for yourself means no disappointment.'

Joseph fulminated at the increasing boldness of ruffians, making perilous the ventures of honest men. Mary, after a comprehensive glance at Santer, said nothing. This surprised me, but then, so much of Mary was a mystery. Only Zeralia sympathised with my ordeal, and held me a little, to say she was glad I was all right. We talked about Acton for a while. She did not know what his real name was, but knew he came from Nubia, which he told her he missed ceaselessly, every day and night.

Though I now returned to my lessons, they were to continue for only a few more weeks: Decius had received word that his father was ailing, and so was to return to Rome. With Santer, I went to Bethany the day before he was to leave, for Martha, with her father's permission, had arranged a small gathering so that all his students and friends could bid Decius goodbye.

I had tried to write a poem of farewell, following the form of Vergil, but nothing I wrote satisfied me, except two lines:

> You fashioned the cup I use in Minerva's river.
> Her water is now my blood.

I read them to Zeralia, who thought they were fitting, so I wrote them as beautifully as I could, added a thank you and my name, and rolled it up. Zeralia found me a deep green ribbon to go round the scroll, and I slipped a sprig of thyme into the knot. The party coincided with a day in which Lazarus found it too painful to stand up, so it flowed into and out of his room. He was cheerful, but his cheeks were bright with a fever and fury lurked at the back of his eyes.

'How are you in all this noise?' I asked him, pulling a chair closer to his couch.

'Don't mind. I hate being shut away. I wish I could go with him. I don't suppose I ever will. Travel, I mean.'

'Why not? Your father could take a villa at Caesarea, like Joseph did.'

He shifted on his pillows, pushing himself a little higher. His arms below his tunic were thin and yellow, the wristbones looking swollen under the fleshless skin. 'To get my father away from here for more than two days would take a war, at least. He can't see the point of going anywhere else. He says there's always too much to do with all the work here, and where else can you be free except on your own land? And always adds, as long as no thief tries to take that from you.' He paused, gritting his teeth. 'If I was older, I would go. Nothing would stop me.'

'You will be older,' I smiled.

'Yes.' His tone was utter conviction. 'I will.'

Decius came over to Lazarus a few minutes later, his face showing the effects of drinking a lot of green wine. He had lost the solemnity which was his normal manner with us. I asked him about his journey, what route he would take to get home.

'Your brother just asked me the same thing!' he cried, and sat heavily in a chair. 'Ask him, won't you? I don't think I can say it all again, the wine has gone to my head. Thank you for the poem. It's —,' he interrupted himself to hiccup mightily, 'it's quite good. You made me feel proud.'

I wondered for a second if he was making fun of me, but he was looking at me so genuinely that I could see he was not.

'You'll be another Sulpicia, if you keep writing,' he smiled, hiccupped again, and frowned. 'What did she say — er — Muses, help me! — uh, that's right, I've got it now — she said "Personally, I would never send off words in sealed tablets for none to read." See? Make lots of copies, send 'em to all your friends! That's what poets do!'

'Am I a poet?' I felt shy, a little suspicious, but very much wanting to believe him.

'You could be. Why not? You seem to have made a good start.' He rubbed the middle of his chest hard, as if to get rid of something, then gave a tremendous belch.

As he begged our pardons, Lazarus laughed and asked him when he would be able to come back. 'Or would you want to? It must be rather wonderful in Rome,' he said enviously. The belch seemed to have sobered Decius a little. 'I do not know how my father is,' he said. 'All depends on him. But if I am truthful, I do not think I will return soon. If ever,' he felt compelled to add. 'Though your home has been most gracious, sir,' he went on, bowing deeply to Lazarus from his sitting position, which caused him to fall from his chair.

Lazarus was delighted, crowing with little high gulps of laughter. Decius scrambled to his feet, flushed with mortification. 'Your pardons,' he said very formally, and would have left, but Lazarus was upset at that, and begged for more talk of Rome. So I poured Decius a cup of water, which soon cooled the heat of the wine.

The little party ended shortly after sundown, other guests leaving then. The rest of our evening (for Santer and I were staying overnight) was spent recounting the more memorable of our lessons with Decius, with fierce teasing from Lazarus, and much merriment. Later, Martha and Santer went off to see what food there was left; Mary yawned and Decius got to his feet. In the light of the firepots and the oil lamps, his skin looked almost golden; his arms were pleasingly muscled, definitely those of a man, I thought. In this light, the hair on his forearms had the shine of ripe wheat in the sun, a dark reddish gold. The studied curls on his forehead made me smile, for they were rucked up into absurd points by his fall, which he didn't realise. He was again saying good-bye to Lazarus, his eyes large with emotion. I became aware of his lips. He turned to me, holding up a hand in the gesture of farewell and something in my gaze seemed to startle him. He coughed, said a general farewell, and left. Soon there was only Lazarus and me.

'You look fevered — are you?' I asked him directly.

'A little. Nothing really. Don't worry,' he lay back, looking as if his bones had shrunk, leaving his skin around them like an ungainly garment.

'There's fresh sleeping water. I'll get some, shall I?'

Relief came into his dark eyes, and he nodded. But he hadn't asked. 'Please.'

When I returned, he was in his night tunic, trying to smooth the coverings on his bed. I gave him the sleeping water and motioned him to a chair, then shook out and freshened his sheets and pillows. He got into bed with a long sigh. I went round his room, removing traces of the party, talking lightly with him, of Vergil, a little, and whether Decius would remember us in Rome.

'Will your father get another tutor?'

'Yes. But I must tell him, if you are to join us again, to make sure he is old and ugly. I do not want my friend to become a Roman bride.'

I paused at the doorway, soiled cups and other debris in my hands. His eyes gleamed at me from under knowing hoods. I was about to disclaim his innuendo with honest indignation, but his look stopped me, and knowledge slid through the gap it made. I felt a blush running up my cheeks, and my eyes were suddenly shy.

'I hope you rest well,' I said lightly, avoiding the whole issue, and left. Martha was already sleeping, but had left two pastries on a plate for me. Her round face seemed mysterious in the half-light, her thick eyelids shut on ancient secrets. I thought of Enheduanna, priestess to the moon. What did being a poet really mean? I wished I could meet some poets, talk with them of a poet's task, find out what steps it took to become one. I could see myself in some high lit, poet-filled room, scrolls everywhere, and we exchanging dignities. Then Decius slid into my mind. Szuzanna had told me of sexual intimacy, but I knew I was not thinking of that when I had looked at Decius. He had said I could be a poet, which was like giving a great gift to me. No mystery then, that he should look pleasurable to me. Outside, a goat yauped and Martha, as if replying, gave a delicate snore, which made me giggle. I thought of the man she would one day marry, then thought again of Decius. My body felt rich and sleek under my thin night robe.

I blew out the single taper and lay down luxuriously on the rustling mattress, first stretching, then relaxing. I felt full of vigour and very far from sleep. Idly, I imagined Decius beside me and was half-surprised by the resulting leap of my pulses. Then I was dismayed. I did not want to marry, to give my life over to the caring of a household and a husband. I wanted to explore my writing, learn more of other ways of thinking and living. There was no appeal in Martha's realm for me. Yet, if I did not, how could I release the promise given by this pulsing of my body? Then I saw I was catching myself in a corner — there was time enough for each of these, in the proper order. First the learning, then the body. Still, I knew I did not want to marry. I thought of Decius again, and wondered if I would change.

'Perhaps,' I whispered, and turned on my side. The stillness of the night rang all around me. Spreading my senses, I went through the silent house out into the starfilled dark. I breathed and mingled with it, heard the wolves howling on the hills, felt the dew falling. Sensate, infinitely wide, I at length came to rest on the dreaming night.

ALEXANDRIA

We went by camel from Jerusalem to Gaza, a small dusty southern port a very long day's ride away. There, we sold the camels and caught a trader ship leaving for Alexandria on the midnight tide. That we could go was Mary's benison: Santer, talking with her of his desires, found to his astonishment that she understood clearly what he meant, and pre-empted the goal of his conversation by asking him directly if he was saying he wanted to leave Jerusalem. Even when he said yes, she did not react as he'd feared.

'She listened carefully and asked many questions, but she did not plead with me to stay,' Santer tells me, his voice perplexed. 'She seems perfectly well, too. And when I told her you were coming, she merely nodded, then asked me where were we going, could she know?'

'What did you say?'

'I said, of course, that I just didn't want Joseph to know because I wanted to walk my own road now, and you did too. She said she understood, and that she would do what she could later to make it all right with Joseph.'

I am overwhelmed by this, but there is more: Mary agreed, on Santer's oath of returning in five years, to help him go, giving him a great deal of money. She said she had saved it over many years, hoarded it specifically for his use. She also insisted we have two companions and would not agree to anything unless they went with us. The first is Hiram, who had some blood-link with

Mary, and the second is Hiram's younger cousin, Stephen, who is older than Santer by only one year. He met us, as arranged, on the roadway in the afternoon of our departure.

My only goodbye was to Mary, and to Zeralia, with gifts of poems I had written for each one and for Zeralia, one of the thin silver bracelets from my wrist. I gave both packets to Mary, who wakened with us in the dull pre-dawn of our going, together with a little note to Lazarus and Martha. I was wordless in the face of actually saying goodbye to Mary. She looked so small and fragile, wearing light cotton slippers inside her sandals, her ankles pointed and slender like those of a young goat. Her face, in the shadows of her headshawl, was dark, closed, the skin on her mouth dry. I wondered how she would stand the brunt of Joseph's vital anger, which would rise in him because his authority had been superseded, and his pride therefore hurt.

'Speak to me in the night,' she said, her voice cracking a little. I nodded, but it was a long time before I really knew what she meant.

I left she and Santer to say their goodbyes privately. Hiram waited, camels grunting crankily by the ochre wall. With only a nod of greeting, he fastened my pack to the smallest of the camels and helped me on its back. Somewhere close by, startling the silence, a donkey brayed angrily. Santer emerges a few minutes later, his head bent. He mounts quickly, heaving his camel up at once, and we begin. The dawn is leaden, the dew still heavy; the hooves of the camels make perfect rounds in the damp dust. We come to the King's Gate and the warmth of the nightguard's fire. Santer exchanges a few words with him and the guard opens the right half of the tall, inscribed gate. Shortly, we are loping south, down the wide road that lay across the flat plain, a trade route hundreds of years old, that leads down to

Gaza, and beyond, into Pharaoh's lands.

The boat is disgusting, with narrow empty cabins that stink of vomit and urine. We board it immediately on securing the passage, for it is to set sail within three hours. The captain, a talkative man with small hard eyes, shrugs when Santer objects to our quarters, telling us there are no others, and that our fare was a bargain in which he had not promised cushions or fine wine.

'We did not expect that,' replies Santer sharply. 'Neither did we expect to sleep in conditions even a dog would refuse.'

The captain scowled, but Hiram pulled Santer away, and made a laughing comment to the captain that this was Santer's first voyage, that he did not understand the ways of the sea. The captain spat and turned away.

'Do not anger him, my cousin,' counselled Hiram when we were in the cabin and alone. 'It is he who controls the ship, and accidents at sea are not unknown. It's very easy to slit a throat at night, and a body easy hidden in the sea.'

'Would he do that?' I asked quickly, and touched my robe, where I was carrying the little twisting dagger. I had not had to steal it. I had told Santer I wanted it, and why, and that I was practising with a kitchen knife. Before we left, he produced it, saying that when Mary discussed weaponry with him, he'd asked for it, and she simply took it from the wall.

Hiram spread his hands. 'Perhaps not, since we are three men, and we will share the watch. But you see how easy it would be — he has the crew to do his bidding, which they would for a share of our possessions. Who would ask questions?'

I saw, with extreme clarity, how right he was and felt a flicker of fear. Was my increasing skill with my knife enough?

'I see,' said Santer to Hiram, his face resolute. 'Thank you. I shall not forget.'

I said to Hiram that I was prepared to take my turn at standing guard. The movement of a smile touched his mouth and the corner of his eyes, and he looked down at his hard, dark hands.

'I think she should,' said Santer, seeing this. 'Not at night. But surely she can help during the day?'

Hiram looked at me in doubt. I brought the knife from my breast and sent it hissing into the wood beside his head. He ducked; Stephen yelped, then laughed. Hiram stared at me as if I'd just grown horns, then wrenched out the knife and handed it to me. 'You must be of Judith's tribe,' he said, putting the knife in my hand.

'Where did you learn that?' demanded Stephen. 'Who taught you?'

'It's just practise, anyone can do it,' I told him, sliding the dagger back into its hiding place nonchalantly. But secretly, I was very pleased with myself, for the movement had been completely automatic, and my aim straight. Both Hiram and Stephen treated me differently after this, I noted. When we discussed future actions, Hiram's eyes included me in the discussion, and the things I said were considered as fully as anyone's suggestions. Stephen was frankly admiring, asking if I would teach him how to throw the dagger, so when we stood day watch together in the cabin the following afternoon, I showed him how to hold it, and how to flick it forward with a fast, hard-checked turn of the wrist.

The journey to Alexandria took only two days and we were never out of the sight of land on our left. But the glorious Sea, which had bedazzled me in Caesarea, spread to a far horizon on our right. Now I came to a deeper knowledge of it, its immense rushing depths and polished swells. Santer and I went up to the deck at sunrise. The sea was flooding gold at the prow and, skittling out from our passing, flying fish leapt on small ribbed wings. Later, to my delight and astonishment, dolphins rolled and arced around the ship, as if inviting us to play.

The clouds also fascinated me, for these were unfamiliar clouds, prestigious palaces which were tinged blue or charcoal near the Sea, but radiantly white at their rounded tops, moving slowly through the silken blue like contemplative camels by a stream. I learned of the wide slanting skeins of grey that were distant rainsqualls, and in the evening, of pink-flushed pennants and small billowings which threw the sun's westering light back onto the Sea.

The work of the sailors interested me too, the spanning ropes seemingly pulled at random, the stained and stretching sails, and all the creaking, blackened wood. The ship was carrying olive oil, huge amphora guarded and trussed with sacks, and oranges in massive straining nets. But I could not watch too closely, for the sailors themselves threw sly glances at me, winking and licking their lips when I was near them. Some put their hands to their genitals, with their thumbs pointing back to me; others rubbed their chests, or made sucking sounds on the passing air. I ignored them, but their actions disturbed and angered me. I felt demeaned and vulnerable, and was very glad of the knife at my breast.

At night, wrapped in our cloaks, we slept in the cabin, Hiram lying in front of the door. I was sleeping furthest from it, amongst our belongings, and in between were Stephen and Santer. There was a narrow closet not far from the cabin where, in a stinking pot, we were to urinate and shit. This was emptied regularly, and swilled, but the stench of the closet was choking. With the gestures of the sailors vivid in my mind, I would not use it unless one of my companions stood guard.

In the late afternoon of the second day, a shout went up. Hiram came to say that the lighthouse of Alexandria was in sight, which the captain had said we could best see from a forward position on the ship. We followed

Hiram, ducking under ropes and spars.

'What is a lighthouse?' Santer asked, a fraction before me. A passing sailor, who understood Aramaic, heard him and stopped.

'The sun at night, it is, the sailor's friend.' He pointed. We leaned out and stared, and then I could see a rising line of black with a curiously shiny top. Some way to its left were two smaller, thinner lines. Smudges spoke of a shoreline and buildings, and suddenly I was tremendously excited, my heart beating violently in my throat. I grabbed Santer's arm and squeezed it, and we grinned hugely at each other. Behind me, I heard Hiram give a little grunt, and pull Stephen away.

'Cabin,' I heard him say. Santer elbowed my ribs and jerked his head. We hurried after them, with me trying to look back at the view until I stumbled heavily and grazed my shin on a massive wooden bole. I breathed hard to shut out the pain and hurried on. The cabin door was shut but the thumping and scuffling inside were plain to hear. Outside, someone shouted what was clearly a warning. I brought out my knife, and stood with my back to the wall as Santer banged on the door.

'Hiram? Stephen? We're coming in.'

'Yes!' yelled Stephen, and Santer set his shoulder to the door.

There was only one sailor, and Stephen was sitting on him. Hiram leaned against a wall, panting, his nose bleeding, a gash along his jaw. I stumbled to my pack to get a clean cloth for him, while Stephen gasped and laughed.

'There were two of them, but one ran off when he saw us, and then I slammed the door,' he said breathlessly. 'The other one had just started pulling our stuff about and was very surprised when the door slammed! Pulled a knife. Hiram went at him — jumped like a monkey and on him!'

Hiram held the cloth to the gash on his jaw, eyes

smouldering. 'Some kind of traveller I am,' he muttered, 'an easy lull. Predictable. Should have known.'

'You remembered in time,' returned Santer and clapped him on the shoulder. 'No harm done, except to your face. How is it?'

'It's all right,' Hiram muttered. 'I'll wash it when we get off this pisspot.' Santer went over to the unconscious sailor. 'Give a hand,' he said to Stephen. 'Where shall we take him?' Stephen asked merrily.

'To the captain,' replied Santer, and Hiram gave an ironic laugh.

They returned in a few minutes, Stephen chortling. 'Mr Innocence himself, our captain! Very surprised to hear of such a thing. Promised to give the man a good whacking!'

'For getting caught,' growled Hiram, and the others laughed.

I laughed with them, but in my private mind, I was very scared. Acton's death-dealer loomed again in my mind, and I could not help thinking of what may have happened to me if I had, for some reason, returned to the cabin just at that moment, and alone. I had my knife, but could I have defended myself successfully with two of them? The answer was clear.

Trying to thrust my resentment and fear away, I gave Hiram a fresh cloth for his cut, and helped repack our bags. We hauled them on deck, where my mood dropped from me at the sight ahead. A wide curving bay spread before us, deep blue water touching, with perfect edgings of white, a sandy shore. Dazzling white buildings were now visible, and palms and colonnades. Two deep red, pointed obelisks stood on either side of a busy quay as if in welcome to us, and at the farthest end of a spit of land which ran out into the waters on our right was a hugely tall narrow building with a shining, pointed tip. The lighthouse of Pharos, harbinger of this city of wonders,

Alexandria.

The ship came to rest against the quay, ropes moving like thrown snakes between deck and pier. I was tremendously excited, but when the captain came to us for the remainder of our fare, he told us we had to stay on board until the Register arrived. My spirits drooped, but we didn't have to wait more than an hour. The Register proved to be a thin man with a querulous voice who asked us where we were from, what our business was, and how long we intended to remain. He registered us to live in the Jewish quarter, demanded an Alien's fee, and gave us a crisp receipt. He told us we were obliged to inform his office of our permanent address as soon as we were settled, and recommended Shalom Inn as a safe place to spend our first night. He came with us as we disembarked, looked over the clamouring group of men who instantly surrounded us, and beckoned to one who had a scarf-wrapped head, broad shoulders, pitted skin and a mouth with several broken teeth.

'This is Gamal,' he said succinctly. 'He is honest and will take you to the inn directly. You can trust him. When you get there, ask for Jacob, who is the owner. Tell him you have been sent to him by Inspector Ephriam.' He told us what to pay Gamal, in Gamal's hearing, gave us the sketchiest bow of respect, and wheeled away.

Gamal bowed several times before swinging four of our bags around his shoulders and back. Carrying the rest of them, we crowded after him. The last of the light was going, the sky a mild lilac, darker where the light of the Pharos boomed out across the Sea. Hiram held the corner of one of our bags on Gamal's back, his other arm linked through the handles of two more bags. We pressed after him. I felt very small between the crowding bodies, and was relieved when we went between the obelisks and out into a very wide, colonnaded street, which paralleled the Sea. Before I had more than an appreciative glance of it, Gamal motioned to a lesser street on our right and, like a pack train, we obediently followed him in. Along this road were plenty of inns, outside tables full of patrons and high on the air, thin musical wails and the crash of tambourines. I could smell roasting chicken, fresh donkey dung, an entrancingly sweet flower scent, and sweat. Excitement tingled down my hands. Rush lamps bloomed behind wooden shutters pierced with patterns, in rooms glimpsed for a moment through clacking beaded curtains behind which was polished brass, and white walls hung with red. Above, the sapphire dark, and already two or three large golden stars. Without warning, laughter rose in me, irresistible giggles rushing up with glee. I felt like dancing, like shouting, whirling round and round. We were not in Jerusalem! We had left all our old constraints behind us, nothing would be as it had been.

'What, what?' shouted Stephen, shaking my hand. But Santer knew, and his eyes were laughing as mine were, bright and dark in the lamplight around our heads.

Gamal turned into a gateway set in a wall of knitted bricks, taking us into a little courtyard in front of a long, low building with a name painted above the door. Shalom Inn. An immense tamarisk tree rose to the left, its leafy dome high above the roof. Purple and white flowers bloomed in wide-mouthed pots beside an open, bead-curtained door, and I heard a woman's voice, raised above a clatter of pans. Gamal and Hiram went through the door, Stephen looking back at us as he followed them. But Santer and I dropped our bags and clutched each other, shook each other by the arms, hugged and, for a few seconds, stamped in the cool beaten earth an impromptu dance of victory.

Alexandria was almost the diametric opposite of Jerusalem: flat and open where Jerusalem was hilly and closed, water on either side, where Jerusalem had only its cherished spring. With its white buildings and wide roads, Alexandria lay shining between a shallow lake named Mareotis, and the beautiful indigo Sea. It had two harbours, one on either side of the Pharos, and everywhere delighted the eye, from the colonnades which lined the two bisecting central streets to the buildings meant solely for relaxation and pleasure: the triple-pooled gymnasium, with its sanded arena for sport; the sculpture fronted theatre, and the walled hippodrome. I was astonished to discover that water had been made to run underground through a series of intricate conduits, and supplies for our house could be drawn from an outflow not far away.

The house we rented was at the edge of the Jewish quarter, and though some of its corners were worn, it was spacious, and perfectly clean. From its flat roof I could see north to the awesome lighthouse, and the double harbours, including the two red obelisks which ornamented the harbour to the east. I could also see the royal quarters of the now vanquished Ptolemies, the graceful white walls and sphinxes gleaming as they did when Cleopatra had walked there less than fifty years before.

Half an hour's walk would bring me back to the wide, colonnaded street we had entered on our arrival night. Its name was the Canopic Way, for it ran straight to Canopus, the city Augustus had had built to steal Alexandria's sea wealth. Cleopatra had been carried down the Canopic Way on her silver-footed divan, her beauty increased with collars of gold, and thousands of people called her name, for she alone of the Ptolamies had learned the language of the natives, and she brought them pride, as a goddess should. So they called her name, proud of her beauty and cleverness, and many were not surprised when their lives became poorer after she was dead.

To the east were vast swamps full of crocodile and hippopotamus, the latter hunted for the feasts of Rome. To the south, as breath-taking as the royal quarters, the temple of Serapis glowed like a royal jewel, and signalled the location of the Mouseion. Beyond, I could just see the line of pallid pink made by the shallow waters of Lake Mareotis. Our house was serviced by two older women, Nawaal and Buphaar, and I was relieved to know that they were not slaves, but women who came and went from their homes, and managed ours, for a sensible fee. They brought food in from the markets, cleaned and cooked. I insisted to the three men that we all treat them with respect, speaking to them as we would to one another, and thanking them for their services to us. Hiram threw me a dour look, and Stephen nodded cheerfully. In practice, they treated the two women as if they were invisible, only thanking them after I had done so, and always without meaning.

Buphaar was small and bent and would not speak with us, but Nawaal spoke demotic Greek, and, since she had long worked in the Jewish quarter, passable Aramaic. Her eyes were merry and sly. She brought us trays of bread and pomegranates in the cool golden mornings, and more than once was discovered riffling through our clothes. Such discovery did not disconcert her: she merely grinned and slapped our arms, as if we were willing partners in her game.

In our second week, after cleansing and oiling ourselves, and preparing our minds as well as we could, Santer and I set out for the Mouseion. I was full of a sort of delicious fear, hoping to be accepted, fearful that our previous learning was not sufficient to gain us entrance into its esteemed courses.

'They welcome all students,' Santer assures me. 'The fact that we have come to study will be enough.' The day is balmy, sunny with a delicious breeze from the Sea. Santer looked very handsome, wearing the lighter tunics which everyone wore here. His curls were freshly cropped, and the tunic suited his lean body, which tended to be swamped by the Jewish robes. In the last few weeks, he had completely stopped biting his nails. He throws me a quick, teasing look. 'They may only wish to take poets, which would make things a little difficult for me, but you'd vouch for me, wouldn't you?'

I wrinkle my nose at him. 'Seriously, Santer, if they accept us, have you decided what you will study?'

We come to the end of our street, where a crowd of women, Nawaal among them, waited at the water out-flow. She pointed to us and chattered to the woman beside her, and flapped her hand in a wave. I smiled at her as we turned into the wide roadway which led south to the Mouseion.

'Yes,' he says with a decided nod. 'Definitely law, definitely philosophy. Mathematics, perhaps. And theology. What about you?'

I sigh. 'I'm not sure. I hope someone there can help me.'

Our way leads past Alexander's tomb, a multi-colonnaded building which held only the veined, marble sarcophagus of the soldier king, dead for more than three hundred years. It was said that inside his sarcophagus, he lay immersed in the white honey, made by the bees in the sacred groves of Greece, which would preserve his body forever and ensure his spirit of peace. In my private mind, the thought of being buried in honey makes me laugh, but outwardly I am respectful as we passed the tomb of the man who it was said had conquered almost all the world.

We pass through the central market, where tents slung their shade over dishes of spikenard, cinnamon and fenugreek. Men with hooded, knowing eyes sit behind piles of richly woven rugs, the corners of their tents hung with cages in which small yellow birds flutter and shrill. There is so much that was new — wonderfully shaped bottles and bowls of glass, a tent wholly devoted to perfumes, and the marvellous bird I came to know as a peacock, dragging its miraculous tail. There are many clothing stalls, piles of white cloth and many galabiehs, the long Egyptian gown.

After several minutes of brisk walking, we come to a tall white marble archway which took us through a colonnaded pathway into a white marble portico. There are gardens on either side, but I have no eyes for their beauty. As soon as I see the entrance to the Mouseion, I begin to shake, and now am conscious only of one thing: would I be able to study here? The question thrums at me, for I am not certain that women are admitted, and my eagerness was tinged with dread.

Santer takes a deep breath. We look at each other and go under the arch. Ahead, many people are walking toward a complex of buildings. Others are walking in the gardens, or sitting on benches beside the bright flowers. Anticipation and longing runs through me, to be part of this centre, to join this throng.

The portico leads into a semi-circular concourse, in the centre of which is a waist-high marble desk. Behind this, several young men are answering questions. We look at each other again, and go to the desk. My shaking subsides as we wait our turn for most of the people asking questions look to be close to our age, and were also obviously here for the first time. And there are several women! I could recognise Greek and Latin, and other syllables of Aramaic. The questions ae all ones we too wish to ask: how do we enrol for study, what are the costs, where will our lessons be held?

One of the young men, hearing we were from Jerusalem, sends us down a corridor to our left, to Registrar Philadelphus. We knock, but there was no answer.

Santer glances at me, then whispers, 'I've changed my mind! I'm too ugly to study. I shall go and brew beer.'

'Idiot,' I hiss back at him, but his ruse works, and I relax.

After a courteous pause, Santer knocks again, which brings a deep call to enter. Registrar Philadelphus stands looking at us, his spraddling eyebrows raised. 'The grace of Serapis be with you — students from Judaea, I take it?' His eyes are light brown and twinkle. On either side of his fleshy, thick-nosed face enormous ears sprang out, hairy with large pink lobes, there is a froth of hair at the base of his neck, but otherwise, he was bald.

'Yes, please,' I say, liking him at once.

The room held a second room to our right, at the doorway of which the Registrar stood. A small desk stood immediately in front of us and further down the room, a low table and four cross-legged chairs. In the far wall, a tall window showed us a portion of the garden outside, and flooded the room with the morning light.

'I am Registrar Philadelphus,' he greeted us, giving us each an incline of his head. 'I usually have a young scribe here as well, but he seems to have found something more pressing to do at the moment.' He indicated the chairs by the window. 'Sit down, tell me who you are and what it is you wish to study.' His breath wheezed as he spoke. When he had seated us, he went into the inner room, returning with a fresh hand-scroll, on which he scribed our names, and the date of our arrival. He asked us for details of our previous studies.

He frowned a little when Santer described his studying. 'Are you being prepared for the priesthood?' he asked. 'If so, this is not the place to be, you should go to the synagogue in the Jewish quarter.'

'That was a thought my mother and foster-father had,' returned Santer equably. 'But those plans have changed and I seek a wider learning.'

'You have put all thought of the priesthood aside?' the Registrar asked again, looking at him keenly. 'Study at the Mouseion is in the Greek tradition, to a curricula also inclusive of Rome. There are some aspects of this that can seem offensive to the Judaic faith.'

'Yes,' answered Santer. 'I do realise that. The priesthood is not for me. When my sister told me of her studies, I realised I wished to have that breadth of learning too.' Registrar Philadelphus turned to me, 'You are Mary — it is good to see that in the matter of learning at least, Judaea may be at last beginning to follow the insights of Plato. You are one of only three other woman scholars from Judaea studying here. What purpose lies behind your studies?'

It seemed a great temerity for me to say I wished to be a poet, to ally myself with that wisdom and beauty. I cleared my throat and said, much too loudly, 'Poetry. I — uh. Poetry.'

'Yes?' the syllable was encouraging.

I took a deep breath, pressing my hands together. 'I should like to try to become a poet,' I said in a rush. 'I want to know how to do it properly, to write the way the great poets write, like Homer and Vergil.'

'How old are you?'

'Sixteen, Registrar.

His eyes seemed to reach into me, to see past my skin and eyes, into my brain. He looked at me so long that I became embarrassed by his gaze and looked down at my lap. He drew a long wheezing breath. 'Yes. All right,' he said. He was about to say something else, but his words were cut off by the tempestuous arrival of an extremely handsome youth.

'Registrar! A million pardons,' he burst out as he came through the door, all rush and eagerness. 'There was — .'

The Registrar cut off the youth's speech with an uplifted hand.

'Spare me your dissemblances, Gratius,' he wheezed. 'Calm yourself. This is not a hippopotamus chase. Here are two new students, for whom I have now inaugurated files.'

The young man greeted us over-heartily, and apologised for his absence. 'The magicians arrived,' he told us in a low voice, as if that explained everything. What are magicians, I wondered. He took the scroll from the Registrar's hand and seated himself at his desk, all with the same intense energetic expectancy. He was so eager that I bent my head to hide a smile.

Registrar Philadelphus explained the workings of the Mouseion and its gymnasia schools while Gratius ostentatiously scratched more details on our file. There was a registration fee, said the Registrar, which guaranteed us each a place for a year. He told us of the lectures available: philosophy, and arithmetic; grammar (Greek and Latin, but not Aramaic) astronomy, harmonics, literature, rhetoric, logic and law, athletics, and the medical study of the body, were the main courses. There were others a little more esoteric, but none of them touched on our interests.

The custom was for students to attend one or two initial lectures to make their own selection of the lecturer which seemed of most interest to them. Once we had decided our preference, we were to pay the lecturers themselves their fees for the year.

Though the Great Library had been destroyed by fire some years before (his face tightened, darkened with the memory of this), the adjacent Cleopatra Library at the Serapeum had been enlarged upon and now offered a 'respectable' resource for students, he said. We should be sure to provide ourselves with sufficient writing materials, for we would obviously wish to record aspects of our lectures for our personal libraries and private study.

'Gratius can tell you where to procure them,' he concluded, 'and also of the mundanities — food and so on.' He placed a thick hand on each thigh and pushed himself up. We stood up, Santer holding up his hand in the Roman way and beginning the formal words of thanks. This he waved away.

'No need, no need. Come if there are any problems. Gratius, be specific. Come to me when you have done.' A final nod, and he went into the inner room and shut the door.

'Shall we pay the entrance fee now?' Santer asked, bringing the money pouch out from the upper folds of his tunic.

'That would be excellent,' encouraged Gratius, unreeling our scroll again. 'I do beg your pardon for throwing you straight to our Rara Avis,' he said, lowering his voice and indicating the Registrar's office with his head, 'but I find magicians impossible to resist, don't you?'

'But what are they?' I burst out. Gratius threw me a startled glance. 'What are magicians? Why, they're — they're — *magicians*,' was his initial helpless rejoinder before he found words to describe them. In time, the magicians and their entertainments awed me as much as they did Gratius, but I also felt a great reluctance to be in their company. Acrobats and jugglers are one thing, but is a man wholly human who can bring snowy birds from empty air and cause fire to leap in the palm of his hand?

I never lost my first sense of wonder at the Mouseion. It seemed that the whole complex had been designed and created solely to express the heights of architecture and ornamentation. All the lecture gymnasia were richly decorated, with curling vine leaves and the figures of the

Muses, with the artful Eros, and Aphrodite in a most beguiling pose. There were busts of Euclid, and the poet Callimachus, together with his inspiration, Heraclitus. Here Alexander lived again, his swift-sailed fleet behind him, there Conon the astronomer, and Archimedes, whose name was too long for Vergil to use. And in one magnificent lintel, springing out of marble so delicately pink that it seemed blood blushed under their temples, were Klotho, Atropos, and Lachesis, the three implacable Fates.

There were halls for eating and drinking, which I never saw empty, the window embrasures a favourite place to sit. The Library was housed in six enormous rooms, each of which had long study tables under the windows, watched over by sharp-tongued custodians who reminded us continuously of the fragility of the scrolls.

The whole complex was linked by colonnaded walkways, with gardens spreading everywhere, complete with wandering pools. Papyrus reeds frilled them, and the five-petalled white verbena, tall spears of asphodel, and the purple tipped strelitzia with its cresting petals of flame. Here the high-shouldered sacred black ibis stepped, and egrets, their feathers white as cottonblossom, pointed and fished. It was, to me, quite simply paradise.

The bane Augustus had set upon Alexandria after Cleopatra held the asp to her lips had gradually lessened the city's power as an influential city of the world. But the Mouseion was still held as a great institute of scholarship and we, as two of its students, came under that same outstretched wing of respect. With the receipt of our entrance fee, Gratius gave us each a Mouseion badge, two sprigs of sage, the herb of Sophia, Greek goddess of Wisdom, to be worn high on our left breast, or clipped to the shoulder, like a tunic clasp. These marked us as students. Proudly, we wore them everywhere.

121

I had one weekly lecture in philosophy, under Hektor, who also tutored Santer. I also had lectures in drama and music, and with two separate tutors, one Greek and one Roman, I studied Poetry. Through my sleep, Poetry gave radiant liberty to my dreams but awake, the hours dissected metaphor and scansion, metre, cadence and form. The vocal onomatopoeia was soon familiar, the running trochee, the satirical iambs. Couplets, epode and epic, lyric verse, the quatrain and the dithyramb, strophe and antistrophe, hexameter and pentameter — all the labelled tools of this illustrious craft. But the most important — and discouraging — lesson was one I learned in the first weeks: that the essence of Poetry, like those essences bound on Inanna's breast, could not be taught. How to find the leaping words, and then how to set them in motion so that their arabesques stir and part, for one brief moment, the veils on Mystery?

For weeks I was too discouraged to attempt even a line. I interrogated myself scornfully, angry with my cowardice, afraid of shallowness, too readily wallowing in despair. I came with humble curiosity to the women Poets we studied: Sulpicia, whom Decius spoke of, and Korinna, who had defeated Pindar five times in competition; Anyte, and Telesilla, whom Plutarch celebrated, and Praxilla, with her cucumbers and glazing stars. Enheduanna was here, and the Songs of the Shulamite. And Sappho, whom Plato had called the Tenth Muse, who made me long to visit her island, where:

> In the spring twilight
> The full moon is shining:
>
> Girls take their places
> as though around an altar
> And their feet move

Rhythmically, as tender
feet of Cretan girls
danced once around an

altar of love, crushing
a circle in the soft
smooth flowering grass.

Eventually, I took up my stylus again, for to remain
dumb through fear was a withering defeat.

Our days assumed a rhythm, and a deeply satisfying
shape. Hiram and Stephen went down to the harbours
or out on the shallow, pink-watered Lake Mareotis or
further afield, to the slipping eastern swamps, where they
were beaters, netters or spear throwers in the dreadful
hippopotamus hunts. They made friends who were part
of their activities, reliving their adventures as they drank
beer at the inns, and sought sexual release from the
long-eyed women who clacked finger-bells at them in
the incense-drifted houses of the dance.

But our friends were all students: Neferenati, sharp-
minded and lovely as any queen, and Julian with his
golden hair. Their desire of each other was obvious and
as satisfying to them as their shared studies of medicine
and philosophy. Lamia, with her smoky braid and Grecian charm, as drawn to Poetry as I; Abdel, whose
family could trace its days back to Rhakotis, the ancient
town on which Alexandria was built, and who was
doggedly studying mathematics and law. Rhiaon, with
his strange green eyes under amber lids, and his ever-
present lyre; and Kharys, studying both drama and
medicine, whose slender dark hands spoke when she
spoke, sketching emphatic hieroglyphs on the air.

We would meet together at the Mouseion archway
when the long afternoon became rose and gold and the
sky lilac behind the metallic hills. We walked in groups
of three and five, to Julian's house, or Abdel's and,

frequently, ours. It didn't matter where we went, all the houses seemed like an extension of one another, where we argued and compared in lamp-filled rooms, eating baked fish or roast duck; or whether we were in earnest dissection on a roof top, away from the flies of evening, the sky dark and high, streaked on the left with the long white bar of the Pharos's light, eating melons and grapes and the sweet honeycakes that were almost tart on the tongue.

The weeks and months passed, our days moved effortlessly whether the winds blew sand dust into our beds, or the thin starved rain of winter fell, whether spring brought days of calm and lilies, or buoyant winds that laughed and pulled at our clothes. We were together and wove between us the rare and lovely fabric of our eight-sided friendship through debate. This was my true learning. The Mouseion gave me knowledge, but through and with these friends, I came to know what I believed of life.

Very early we discussed pleasure, the ineluctable attraction of sex, with its lethal limbs and tongue. I was often the instigator of this discussion, for Love and passion had come to haunt me in my studies, shaking my mind with their syllables, their images sweetly entering me, trembling my body and arresting my thoughts. Like Archilochus, I felt 'such desire, for love, coiled at my heart, shed a thick mist over my eyes, stealing the tender senses from my breast.' Everywhere I turned I ran into Love: Theocritus, piping of Pan and goats, and 'breasts far brighter than you, O moon'; Meleager and his plaints for Heliodora, and Ovid, with his long list of places where Love's kisses can be plucked. Here too was Pindar, reaping 'the harvest of soft youths blamelessly upon alluring beds,' and Sappho, O Sappho, with her garlands of violets thrown around sapling throats and nights when 'on soft beds, gently, our desire for delicate girls was satisfied.'

Everywhere I turned, sex and love and passion were there, in the curve of a neck, or lips wet with wine, where felucca sails triangled summer-placid waters, and in the gardens, surrounded by the swooning scent of peach. Rhiaon wooed me with his leaf-green eyes, looking sideways at me while his supple fingers stroked plangent notes from his lyre; and Kharys, who slid her brown hands up my arms and whispered Vergil to me:

'Love overwhelms all things. We've got to give in to Love ...'

So I insisted and insisted, until through debate, my thoughts on Love and passion were finally clear: that celibacy brought utter cessation from worry, but did not assuage the flesh; that Love dwelt briefly there, but long in the temples of the mind; and that wherever it blossoms truly, no matter what its shape, Love is an essence of that intangible we call divine, and passion its earthly tether in the amusing dance of sex. That I loved Santer was as unquestionable as the love I bore Szuzanna, but we were not lovers; when my mind exalted my body with its pictures, it was with strange fingers at my nipple and thigh, and an unfamiliar sweet-breathed mouth on my lips. I had tried to talk out this aspect of it with Santer, but some indefinable barrier seemed to obscure my intent. I would state, so clearly to me, the skeins of my understanding but within a few minutes, these would become impossibly tangled by his replies:

'What tyranny is exercised by eyes and ankles, Santer! Have you noticed that? That just a memory can hold you in one place for half an afternoon?'

'Desire, are you talking about, or the more simple lust?'

'No, neither — it's more — more gossamer than that. Like a gossamer trance, perhaps, so that without your notice, you can stand in a perfectly ordinary hallway not seeing the pattern of the door, nor the dead flies by the wall, but a figure running, or a certain slant of light springing colours from newly washed hair.'

'And then the sweat, and the breath coming quickly? Grunts and urgent movings, and salty rising smells!' he said, amused.

'Aphrodite nights! No,' I mused. 'I mean something quite different. Something placed obliquely between that, for instance, and the love I have for you.'

'Or someone, do you mean?'

'No! This is a feeling, an experience, a reality that floods over you, lifting you to another realm, and a new clarity.'

'Perhaps you're not certain of what you want? That kind of indecisiveness can blank you, hold you motionless until you realise you must make up your mind ...'

I looked at him, love and exasperation mixed, sure he was deliberately trying not to understand. He had grown taller, though he would never be tall, and there was now substance to his neck. He kept his quick-springing black hair cropped and his mouth, so like Mary's, was firm above his so-dear clefted chin. His voice had found its timbre, strong and mellow, like Rhiaon's lower strings. He met my eyes, his glance open and inquiring, without a shred of tease. I couldn't answer. The words bumbled at my lips, but none were right. For a moment, the gossamer shadows of lovers slid between us, so that I saw him through them, as they urgently stroked and moaned; on that hot air of afternoon, I smelled sweat and the salt-tang of private seas. All the tiny hairs of my body lifted in response. Involuntarily I pressed my thighs together, laid my hand across my breasts. Still his glance was steady, inquiring. What I saw was invisible to him. I gave a little chuckle and slowly shook my head.

It was in the middle of our second year that, through business interest, curiosity, and a desire for first-hand information, Joseph came to visit. He knew where we were, for after our first six months, when we were well settled in our studies, we had begun to send quarterly messages back to Mary. I was surprised how pleased I was to see him, and how warm he was both to me and to Santer. He made no reference to our surreptitious flight, and when I alluded to it, he shook his head. 'It cannot be changed,' he said briskly, 'and showed enterprise and will!' His eyes were warm as they lingered on Santer. 'Fine qualities in a man!' He turned his glance to me. 'It can't hurt your prospects, either, so there is no harm done. What more is there to say?'

So we talked about his business, a little, and what sorts of artefacts he was seeking; and of Mary, and James, who was now a sturdy boy. I asked after Zeralia, and Joseph looked puzzled until I remembered that, to him, Salome was her name. He gave me a blank look, but told me that Mary had no complaints of her.

Our friends were captivated by him at once; he was tall, handsome and assured, with an interest in all of Alexandria's wonders. He also had letters of introduction to eminent members of the city, through whom he arranged a visit to the Pharos and the holy huts where the Septuagint supposedly was copied, with further permission to visit the interior of the colossal lighthouse itself. All of us were impressed, for usually the public were not permitted on the island, at once so sacred, and so awful a hive of activity.

The island of Pharos was connected to Alexandria by a quarter-mile long causeway, which was perhaps two hundred feet wide. A road ran down its centre. Donkeys trudged in file, laden with wood and oil, accompanied by drivers carrying long switches of green bamboo. Waves plashed on either side, and in several places on the sunny rocks were inquisitive, whiskery seals.

'Their barks sound like questions!' I cried, and Stephen at once became their interpreter: 'They want to know who the three beautiful women are, are they new goddesses come from other lands?'

'Say I am too young to be a goddess,' murmured Neferenati, with one hand to her blowing hair.

Joseph looked all around, seeing everything, curious about it all. Abdel walked with him, and, with Neferenati, Kharys also walked with us.

The holy huts were no longer standing; only four incised slabs of marble, set into the ground, told of their construction and mooted where they had been. Joseph went separately to each slab, an oddly humble look on his face. 'The scene of our greatest gift to Greece,' he said quietly. 'The very words of our God.' Neferenati looked at him thoughtfully, but said nothing.

The shadow of the lighthouse reached out into the harbour with its unbelievable height. From its top issued a vast plume of smoke, which seemed almost menacing to me. By mid-morning, we stood at the entrance to the colonnaded court in which the lighthouse stood. Here we were to be met. The base of the lighthouse, with the courtyard that held it, reached virtually to the promontory's edge. It was a colossus against whose bulk humans were made tiny, inconsequential. The first two hundred feet of the tower was built of whitish stone and formed its vast, square base. The walls of this base were punctuated with windows, for this structure was also home to the hundreds of people who were the blood of the lighthouse, making it live: those who looked after its mechanics, both crude and precise; those who went to the very tip and manipulated the great light; those who hewed and repaired, and all the carriers, cleaners, herdsmen and cooks made up the rest.

A wide cornice separated the base from the second

story, which was a white octagon. On the cornice stood huge figures carved from marble, with upper bodies like men and lower bodies like the tails of monstrous fish. They held enormous conch shells to their salt-eroded lips.

'The Tritons,' our guide said, pointing up to them. 'Sons of Poseidon and Amphitrite, god and goddess of the sea. They blow warnings, to keep the waters and all upon them safe. And see, up there,' he pointed, 'the name of Sostratus, the architect of this wonder, which has no equal anywhere.'

The letters were thick and dark against the white marble of the cornice, and gave credit to the architect 'Sostratus of Onidus, son of Dexiphanes.' I wondered if anywhere there was a world that would credit the architect's mother as this pillar credited Dexiphanes's father, watching the smoke which, far above, trailed on the morning sky like an unreadable sign. The whole edifice made me feel cold and small. Inside the white octagon were scores of spiralling stairways creeping round the walls, where the steady burdens of wood and oil made their way to the massive pyre held in the circular room which stood on top of the octagon, and was built of reddish-purple stone. The narrow tip held the great angled mirrors which flung the light across the Sea. The whole structure looked unbalanced to me, its dark tip seeming heavier than its white base. Poseidon stood on top of the lantern, looking over his domain.

'It's exactly five hundred and eight feet high, to the top of Poseidon's head,' the guide intoned importantly. 'The Caesar Julius proved his stature as a strategist; he occupied the Pharos first when he came to conquer us.'

Most of our party was disappointed not to be able to climb up through the entire structure, but secretly I was glad. The lighthouse intimidated me, seemed full of hanging menace. The streaming smoke told of the fire overhead, where fire should never be, flaming oil and wood tended by near-naked slaves. Just to be in its shadow made my skin shiver. The parade of laden donkeys plodded to the tower. In the courtyard, children played and screamed. Women peered at me from high dark windows and on the breeze was the smell of burning oil. I walked backwards, as if to see the tower again in its entirety, but really to get away from it. Kharys followed me, waiting with me at the gate. We watched the donkeys and the children and the shadowed streaming smoke. 'What do you think of it?' I asked her.

'Extraordinary, but ugly,' she declared. 'I know it saves ships from cracking on the rocks and supplying the kitchens of Amphitrite, but no one would call it beautiful.' She tilted her head back, looking up the tower with slitted eyes. 'What do you think of it?' she asked Neferanati, who had joined us.

'I think it looks diseased,' pronounced Neferenati. 'Like an infected finger.' When the others rejoined us, all praises for the lighthouse, we went back down the crowded causeway, Joseph enthusiastically describing the system of shutters in the lantern of the tower. 'They allow the light of the sun to shine directly on them, and so they are able to flash messages along the coastlines all the way to Cyrene, or to the watchers at Abousir, where they have another such tower. Amazing!'

Abdel shook his head. 'No — there is not another Pharos at Abousir — only a much smaller tower, from which the light of the Pharos can be seen.'

Joseph took Abdel's arm. 'I did wonder if I was mistaken — if there were two such lighthouses, we would have heard of them, even in Jerusalem. Tell me what else I should pay attention to in your city.'

With such an invitation, Abdel took Joseph to re-enter Alexandria under the Gateway of the Moon. This was an archway over fifteen feet tall, with a spanning arch of twelve feet. The supports were statues of Artemis, Moon Goddess, whose Roman name is Diana. Along its crowning span were the moonshapes, from crescent to orb and back to crescent again. The statuary was finely done, picked out in silver and touched with gold, and the neck and hands of the goddesses were dressed with stones of lapis, and the moonlight-coloured pearl.

'Why is it called the Gateway of the Moon?' Joseph asked Abdel.

'Because, ten miles straight ahead, at Canopus, is the Gateway of the Sun,' replied Abdel in his meticulous way. 'The builders thought to imitate the passage of the two celestial lights.'

We passed under the arch and strolled into the imposing Canopic Way. There were knots of people, and somewhere, a small insistent drum. Under a tent top, people clustered avidly around a young leopard at its meat.

'I most certainly will go to see the Gateway of the Sun,' declared Joseph to Abdel, 'and also the greatest wonders of your Egypt, which I have heard are older than time and huge in majesty.'

I resisted looking at Santer, but could not resist a smile. This was a Joseph I'd never seen, Joseph the charmer, Joseph the ambassador. His interest was not feigned, nor was his attentive attitude. It is his passion, I thought, and wondered why I was surprised.

'You are talking of our Pyramids?' Abdel glanced at him to search out Joseph's intent. At Joseph's nod, Abdel smiled. 'It is some days' travel to reach them,' he murmured. 'I would be pleased to help in any way.' He bowed. 'I am honoured that you know of them, and still wish to see them, even though Alexandria is a city founded on the strengths of Greece.'

'All the world knows of your Pyramids,' returned Joseph deftly. 'They were old when our people were exiled to Babylon.' He looked round at the rest of us. 'That makes them the first philosophy, does it not?'

'How does it?' asked Neferenati. 'They've not been named in my lectures.'

'Or mine,' said Santer with a quizzical look.

'They are indisputable proof of great knowledge and right conduct!' replied Joseph, his eyes sparkling with his triumph. 'Ask your tutors if I am not right,' he added.

'How can you assume right conduct?' inquired Santer, motioning to the smaller road that led back to our house.

'Your foster father wants to debate!' exclaimed Kharys in a low voice, slipping her arm around my waist. 'What does he know of drama?'

I thought of the holiday in Caesarea, and the plays of Aristophanes. 'Quite a lot, I think,' I told her. 'And of medicine?' asked Neferenati. 'No, you'll have him there,' I said, and both of them grinned.

During his visit, we went en masse to the theatre, and out to Lake Mareotis, to a small public amphitheatre to see a display of Greek wrestling, and several concerts, in one of which Rhiaon played. He also went with Hiram and Stephen on a crocodile hunt, returning three days later with a massive skin and a bowl full of black claws.

Though he did visit the Pyramids, Abdel did not accompany him, Joseph having decided to make them part of his homeward journey, going down to the Pyramids then back up to Jerusalem overland, along the old, well-travelled trade route.

Before he left, he gave Santer and I more money, and asked Santer to verify again his promise that he would return to his mother in another three years.

'I do so willingly,' replied Santer. 'I have never intended to live permanently here.'

'And what is all about you has not changed your mind?' probed Joseph.

'No.' He did not enlarge on this answer, but Joseph

seemed satisfied. I was puzzled and mulled the conversation over in my private mind. What made Santer so committed to returning to Jerusalem, when Alexandria and its freedoms could clearly be our home? Nuances of his opinions expressed in our debates began to return to my mind as I pondered that question. How he was light, sometimes even glib when the subject was the Muses and their inspirations for theatre, for architecture, statuary, Poetry and the dance. How the ills and humours of the body left him unmoved, almost silent, though once when Neferenati talked about the known perils of birthing, he questioned her roughly, with a sort of horrified awe. He was disinterested in astronomy, and even the daily gift of nature's loveliness, unmindful of the traceries of wings against the sky, the throbbing green of reeds beside the still waters, the exclamation of oryx horns as it thrust against its mate. What seduced his interest always was behaviour and human actions.

I thought of particular questions he had thrown into the debates: 'What brings about the state described as happiness?' 'To whom does a person owe unquestioning respect?' 'Is there an absolute duty one owes to oneself?' He was also consummately interested in the dissection of power, in all its forms — of knowledge, of law, of utter sovereignty. At our last debate, he offered as a subject the power of work. He held there was an intrinsic power in work that was eternal, the drawing of water, the planting of seeds, the reaping of the seed harvest, the preparation of the daily bread. In this, I recalled, few of us had agreed, saying there was no power here, mere rote, the humdrum of survival. Or, if it was something, it was not power, which could be authorised and transferred, but something by another name.

'But it has just that,' he had said passionately, 'every day, regardless of what the ruling state is, all people feed themselves, relieve themselves, make love, sleep. This is

a truth known to everyone in the world, and a common-
ly held truth has an awesome power, power that always
has been and always shall be, power that you can
absolutely depend on! What's the first thing a great army
leader has to do when deciding on a campaign? Work
out how to feed his troops. What does a mother do each
day? Plan how to feed her children! Identical actions,
demanded by the power of being alive!'

'I disagree,' said Abdel. 'To me that is not power, it is
need.'

'What about the power then of music, which everyone
also shares?' interjected Kharys.

Rhaion shook his head. 'There is a kind of power
there,' he countered, 'but it is the power of one, exercised
(and we cannot know how similarly) only within the
autonomy of the skull.' He looked around our faces,
plucking notes from his lyre. 'All here would agree that I
have talent, and all here can agree that something I play
is pleasing; but can you decide among you that what one
of you heard, all of you heard?' He smiled into our faces
and picked up his cup. 'To the skull's autonomy!' he
cried, and we drank the toast.

'Irrelevant,' said Abdel decidedly, putting down his
cup. 'The power exercised by music is not demonstrated
by the musician, but the audience, and is a demonstra-
tion of an eternal power, if you like, Joshua. One person
can hold many silent, and also in the grip of some emotion, regardless of whether that emotion has been
named. That is power, clear, objective power.'

'Is music work?' asked Santer thoughtfully.

'If you define work as labouring over a specific action
to achieve a certain goal, it definitely is,' Rhiaon declared
roundly. 'How many of you work at your subjects until
your fingers blister?'

'I do,' murmured Lamia, but her voice was over-
shadowed by Julian, who said to Rhiaon with mock

sympathy, 'Poor you, how you suffer for your art. Let's kiss his fingers, shall we, make them feel better?'

And we had devolved into teasing laughter, and comparing body pains our studies brought us. But, before he joined in, I remember being surprised by the look of exasperated despair on Santer's face.

One summer night during our third year in Alexandria, Santer brought a new participant to share one of our debates. Philo was four or five years older than the rest of us, thin and tall, with a weak-looking body and a ready frown. Santer had met him at the Jewish Sabbatical lectures on ethics that he had begun to attend, and had become intrigued by Philo's lines of thought.

'He talks a bit like I imagine a camel would, if a camel could! Sort of chewy, and offering lots of words to choose from! But he thinks, Mary, he really thinks!' He leans toward me, hands flat on the table. I am looking over the food trays Nawaal and Buphaar had prepared for our rooftop meal.

'Tell me,' I invite.

He takes up a fig, rubbing at its bloom absently. 'He follows Plato, of course — who does not? — but he dares to go further!' He brims over with enthusiasm. 'You know Plato's Ideas, his Forms, as he calls them?'

'Yes — help me take these up to the roof. What about the Forms?' I pick up one of the trays and Santer, putting the fig on top of another, picks it up and follows me. We go up the stairs jutting out from the inner wall. 'Philo advances that these Forms are God's eternal thoughts, which were real Beings before God created the world!'

We emerge onto the roof and put the trays on the long table. The sky is a delicate lime green behind the

Pharos, and in the east, the crescent moon lies on its back as if to catch the three stars aligned above it. The moon is a faint, coppery pink. 'That's an interesting concept,' I reply. 'Does that mean that God also underwent some kind of transformation after the creation of the world? Or during it, more likely, as a woman is transformed by birth?'

'You'll have to ask him,' he returns happily.

I survey the glory around us. 'If Plato's Forms are God's thoughts, I have to say I think evenings like this are God's dreams,' I tell Santer. He looks at me, eyes warm and smiling, saying 'Incorrigible poet!'

'It's as likely as Philo's idea,' I retort, motioning him to come and help me with the other trays.

'What, that God dreams?' His voice holds the merest hint of a laugh.

'Why not? It's as provable as saying that God thinks!'

'Aren't we the proof?'

'Perhaps,' I counter. 'And evenings like this proof of dreams!'

'Point,' he admits and swings up another tray.

In my private mind, I wished Philo wasn't coming, for I had decided that I would try to begin to illuminate my future through the debate, and was going to begin tonight. My decision to do this had occurred several days ago, when Lamia had read out to us the newest of her poems. It was a lament to Crete, which she called the 'cradle of thought slung between the horns of Isis.' She brought against this image another, of the legendary Cretan bull leapers, swinging the theme backwards and forwards through the lines until they were clearly a metaphor for human endeavour against the might of gods and time. It began:

> Heel, horn, leap and swing
> The unimaginable yawns below —

I knew she had been working on the poem for several weeks, and thought it was well crafted and very good. It also disturbed me, in a way I could not immediately identify. The feel of it stayed in my mind and later, to her pleased surprise, I asked for a copy of it. This she gave me, beautifully inscribed on a miniature scroll. She had added a dedication: for Mary, leaper in the face of challenge.

The inscription, so personal and yet so connected to the poem's intent, made me realise more clearly its effect on me. Was I leaping towards my challenge, could I be if I wasn't aware of doing so? From his abrupt conversation with Joseph, I had seen that Santer had an idea of what his future life would be, but I had none. Before we began our studies, I was sure about my goal — to become a Poet, as I had said to Registrar Philadelphus. I had not wavered in that desire. But when I'd voiced it, I had thought becoming a Poet was something to be achieved with finality, in the same way that one became a teacher, astronomer, or practiser of law. I knew now that there was no surety that I could come to be a Poet, that I could achieve the wit or elegance of Ovid or Homer, Vergil's passion or even Sappho's grace. The opinion of my tutors was that my work showed merit. Slender threads for a future, and that was not all.

For hundreds of years, women of other countries had stood tall within their cultures. In Athens, Korinna could enter competitions and vanquish Pindar, and Sulpicia could publish her work with Tibullus of Rome. But where in Judaea was it possible to do so? Where, supposing I found something I felt worthy enough, could I find outlets for my work? The women of Judaea were not only without souls by male decree, they were also barred from the life of the mind. If I had known these two things fully while I lived in Judaea, they alone would have been enough to force me to leave. Now I shuddered with revulsion at the thought of returning, at once more living there.

When I had applied my mind to my situation, I could see it was not attractive: I thought about staying in Alexandria when Santer left, but several problems immediately presented themselves: what was I to do for money, how could I support myself? Even if I were to feel I was a good enough Poet to be published, would that bring me enough to live on? If not, what else was I to do? I thought it likely that I would have great difficulty having someone hire me even to do the work that Nawaal and Buphaar do. The only avenue, it seemed, was marriage, and I did not want to marry. But even if I cast that aside, there was the unsolvable riddle of my blood. What family would want me, a woman whose antecedents could not be proved? Even if I were to marry outside Judaic culture, this would hold true, and I would have the added burden of continually being an outsider. And lastly, I could not even imagine my life without Santer. Philo would bring an unknown element to the debate, but I decided there was no reason I should delay. I hadn't intended the discussion to be personal.

By the time we were all gathered, the moon had swung away from its lance of stars. The air was mild and sweet, with fireflies blinking close at hand. The last of the ducks had long since whirred their way to the lake. In the distance came the curl of a voice, nasal and high, winding around an instrument's reedy notes. Our table was crowded with food, with jugs of water, beer, and wine. Rush lamps flickered on the table, two more throwing light down the stairwell. We all wore white except Abdel, whose galabiah was dignified stripes of bronze and cream. In the rush lamps, gold winked: in the lapis-studded collar at the base of Neferenati's throat, from Julian's curls, and on the braided belt at Kharys's waist. Lamia had banded scarlet ribbons in her smoky hair. Rhiaon was, as always, carrying his ivory-inlaid lyre. Philo wore the crowding Jewish robes, as did Santer, perhaps in deference to him. I had added a bracelet of jade and pearl to the silver bangles on my wrist.

We ate roasted duck and wheat bread, olives, and lemon-soaked goose. Santer introduced Philo and spoke about Philo's brother, who was a tax official and who had recently adopted a fully Grecian name. 'So our friend wears the robes to remind his brother of their heritage!' Santer concluded admiringly.

'My brother was, is, will always seem quite young. He refuses the house of our father, and declines to return,' said Philo, a haunch of goosemeat greasing the fingers of his left hand.

'The son is the enemy of the father, the myths say, until he leaves the father's home,' offered Kharys, leaning forward to meet Philo's look. Her lips, unstained by plum or pomegranate juice, were very red.

'Is it the same for daughters leaving their father's home?' I asked into the pause.

'No, for daughters must stay, remain, continue in the house of their father until they go to the house of their husband,' answered Philo at once, uncomprehending. But the others shifted and rustled, and the air swam with tightening lines of argument.

'Why?' I made the word airy, almost dry.

'It has always been so,' he evaded. Everyone remained silent. 'To keep them safe, protected, unharmed, until they are passed on,' he elaborated. 'So that the husband has no worries, nor the father none.'

'Worries?' Neferenati inquired.

'Yes. The bloodline is without stain.'

'And what about a daughter's mind?' I asked swiftly.

'Her mind?' asked Philo blankly. 'That does not matter. Unless she is too simple, or in the grip of demons. But even then,' he went on, settling in. The haunch of meat

139

waggled in emphasis. '— even then, the blood would be certain. There just would not be a crowd of suitors, contenders, claimants for her hand.' He gave a quick bark of laughter, pleasedly looking round the table.

'Breeding tells,' murmured Kharys softly, which I knew was a quote from a play she was studying.

'Suppose there was a father-approved suitor for his only daughter,' began Abdel, 'and one other man. This other is a man of cunning, a thief. One day he sees the daughter perhaps in the fields, perhaps at the market. He falls into desire for her, he must have her. But he doesn't want her violently, he wants her open with desire, to match his desire, which is genuine. He knows he cannot come to her father, for he is a thief and everyone knows he is a thief. He watches the house, at dusk and at other times when he can't be seen. Soon he realises this woman is not like other women, her movements and speakings are different. She is a natural, a creature of the bridge. He realises that because of this, if he is clever about it, he can have her and no one will know. He is clever, and comes to her when she is drowsy with sleep, perhaps in the wheatstraw, perhaps in her bed. He strokes and murmurs her and they couple, with passion, with tenderness, and much, much pleasure. He steals away, content.

As for the woman, it was a pleasure, a happiness, almost like a dream. Two days later, her father agrees to a bride-price offered by the chosen suitor. Within a week, the bride is given over, the sale complete. In nine months, a child is born. All believe the bloodline is carried, purely, without stain. But it is not so.'

His voice, deep and lazy, lingered a little after he finished. He put his elbows on the table and his hands under his chin. His gaze was an inquiry as he met Philo's eyes. Philo shrugged and spread his hands. 'Of course, under such circumstances, no one would know.'

'Except, perhaps, the daughter?' Lamia delicately sighed.

'The daughter, yes, of course, surely,' shrugged Philo. 'But we are postulating, isolating, supposing that she does not bring her knowledge into the open?'

Lamia nodded slowly. 'Yes.' Santer nudged my ankle, and Julian smiled.

'But the bloodline would not be pure,' I advanced.

Again Philo's shrug as he plucked off another swath of dark meat. 'No. But they believe it so, so there is no fuss, no outcry, no war.'

'So what is important is the belief, not the actuality?' I pressed.

'We are human, and imperfect,' he nodded, his voice friendly, mellow. Laughter rippled. Rhiaon played a conclusive chord. I drank some wine, waiting, but perhaps because of Philo's presence, no one seemed eager to offer another gambit. So I offered one again. 'Suppose — since a daughter is the person with the highest likelihood of knowing the full truth of it — suppose the certainty of the bloodline was the lifetask of daughters? What kind of society would then evolve? Would it be very different from the societies we already know?'

'Each of them treats its daughters differently,' observed Neferenati. 'We have to have a common base.'

Several suggestions were tossed in:

'Allegiance to the bloodline,' from Santer.

'No — the state,' cried Julian.

'It must be the gods,' stated Kharys, looking at us as if the whole thing was clear. 'Anything temporal is too small.'

'Yes, of certainty it must be God,' chuckled Philo.

'Let's not use the obvious,' objected Neferenati, 'It will only cloud us. Let's take something completely new.'

This was the place I'd been waiting for. 'I propose — weakness. There is a society in which the certainty of the bloodline is the responsibility of the daughters, and its central tenet is a belief in the importance and protection of the weak.'

'Weak in what ways?' asked Abdel.

'All ways. Any way. Weak and vulnerable in body, as babies and ailing adults are. Weak in mind, or spirit.' I had an inspiration. 'The society believes that the weak are the thinnest of veils between this life and a parallel one which is the provenance, perhaps, of the gods.'

'Don't make it a perhaps,' warned Julian.

'No, you're right — the parallel life is where the gods dwell.'

'There would be no war,' said Kharys at once. 'The first victims of a war are the weak.'

'On the contrary,' Abdel replied, 'I think war would increase, because there would be an awful pressure to keep those weak ones safe.'

'Flawed, I'm afraid,' interjected Philo critically. 'Any war, no matter how conducted, managed, run, will obviously increase the difficulty of protecting the weak.'

'Not if you have it in another country, like Alexander,' commented Rhiaon lazily, loosing a minor note.

'Even so,' Julian reflected, 'you do increase the danger, because any traveller from the one country to the other can become hostage, and therefore immediately becomes one of the weak.' He picked up a flagon and refilled his cup. 'Kharys is right, there could be no war.'

'You would have to be ready for one, though,' objected Philo strenuously. 'Plato clearly surely, certainly shows us that. It is necessary to keep strong borders, boundaries, perimeters of your state, or soon you will not have one.

'What if you made it clear everyone was welcome there, they could have anything they wished, without resistance,' mused Santer.

'But then where is your society?' demanded Philo. 'It is diluted, irrigated, mingled.'

'Would it be?' countered Santer. 'The daughters of the society could easily continue to take responsibility for the bloodline, and the society's members continue to cherish the weak.'

'Inclusive of the "new" weak, people who now live at hand, even though they were not part of the original society, and do not share their beliefs?' probed Julian. 'Or does the society's belief extend only to themselves?'

'It would include all who believed it, surely,' Kharys declared.

'Yes,' exclaimed Santer. 'Don't you see? It can exist wherever it is, in more than one place, among even violent strangers. As long as there is belief.'

'That means the membership of your society lies in the mind,' murmured Neferenati. 'So why are the daughters still busy protecting the line of the blood?'

Santer opened his mouth to answer, but Philo spoke first: 'Suppose one of the strangers did not agree with the society's beliefs, and violated, raped, possessed one of the daughters, and impregnated her? Without an understanding of defence, let alone war, your society is soon gone,' he said decisively.

'Not at all,' I rejoined. 'As you yourself show, it's the belief that's important, not the fact. And in the situation you outline, the decision rests with the daughter, not with a phalanx of soldiers. She could leave the society, either physically, or through death.'

'Mmm,' said Santer. 'If she has belief, she will choose one of those.'

'Ah, but can you trust her to do so?' demanded Philo.

'Why would she not, since it is central to her belief that the bloodline remain pure?' Neferenati's voice was casual.

Philo heaved his shoulders up once more. 'Because we are human and therefore imperfect,' he said with a triumphant grin.

'How many societies do you know of, Philo, in which decisions are in the hands of the daughters?' I asked.

Philo pursed his lips, considering: 'Plato speaks of the Sarmatians, who live around the Black Sea,' he said slowly. 'But others? I can think of none.'

'So we can agree, that for the purposes of a debate, that a daughter society is — mythical. Yes?' I looked around the table. People nodded. Santer was looking at me with frank curiosity in his eyes. 'So. I postulate a daughter society in which young men are mere ornaments, with no power, and no duties other than to do what the daughters ask. Suggest plausible and effective actions for one such youth who is vigorous in mind and body to take within such a society, to gain for himself autonomy — an autonomy that is not desirous of causing division or war,' I added hastily.

'There is only one such youth?' asked Abdel.

'Yes.'

'What is his position?' asked Julian. 'Son of a queen or son of a peasant?'

'The daughter society does not have these distinctions,' I replied, eliminating this distraction.

'You do not say to gain for himself autonomy within the society,' Kharys pointed out, 'so presumably he could leave.'

'Apart from leaving,' I countered.

'What does he mean by autonomy?' asked Lamia, and Philo harrumphed in agreement. I seized her question. 'He is a singer, and it is forbidden for youths to sing. He is very fleet of foot, and it is forbidden for youths to run. He desires autonomy in order to sing and to run.'

A melancholy cry of notes was hung upon the air. 'Pray,' said Rhiaon. 'He'd have to pray.'

Philo sliced open two eggs, sprinkled them with salt and sesame seeds. 'A plausible action which has the chance, possibility, likelihood of being effective for the youth is to persuade, convince, induce others to his point of view. The more people he does so, the larger, greater, better the chance he will be successful.' He popped an egg half in his mouth. 'You do not say why it is forbidden,' he said somewhat thickly, then, seeing my mouth opening to say that was irrelevant, he held up his hand, continuing: '— and I know it is not relevant, except to say that if he could attack, strike, fight the bans at their root, this also would be a plausible action with a possibility of effectiveness.'

Abdel chuckled. 'It is also plausible that his voice would crack in his throat and his legs crack at the knee before he was successful.'

Philo agreed, and ate the other eggs. A little silence fell, which I would not break. Neferenati watched Philo impassively, her back and head erect. Her hands, graceful as reeds, toyed with a spoon. I could tell Philo offended her sense of order, but Philo would never know. Beside her, Julian was carefully cracking almonds and separating the nutmeats from the shells. 'Death would give the youth ultimate freedom,' Neferenati observed, 'and when the gods had weighed his heart well, Osiris would grant him the freedom to run and to sing.'

Julian chuckled. 'Only if they were the daughter society's gods.' He brought the nuthammer down on an almond with a decisive tap.

'No autonomy either,' added Rhiaon mournfully.

I looked at Santer, who met my eyes and gave me a little shake of his head. Either he had nothing to offer, or chose not to enter the debate for some reason. I wondered if he knew my goal. Then Lamia, who seemed to have been studying her hands, now raised her head. 'I think the most effective action for the youth is to live what he wants,' she announced. 'Let him run, and sing. You do not say if the penalty for doing these things against the rules of the daughter society is death, but it doesn't matter. If he runs, sings, then is killed, at least he will have had autonomy, will have moved freely in his being. If he is not killed, and continues to sing and to run, then he will increase his autonomy each time, move more and more freely in his being, and by doing so, it is possible he could achieve all the other things — change the dominant points of view, remove the bans, convince others of the rightness of his actions.'

After momentary reflection, we broke into spontaneous applause. Rhiaon lifted his lyre and played some grandiloquent riffs to her. As if in response, the house gently trembled.

'Did you feel that?' cried Kharys, jumping to her feet. The house trembled again, as if it was trying to wriggle, or shift its position. The oil in the rush lamps on the table rippled and one of the two at the stairhead fell. I was held utterly motionless by two conflicting things: the emotions raised by Lamia's words, and the sensation beneath my thighs and feet. In a state of confused ecstasy, I did not know whether to believe what my physical senses told me, that this substantial rooftop had briefly moved like water. Julian said calmly that perhaps we should leave the roof, Santer went to pick up the fallen rushlight.

'There is no danger,' Neferenati stated. 'It is merely that Nut has put her fingers on the earth. She wishes us no harm.'

'Sometimes the touch of the Great Mother can be overwhelming,' protested Abdel, who was standing poised by the stairway's top step.

'Not tonight,' said Neferenati with magnificent assurance. In the face of her composure, those who had gone from the table came back again, though Abdel did so most reluctantly. Julian put the almond nutmeats in a dish, sent it round, and resumed his task of cracking more almonds. 'Shall we have the godgame?' he inquired thoughtfully, 'It might be amusing to Nut.'

'What is the godgame?' asked Philo, taking some grapes.

Julian gave him a swift, bright smile. 'It's a game in which we discuss the purposes of goddesses and gods. Or, in your case, a single god. Interesting?'

'The purpose of God? Surely it is not for us to know the purposes of God!' Philo answered, genuinely shocked.

'Why not?' asked Julian. 'There is obviously a relationship between us.' He looked around. 'Shall I use the non-inflammatory word SIL in place of the g-word?' Philo was frowning deeply, but the rest of us cried yes.

'Thank you,' said Julian happily. 'So, as I said, there is obviously a relationship between Human and SIL, do all agree?' He looked round quickly, then longer at Philo, who gave a brusque nod.

'Right,' said Julian. 'Each of us here can say what our own culture believes that relationship to be, but since the *interpretation* of the relationship is only a human one — and we are all human — then, to add to the knowledge of what the relationship could be — for we, being human, are imperfect — ,' he dipped his head at Philo. 'we have decided to try to find insights into what their purposes, or goals, or desires are. For instance, could they want us to discuss the relationship we have? What is their purpose in having rules for us — or do we believe they do have rules for us? You see?' He studied Philo, who seemed mesmerised. 'We thought if we could gain insight into their purposes or goals, it could affect our choices, our actions.'

'A moment,' requested Philo, putting up his hand, forefinger raised. 'We Jews are not dependent on only human interpretation for that relationship. We have the Book, which was given to Greece — and the rest of the world — ,' he dipped his head at Julian, 'here in this very city.'

'Your book was still written by humans,' put in Abdel.

'They were recording what God said!' Philo was very stirred.

'But how do we know that?' I asked, my voice very casual. Philo glared at me, but I was not intimidated by his gaze. 'The most we can know, absolutely, without any question, is that the Book was written by humans. And humans are — '

'Imperfect,' burst in Philo with a gush of annoyed breath. 'But those humans had only God as the centre of their lives. They were devoted to God, and their purpose was the writing down of God's Words.'

'But not wholly, I think?' said Julian, glancing at Santer and at me. 'If my friends have informed me correctly, the writings speak of the doings of certain humans and also the doings of other humans who were declared their enemies? What is more natural — particularly for imperfect humans — that they write also of a SIL, say, omnipotent and invisible (two very impregnable qualities) that not only urges them to smote their enemies, but also says that such killing finds favour in the eyes of the omnipotent impregnable SIL? The purpose or goal of that action is clear to see.'

'God chose our people to be His people,' uttered Philo, face purple with rage.

'So you say,' drawled Julian, 'but you are human, and therefore imperfect.'

'Can you explain to me,' asked Lamia sweetly, 'why your chosen god is a he? Does that mean your god has sex? If not what is the reason for his gender?'

Philo pushed himself away from the table so violently that two cups of wine slopped their liquid out. 'This is the utmost blasphemy,' he stated, his voice compressed with anger and dislike. 'I will leave.'

Santer made an inarticulate sound, his face distressed. 'There is no insult intended, Philo,' he said urgently. 'It is only to get closer to the truth.'

'What it gets close to is blasphemy and disrespect,' thundered Philo and swept down the stairs. Santer hurried after him, his face worried, but I thought Philo quite inflexible, to be unable to take part in such a crucial debate. If gaining more and more knowledge about the Divine Mystery was not debatable by Philo, then he had begun to close his mind. Santer came back a few minutes later, a resigned expression on his face.

Philo's departure ended the evening, though I knew it was not late because Hiram and Stephen had not yet come home. First Rhiaon left us, with Kharys, saying they were to look in at another celebration in the home of other friends. Then Neferenati touched Julian's shoulder, and they both rose. Abdel and Lamia drank a little more, but the conversation was desultory, and they soon left. I stayed on the rooftop as Santer escorted them to the door. The moon was now high on the shoulder of the sky to the west, its brightness dimmed by the Pharos light. Only in the east was the light true night; above, the stars had a brilliance that compelled the gaze, their colours sharp, blue-white pulsing red, yellow, and a flicker that was sometimes green. The air was warm on my arms. I heard Santer's voice raised in goodbye, shouts of laughter from the next house; I could hear music, a shake of bells and the shiver of a tamborine. Slipper footsteps quick on the stairs. Then, 'Ooops, I think,' said Santer.

'I thought he was rather rigid. What scholar refuses a debate?'

'Mmm. I should have sounded him out a bit more,' he says thoughtfully, 'made it clear our talks were completely open. I'll try to talk with him tomorrow, and apologise.'

'Will he apologise to us?' I ask.

He looks surprised. 'Why should he?'

'I thought be was quite dismissive, and very rude to leave without a word to me. He ate half the goose, I hope you noticed! He could at least have said thank you for that.'

'He probably didn't even think of it — I know he's accustomed to much more lavish suppers, he told me about them. Ones with jugglers, and dancers, and thirty or forty guests. I don't suppose be paid much attention to what he ate.'

'That's no excuse. A considerate person says thank you even for a sliver of stale bread.'

'True,' he admits, and took a few almonds. 'Good debate though, I thought. One of our best. I was really interested in some of the ideas that came into the daughter society bits, weren't you?'

I lean on the table, picking at the grapes. 'Yes — I liked the idea of living one's autonomy, one's freedom of being.' If dissimulation is a form of lying, I was lying mightily with this casually spoken sentence. I had felt Lamia's words as a mouth which had been laid on my mouth and which blew new life into me. How simple it was, after all. I could see there would be difficulties, but when she spoke her idea, I saw immediately that that was the way.

'Mmm, it would appeal to you,' he replies, 'it's how you already live.'

I am considerably startled. 'It is?'

'Mmm. The thing that took my attention was your postulation of the importance of the weak. Even just the words of them, listen to them: the importance of the weak. Is that a paradox?' He slews around to lean his back on the table, his legs stretched in front of him. He laces his fingers at the back of his head. 'The importance of the weak. I like it.'

'I don't think it's a paradox,' I observe. 'What are babies but weak, and what is more important? Or people who are experiencing life in a different way than we are, like people who are dying, or people who are blind.' He listens attentively. 'Look at slaves,' I went on, and he gives a groan. 'Yes, but look at them — it's like babies, the future depends on them.'

'Clarify!' he shoots at me.

'As if you didn't know,' I say scornfully. 'Who are the weakest adults, in terms of power? The slaves. Yet the society depends on them, because it's fine to have the ideas, but they are useless if you don't have the labour. They are humans at their weakest position, yet like babies, the future depends on them.'

'Yes,' he says with the greatest satisfaction. And then again, 'Yes.'

A few days later, Abdel — to Nawaal and Buphaar's incredulous delight — brought me a cat. I had seen many carvings of cats and knew that it was considered a sacred representation of the goddess Bast, who was beloved of their principal female goddess Isis. One of the things I most liked about Egyptian society was their beliefs — their goddesses and gods had such dignity. Decius had told me a little of Isis, for her worship was popular in Rome. But he had said nothing of cats. It was one of those days when we did not go to lectures. Santer was away somewhere with Hiram and Stephen, and I was in the courtyard attending to my pots of herbs. The courtyard scarcely deserved the name, it was a scrap of space which held my several pots, a long bench, and a thin-boled casuarina tree. Clustered against one wall were smoke-blackened cooking pots and huge-bellied red amphora, one of which held water, the other oil. The kitchen door was open beside them. Along the farthest wall, a line of chamber pots were placed in the sun.

Nawaal came to me, saying 'The second most man has arrived,' which was her way of naming Abdel, since be was the second man of our friends she had met, Rhiaon being the first and Julian the third. I went to the doorway and beckoned him to join me.

'Abdel! How lovely! You look splendid — are you going somewhere?' He was wearing a very fine galabiah, a beautiful thick creamy colour, with subtle embroiderings in the same colour at the cuffs and around the neck. He carried a small basket. 'One must wear one's best when one is consort to a goddess,' he said with a flourish.

'What's that?' I laughed, brushing soil from my hands.

He sat on the bench and put the little basket beside him, then looked up at me.

'I've brought you a goddess,' he smiled and removed the basket's lid. Out curled the head of a young cat, perhaps four or five months old, with inquiring amber eyes and fur the colour of shadowed sand. It was like a jewel come to life, delicate and vivid. It stretched its neck, smelling the air, then with a quick, graceful twist, jumped onto the bench and then on the ground. I was at once enchanted.

'Mau!' exclaimed Nawaal, watching from the kitchen door. She called excitedly for Buphaar and, presently, they both came out and squatted down to watch the beautiful little beast. She called out a question to Abdel in their language; his answer made her smile.

'What did she ask?'

'She wanted to know if it was mine. I told her no, it was yours.'

He was beautiful himself, hair so glossily black and curling, high-arched nose and rich brown shining skin. The neck of his galabiah parted whitely against his strong brown throat, black hair sprinkled below. I saw other shades of meaning in his eyes. Nawaal giggled, drawing my eyes to the little cat. Its ears were pricked forward, head making the smallest movements as, with one paw raised, it followed the movements of a droning fly. The fly settled, the cat pounced — but not quickly enough. The fly sailed upwards and the cat leapt after it, paw outstretched, eyes intent. When it fell backwards, Nawaal laughed aloud, then nudged Buphaar and murmured some words. Buphaar went into the kitchen, returning with a little saucer of milk.

'Mistress,' called Nawaal. 'Give this.' She waved to the saucer and I took it from Buphaar's hand. I knelt on the ground, looking at the cat, which was now investigating the dirt around my herbs.

'How do I call it?' I asked Abdel.

'You will find a name for her, but in the meantime, just mau, like this.' He knelt beside me, calling, 'Mau, mau.' The scent of his body was cinnamon. The cat stopped its investigations and looked over to us. Abdel called again and scrabbled his fingers on the ground. The little thing bounded toward him; he brought it to the dish. It sniffed the milk, then eagerly began to lap. Nawaal and Buphaar gave soft exclamations. I kept my eyes on the cat, widely aware of Abdel.

'It is so beautiful, Abdel, thank you very much. Where did it come from? How did you come to think of giving it to me? Are you sure it's all right? I am an alien, you know.' I knew I was gabbling, but I couldn't stop myself. Involuntarily, I lifted my eyes to his, which were dark as noon shadows, and warmly intent. My skin tightened, my tongue became confused. The vein under my jaw throbbed. His hand lay on his white-clad leg, fingers with square tips, a graceful intersection marking the supporting bone of his thumb. He lifted his hand and touched me.

'Clear your mind,' he said gently 'No law is broken if a cat comes to your home.' But he was really answering the under questions, the hidden shafts of light that were dazzling my inner eyes. Suddenly, I wanted to feel my body on his. The hollows between my fingers ached to be threaded, my robe stretched my nipples, my legs felt wet. The cat had finished drinking and was now grooming itself in the sun. Nawaal sat watching it with a fond smile, one hand on her ankle.

I stretched out on my belly to study the cat, thankful for the hardness of earth. I pushed my senses away from Abdel, focusing on the cat and soon became riveted by it, the pink tongue, the glossy fur, the little pads at the bottom of each paw. The creature was utterly, satisfyingly beautiful. My heart opened with love. The cat paused, looked directly at me, and sniffed the air. It was very still for a moment, holding me with its gaze. To my amazement, its image appeared in my private mind. It seemed to give a miniscule nod, the barest movement of tucking in and downwards with its head, after which it continued its grooming.

'Did you see that?' I cried, looking up at Abdel, who swiftly smiled. Nawaal chattered something softly in her own tongue, and Abdel laughed.

'She said you are very lucky, that you now belong to East,' he told me. His eyes were fully on mine, tenderness in their depths. We looked at each other for a long moment before I turned away. 'But not to Egypt,' he whispered gravely, with a little shake of his head. The skin between his neckbones quivered like a beaten drum. He got to his feet as I sat up.

'No, no, stay there, Bast will want your soft lap soon,' he smiled, putting out a hand to stop me rising. And indeed, the cat had finished its work and was coming to me, lifting its feet high, tail erect as it came to investigate me. 'I will see you and Joshua tonight?'

'At Neferenati's, yes,' I said as Bast jumped on my thigh.

'Until tonight then,' Abdel murmured, and went into the house.

I thought of something and called him back. 'Is Bast a female or a male?'

'The goddess herself,' he replied, with a half bow to the cat, which was now beginning to knead against my leg. 'What will you call her?'

'I cannot call her Bast?'

'The name of the goddess is not dignified in such a way,' he said gently after a considering pause.

'Of course not,' I accepted. 'What do you suggest?'

'No — you must find its name yourself,' he said. 'That ties the bond between you.' He came down on his haunches and put a finger out to caress the lovely line of its neck. 'You won't find that hard to do.' The cinnamon smell of him was aromatic, close and strong. I put my forefinger on his hand, near the vee of his thumb. I could feel his eyes, but could not meet them. 'Thank you Abdel. I'm sorry,' I whispered obscurely. But by the half-quashed grunt in his throat, and a light clasp of his fingers, I could tell he knew what I meant.

I sat somnolent in the courtyard for a long time after he had gone. The cat in my lap was asleep, as were Nawaal and Buphaar on the cool of the kitchen floor. I thought of Lamia's freedom of being, feeling again the release that this gave to me. But I dared not live a freedom of being with Abdel, for in its recessed reaches lay the shapes of gods, babies and wives, waiting in the twilight corridors to be released. I knew my life was not futured with Abdel's, nor did I wish it to be. But if my future was to stay in Alexandria, perhaps I might have to turn to him. I stroked the dreaming cat, my hand sliding over its soft rump and onto my inner thigh. I smelled the fragrance of my desire.

The cat stirred, flexed out the delicate scimitars of its claws. Raked, my flesh shivered, and I gave a shallow laugh. The translucent ears were the pink of curled shellfish, hairs of gilt curving at the tip. What should I call this small loveliness, curled and curving, with its lambent eyes and exquisite fur? I thought to my poets, slid lines through my mind, and came to Sappho's incomparable flower, grown in the grove among the apple trees and casting shadows on the frankincensed air. The cat stretched sleepily, murmured once in its throat. 'My name is Mary,' I told the sleeping beauty, 'and your name now is Rose.'

Over the following months, Santer became more immersed in his studies than ever and this in turn was reflected in the questions he threw into our debates. Such questions began to form most of our ordinary conversations too, whether we searched the shore rocks, read aloud in the Mouseion gardens, or waded through reeds and lilies in the warm shallows of the lake. He seemed semi-obssessed with the concept of 'absolute duty to oneself', examining it in the context of one's family, and then one's friends. (Which allegiance has precedence, he had asked, and Julian had replied that only circumstance could know.)

Another time, he challenged us to try to create a test or tests 'that will reveal truth, especially unrecognised motivation.'

'Trying to catch the underside of a shadow!' glinted Rhiaon with half-closed eyes. 'Is what you are after so elusive?'

'Self-deception, that's what you are talking about, not things like the truth of beauty,' put in Neferenati. 'You really want a test for self-deception.'

Santer rubbed his cheek and slid his hand over his mouth, staring at and through her, mulling over her words. 'Perhaps I do,' he said.

She laughed at him, lightly drumming her fingers on the table, nails gleaming. 'That's easy,' she teased him. 'Ask an enemy. Or better still, a brother!'

I could see he was looking for some kind of certainty, but I couldn't see what it was, or why.

In the deep of the summer, the major festival of Bast was held. Since Rose had come into my life, I had often danced her honour in the little street festivals which took place almost every week. But this was the festival that included all the city, with a gigantic statue of her specially built and mounted under the arch of the Gateway of the Moon at the mouth of the Canopic Way. By the time we arrived, an immense crowd had already gathered. Jasmine and patchouli mingled with smoke and sweet oil on the still air. Dancers, their skin oiled and gleaming, were slyphs of gauze and fingerbells, dark eyes triumphant and arms bent with pride. The rattle of the sistrum pointed the beat of the drums and the ringing of scores of little bells. Rhiaon immediately joined a group of musicians and with them was now playing a fast-fingered tune.

Lamia and Kharys pulled me into a dance, though I protested I did not know the steps. 'Listen to the music then!' shouted Lamia, her braid bouncing wildly and, when I did, I found my feet knew what to do. We called and beckoned to the others, and soon were all swaying and pattering to the music, laughing under the deep lavender moon-filled sky.

More and more people swelled the crowd, which at a certain moment took on a presence of its own, amiable and huge. It parted to reveal fire-eaters at its fringe, and the flashing of juggled swords. Mendicants held out their hand, and more than once I felt the flutter of searching fingers at my waist. The crowd continued to move and we with it, effortlessly keeping to the dance. I felt exhilarated, wildly happy, as if I had become part of a radiant breadth, a thrumming current. The whole festival roared and flowed in one direction, the music made from many instruments and voices shouting and calling, singing Bast refrains. Then we were at the Royal Courts, where swans arched their necks at our noise and moved to the centre of the wide pools, parting the stems of the furled lotus in an attempt to hide.

Then it seemed as if my sensory boundaries fell away. Not only could I hear the shouting songs of the crowd, the finger flip of hand on drum and the slap of dancing feet, I could also hear flutes somewhere inside the palace, two lovers panting under a moon-striped palm and, at the very edge of it all, the night crash of the Sea. My body moved to the will of the current, every step I took fitted exactly. I could see colours rippling just above the crowd and as I looked at my friends, each moved in their own glow: Neferenati bronzed viridian, Kharys purple rimmed with deep red. Rhiaon seemed yellow bright silver, Abdel an indigo-shot seagreen. Julian shone both sky and night blue and there was a flame of persimmons and sunlight around Lamia's braided curls. I didn't think or wonder about it, there was no thinking, only being. I looked down at my body: over my arms and hands there seemed to be a glow of violet shimmering at its edge with a milkiness like pearl. I turned to look at Santer, who from head to jigging toes was clothed in iridescent scarlet, vivid as living blood.

The sound of the festival moved away from me — a ring of quiet expanded between my hearing and its sound. The quiet of the sky drew my attention, the soft gleaming dark almost blotted out by the patterning cluster of stars. I felt joined to the sky and to the earth, fully part of the whole, completely right and perfectly fitting. I was the whole, and it was me. It seemed as if that avenue of quiet that surrounded me was alive with a great awareness. I thought I heard the breath of the serene world.

Then the quiet collapsed; sistra and tambourines spoke in my ears again. When I reached my pallet, hours later, my exhilaration was undimmed, but I was completely tired.

My body was heavy in its need for rest, but my mind blazed still. I seemed not so much to fall asleep as to move into other halls and doorways, lit by a clear sun and with known voices calling from other rooms. Santer was somewhere about, I could hear his voice with the voices of other men, and I smiled as I heard Szuzanna laugh. There were steps down into hidden gardens, through shadowed cellars out to a cooling sea. Santer called my name, said the dance was beginning. I stood looking at the shore, thinking I must hurry, looking at the bones of a small beast lying whitely beside a knobby, spiralled shell. Then Lazarus took my hand and spun me into the rhythm and the whole throng clapped, though Mary frowned and bit her beautiful lip.

I came awake quite early, aware of my body, of a sort of sleekness, fullness, of immeasurable strength. Almost before I realised Rose was not with me, she trotted into the room and laid a dead mouse at my feet. I laughed and praised her, nudging the still-warm little body to please her, edging it to a corner where I hoped she would then make it her morning meal. The water in the ewer was almost warm, delicious on my skin. I put on a favourite tunic, one with bronze shoulder rings and a girdling belt.

The cries of the morning bread sellers and the lifting seagulls were crisp on the fresh air. From the market, I heard a peacock scream. I felt excitement running through me, a sort of pleasurable expectancy, as if the day held something momentous and wild. I heard Hiram's voice, Santer's answering, and went light to join them at breakfast, still feeling that every step I took was part of a pattern complete.

'Ah, the endless dancer,' Santer greets me. 'Are you still dancing this morning?' He said to Hiram, 'She danced last night as if she had been training since the cradle! She wouldn't be stopped either, and danced all the way home!'

'Seems to suit you,' says Hiram, pushing the bowl of oranges closer to me.

'It does, thank you,' I say cheerfully, taking an orange. 'Did you get to the festival?'

'We caught the very end,' he replies. 'We'd been to Canopus, to fetch wood for a merchant. Thirsty work,' he added with a meaningful smile. Santer stacks passionfruit skins one inside another, and reaches for more fruit.

'Has Stephen left already?' I ask, splitting off the last of the peel.

'No, no — still sleeping, I'd guess,' says Hiram.

'Good,' interjects Santer, 'because I'd like us all to talk this morning — if you haven't any plans?' He raises an eyebrow at Hiram.

'No,' returns Hiram. 'The wood job is finished. Next job starts in two days. What do you want to talk about? Money?'

'Money? No — is there any reason why we should?'

Hiram shrugs. 'It's one of the few things that concerns us all.'

'I suppose money is part of it,' Santer answers, then shocks me as dreadfully as if I had been swung through the fires of Pharos. 'No, what I want to talk about is the future. My studies are almost ended, and I'm thinking of our return home.'

I could feel myself blinking idiotically, my mouth muscles stiff. 'What?' The syllable came from me like a puff of dead air.

'Mmm,' Santer nods, wiping his lips. 'Seems impossible, but my courses will be finished in two more months.'

'What about my courses?'

'Yes, when do they end?' he asks, crossing his arms on the table and smiling at me.

'What if I said next year?' I fling at him.

His eyebrows lift in pure surprise. 'Surely not,' he counters after a moment. 'Each subject spans the same months at the Mouseion. The teachers cannot work continuously.'

'But what if they did,' I insist, my voice high and rough.

His eyes are on my face, objective, intent. 'Then we would have to make arrangements taking that into consideration,' he answers quietly. 'As we would if it was you who were finishing, or Hiram who had undertaken a project that required him to stay. Everyone's plans are important.'

'Of course I know that,' I say sarcastically, getting to my feet. Rage is smashing against my bones, shaking my throat and leaving my breasts cold. His voice is rational, reasoning, but the shock is too much, and I cannot contain myself. 'How could I possibly have misun- derstood you when you talk about going *home*.' My emphasis on the word was withering contempt. I almost spat the words out at him and swept from the room, going to the courtyard to the company of Nawaal and Buphaar, who were cosseting Rose. They drew back a little but I shook my head and turned away from them, looking up into the skimpy feathers of the casuarina's leaves, black against the morning sky. Its bony trunk seemed like the shoulder of my one friend, on which I laid my head and cried. How could I calmly return to Jerusalem, go from the freedom of this house and this city, from the joy of my friends? How could I bear to consider going into the captivity of Joseph's home, a much worse captivity than when I had been a child. Did Santer really see me donning the doubled, ribboned headshawl and being content to keep within? Were my studies mere decorations of time, fillips to his more urgent reality? Desolation settled round me, grey and thick; pain cracked under my ribs as I sobbed against the tree.

I felt I couldn't stay in the house, couldn't see Santer. I went to my room, heedless of Santer's call, and put some clothes into one of my woven bags. Then quickly, quietly and unseen, I went out of the house and hurried through the bright morning streets to the statue-bedecked Greek quarter, past the public pool and corner fountain, to Kharys's home. I wanted the comfort of Kharys, but I also wanted Santer to find me gone, to be alarmed and concerned, to feel some of the hurt he had given me.

There were people crowding to one side of Kharys's house, which disconcerted me until I remembered that her father was a doctor and people came to see him in the medical annex he had built to the left of the house. The people watched as I knocked on the door. With my swollen eyes and cheeks, I thought I probably looked as if I should be in their queue. A servant opened the door and recognised me, gesturing me to enter. He told me Kharys was at breakfast, and led the way.

Kharys and her mother, and two younger daughters, were eating fruit and bread on the wide terraced roof. Kharys's mother was heavily pregnant and did not rise from her lounging chair. Spread out to the left, as if for their personal delight, was the light-cobalt sea. Kharys smiled her surprise, saw my face, and jumped up.

'Mary! What's the matter?' 'What sorrows rush with an impetuous tempest on thy soul?' The book in her hand was Medea, which she was playing in the final production being presented by their drama class, but I couldn't respond, my emotions lost to control. 'Nothing. Everything. Joshua —.' Up came desolation's tears.

'He's not hurt?' The quick fear in her voice steadied

me. I put my hand on her arm and took a deep breath. I tried to smile. I could feel my lips twisting with the effort. 'Your other companions? Stephen and, and — '.

'Hiram,' I supplied wearily. 'No, they're all right, it's not that, Kharys, it's — .'

'Where are your wits, Kharys,' put in Kharys's mother, 'give your friend a chair, get her a little wine. You can see she's most upset. Leave the questions until she has once again become calm.' Her voice was deep, soothing; under its kindness, tears again closed my throat. Kharys apologised, ran to fetch wine, and a cushion for the chair. Her mother sent the younger daughters away. I sipped and sniffed, Kharys trying not to watch my face. I looked out to the Sea, watching the progress of two ships leaving the great harbour. Three others interrupted the skyline. Gulls held their wings steady as they slid down the wind. There were massive pots of geraniums, scarlet and white, and a dozen clustering pots of herbs. The sun touched my arms like a lover. The beauty and peace of the rooftop was pure anguish. Once again, I cried.

Kharys's mother called to her, asked a short question, then called to me.

'Mary? Mary. Come here, come to me, it's difficult for me to get up or I would come to you. Please. Come over here to me.'

I stumbled up and went to her, stifling my sobs, trying to wipe my eyes as she murmured wordlessly, pulled my hand and brought me to kneel beside her, put one strong warm hand on my shoulder and with the other, wiped my face. 'Now,' she said firmly, 'you tell Mama what is hurting you. Mary. Come, yes, you can tell me.'

I heaved and shuddered, sat back on my heels. 'I have to leave Alexandria,' I said baldly. I looked across her belly to Kharys, whose face was drawing into sympathetic shock. 'I have to return to Jerusalem.'

Kharys's mother put a hand to my chin and turned my face to her, scanning it intently. 'It is known as a fearsome city,' she nodded. 'Are you betrothed? Is it not the custom there to betroth the girls before the blood of womanhood arrives?' Her hand slid to my shoulder, patted it.

'It is a common custom,' I admitted, 'but my circumstances are different. But betrothal will be all I am permitted when I return,' I added bitterly. Once more, tears flooded my eyes, this time silent, without hope. Kharys recited, half under her breath, 'a deed of more than common horror'.

'It is customary for women to marry,' said Kharys's mother dryly, giving Kharys an admonitory glance. 'It is not so terrible, if you have a decent man.'

'You don't know our marriage rules,' I said vehemently. 'I want my life to be my own!'

'What does that mean?' asked Kharys's mother, genuinely puzzled.

'It means I want to do what *I* want to do, live a life *I* want to live, not do what someone else tells me to do, live where he wants to live.' I scrubbed the tears from my cheeks, furious now that I should cry.

'Have you money, property, perhaps a house?' she asked casually. I shook my head. Her eyes, brown and scored underneath with dark stains of tiredness, regarded me steadily. She gave a tiny shrug. 'Then you must marry. You would not wish the alternative, to go into harlotry?'

I scowled, and threw out a hand. 'Why does it have to be either or?'

The fabric covering her belly gave a discernible ripple, over which she laid her hand. She let out a long breath. 'Why is water wet? A woman with money has certain choices, a woman without money only two. That is how it is.' She beckoned to Kharys and held out her hands.

Kharys pulled her to her feet. Standing, she was tall, the loops and coils of her black hair increasing her height. My head came only to her shoulder.

She put her hands on my shoulders and kissed each of my cheeks in turn. The fragrance of her pregnant body reminded me suddenly of goats. 'Do not waste energy in trying to change what is,' she advised, holding my gaze. 'I tell you, there is power and pleasure in marriage, even for a woman. Put your energies into making sure you are married to a good man. You can find freedom in that, and will be safe. Excuse me now, I must have a little rest.' She patted my cheek as if I was nine instead of nineteen, told Kharys to stay with me and slowly descended the stairs, her left hand curved under her pregnancy.

Kharys and I stayed on the rooftop as the sun arched across the sky. It eased me considerably that Kharys completely understood my point of view and was horrified at the life I faced in Judaea. 'Never mind what Mama says,' she said confidingly, her arms around my waist. 'You'll find another way.'

I held her away from me so I could look into her face. 'Do you want to be married?' I demanded.

She wrinkled her nose, pulling herself free and, as usual, turning the coppery bracelet which she wore high on her arm. 'I suppose I do,' she said finally, 'if only to have my own house. This one is Mama's, and I am always her daughter here. But it is different for me, Mary. My parents will let me choose who my husband is to be.'

'What if you could have your own house, without marriage?'

She turned her face to the dying sun and quoted again from Medea: '"Rather would I thrice armed with a target in the embattled field maintain my stand than suffer once the pains of childbirth." When I read that, I thought of Mama. She says not to think about childbirth, that

Medea was written by a man, and what does he know? That yes, there is a pain, but it is natural pain, pain which the body is prepared for, not pain because the body is ill.' She smiled delightfully, her eyes still on the west. 'I think I would like to have a baby, have a child.' She turned to me, the pleasure of her thoughts still on her face. 'I guess I want everything that a woman can have. You do too, don't you? I'm sure you'll find a way.'

'What do you mean by that?'

'You are different,' she said consideringly. 'You don't have a father or mother or anyone whose authority you *must* obey, have you? Even Joshua is not really your brother, is he? And you are quick thinking, clever and brave. If any of those qualities can help find another way, you'll find it.' She pressed her lips together and her eyes were wistful. 'I am not sure that I ever could. I am only able to study drama because I am also studying medicine. I am to join my father in his work, because he has no son.'

'Did you not want to study medicine?'

'What I really want to do is be a travelling actor,' she told me with a quick half-smile.

'O, Kharys,' I said and took her hand.

Blue dusk was drifting in and the sky darkening, but light welled up from the street below, from the outer torches flaring in their sockets, and from the lamplit windows Some lambency of the dusk made bright the tunics and robes of people below, those passing by, and those still waiting by the annex gate. In the house across the street I could see into a room, where a small brass table with a pierced edge stood on a figured maroon carpet, many cushions at hand. On the table was an oval dish of olives, wet and plump. I knew what was going to happen in that room as if I lived there, people coming in, eating olives, drinking, talking. Loneliness pricked at my eyes.

'I'd better get back,' I said and let go her hand.

'You can stay if you want to; Mama has said.'

'Thank you. But it wouldn't solve anything, I realise that now. But thank you. I don't know how I would have gone through this day, without you.'

She moved her head a little as if to deny any debt, and simultaneously, we hugged. I sought out her mother, to say my thanks and farewells. She acknowledged me with a delicate grunt, looking keenly in my eyes. She nodded and smiled. 'That's very good,' she said obscurely. Then, to Kharys, 'Call Hektor to escort her home.'

I protested, but she gave me a sharp look. 'I am sure you do not plan hardship into your future,' she said dryly. I flushed, embarrassed, and thanked her again. Then I was on the street walking through the dusk with Hektor, who was massive bodied, with heavy muscular legs covered thickly with pale hair.

Near the market square, some twenty or thirty soldiers lolled on the steps of Alexander's tomb, drinking and watching passersby with jocular remarks and frank stares. Several bare-footed women were with them, their laughter deliberately loud on the young night. I was glad of Hektor's presence for without it, I would have been too visible, perhaps even taunted by the group. As it was, I was merely an ordinary female being taken back where she belonged. I remembered I had grown so accustomed to my safety, to being always with our group of students, that I no longer even carried my knife. Hektor padded on my right, silent and alert. On our left, the day's heat radiated from stone walls. I felt sticky and tired, and very much alone. Hoofbeats sounded; three high-necked horses flashed past, each ridden by a dark-faced man wearing voluminous robes and cloak. In their wake came dust, the smell of leather, horse-sweat and spice. And an impression of strength, of them riding together united in a single purpose. I wondered if it would be the same if they were hurrying for their evening meal or on some more serious intent, and knew it would. It struck me that their strength was like the strength I felt from our group debate, joined by each of us not only to test our individual knowledge, but also to reach for a higher understanding, to try and discover a great dressed stone which would prove to be the threshold of Truth.

For a moment, I saw the eight of us carrying that stone to a place of public exhibition where we were cheered by a toga-and-tunic crowd and consulted on all manner of questions for the rest of our lives. I almost laughed aloud at this, then was a little appalled. Was that what my desire was? Public acclaim? The search for the stone of truth was all in my mind: no such comradely undertaking had ever been voiced in our gatherings and it was taken for granted, even by me, that when our studies were ended, we would go our separate ways.

If I was to have the life I wanted to have, I must do it myself, live my autonomy, as Lamia had said. So what did I want to do? In Judaea, nothing that I could see. In Alexandria, some possibility lay that I could write, could publish my work, could perhaps even teach. That would be privately, of course, but the possibility was there.

But when Santer went back to Jerusalem, I would be alone. My mind sped among the avenues. Stay with Kharys and her parents, turn to Lamia, Neferenati? Could that be? But I was seeing clearly now. At best I would be a moneyless adjunct to their lives, an unacceptable thought. Marry Abdel? My breath came quickly. He stirred me, that was undeniable. But that was merely joys of the flesh, he was not offering marriage. And if he did, would I be able to teach, what would be my position as wife in his family, alone, moneyless, not even familiar with their traditions?

I saw then that the decision I had to make was simple: stay with Santer, or go? Then the afternoon at the inn slid into my mind, with Szuzanna giving Santer halvah and figs, and asking him to grant her a boon. It was because of her farsightedness that I was now in Alexandria, walking beside a guardian and turning into our familiar, night-filled street. Torches had been lit and flared at our door. Two things were very clear now: that I could not readily leave Santer; and Alexandria, white dream city, was not a place I could readily stay. 'Help my baffled virtue,' I muttered, perhaps even to Medea's gods.

JERUSALEM

The journey back to Judaea was a deliberately long and circuitous one, for we were to go via Greece. Both of us saw it as a kind of homage, a journey of respect, Santer to Socrates and all the thinkers since, and I to the writers who had stirred my thoughts. So we boarded a ship in the western harbour one bright morning, the sky a radiant pale yellow behind cloud bars of grey. The ship was very different from the one on which we had arrived, though it too was a merchant ship; but this one was larger, very clean, and Greek. It was bound first for the island of Crete. Rolls of papyrus were our cargo, and great mounds of cotton, and nutty piles of wheat.

Neferenati and Julian walked with us to the boat, and we were joined by Kharys, Lamia and Rhiaon. Abdel stayed away. He sent parting presents, one for Santer and another for me. Santer's was a miniature scroll, one of those made for a private library, on which was written the final Socratic soliloquy. To me, he had sent a broad armlet of beaten gold on which had been embossed the silver leaves of the Mouseion studentcy, surmounting the eternal Eye. Other gifts soon appeared, Neferenati giving me a wisp of cotton that was an under-robe, Kharys a vial of patchouli, and Lamia her latest poem, bound with a violet cord.

We seemed to leave so quickly, their figures indistinct and soon dwarfed by the sweep of the red pillared harbour and the shining white city beyond. I thought of Rose now in Nawaal's charge, and wondered if she would miss me. The thought of her, of the marvel of our Mouseion days, of our debating nights — so much lost, including the joy of the city — brought grief running like a river.

When I had cried for many minutes, Santer looked into my sodden face. 'Here,' he says quietly, 'come and look here.'

He takes my hand and leads me across the deck, through a maze of coiling ropes, ducking under the round, sail strung beams to a small open space near the ship's prow. 'Look, look ahead. You cannot see any land, no other ships, no other human thing. But there — ,' his hand makes an arc to the right, 'there lies Greece. And Rome is crouched beyond the horizon to our left. Now tell me it is right to dwell only on what is behind.'

I manage a half-hearted watery smile. 'It just seems so much to have lost.'

'Lost? How could you lose any of it — it's part of you.' He laughs and taps my forehead. 'They are all in there, forever, aren't they? And always as they are now — which would please Rhiaon, you know!'

That makes me laugh. Rhiaon, so pleased with his beauty, would certainly applaud everlasting youth. Something splashed, and Santer touches my arm. 'There!' Not far from the ship, scores of dolphin had begun to leap among the waves. They are so lovely, flashing silver backs in the lapis blue that I clap to see them, and am lessened in my woe.

'Is the future to you really as blank and open as the Sea, then?' I ask Santer after some minutes of watching the leaping bodies.

'Not quite,' he returns after a long pause.

'What is it, can you tell me?'

'No,' he replies, almost absently.

'Am I part of it?'

At that, he gave me a curious look, one eyebrow lifting quizzically. 'After all this, all we have done together, do you doubt that we will not always be part of one another's lives?'

The water soughs beneath us, smacking the blackened wood. A sailor shouted to us to stand away from some ropes.

'Why won't you tell me what's in your mind?' I demand.

'Because I don't know myself yet,' he said patiently. 'What is the hurry? We have all the time in the world.'

'Have we?' I say furiously. 'Perhaps you have, but if I don't have a plan of action long before I reach Judaea, I might as well fling myself into the Sea now, while I still have some control over my life.'

'It's your choice,' he answers, almost coldly, and draws away from me.

I look down into the water, the flexing waves like the back of a humping beast. I imagined falling into that immense wetness, dark depths full of eager mouths. A shudder runs over me and I quickly lift my face to the sun.

'Exactly,' says Santer.

We sailed into Iraklion, the port above Knossos, two days later, on a calm, rose-coloured evening, the dolphins still leaping at our prow. The violet sea was overlaid with carmine at the horizon, and all the lovely houses flushing pink. Lamia's poem, inspired by the ancients of this island, came vividly into my mind. In the three days we stayed on Crete while the ship offloaded cargo and replenished water and food supplies, Santer and Stephen and I walked the shrub-clad hills with Tyander, a Cretan who became our guide. Spurred by my questions, which themselves came from Lamia's work, he tells us of the ancient Cretan days of glory, of the magnificent palaces of the queens, where young girls learned the strength of their bodies by leaping down the backs of sacred white bulls long before Theseus arrived.

From Crete, we threaded our way through the Kyklades, islands a dreaming blue in the distance, bright fawn and green close at hand. This seemed the birthplace of statuary; every island had its complement of pillar and figure, some clustered as if in discussion, others white and singular on promontory or point.

We were a month in Athens. We became familiars of the Parthenon, with its moon-shafted columns and altars dedicated to the Virgin Athene. On the full moon, there was a festival in her honour, and a ritual blessing of honey and wheat in the Erechtheion, the smaller temple with its porch formed of statues of women, their garments seeming to need only a breeze to make them move. We listened to impromptu lectures, and Santer was delighted to find that we could purchase scrolls which contained salient points from the philosophies of Aristotle, Epicurus, and Zeno of Citium, propounder of the emotionless philosophy known as Stoicism.

In one theatre we watched the miseries of Hecuba, whose travail reminded me strongly of Zeralia's; in another, the forbearance of Alcestis, and the dignity of Hercules. I wished for Medea to be presented, because Santer had not yet seen that betrayal tragedy, but no players were presenting her during our stay. In the amphitheatre, we watched gymnasts, and youths with glistening bodies wrestle and toss.

Twice we stood in a crowd around a magus. They could not have been more different, the first wearing robes of high quality, a chain at his neck suspending an intricate jewel. There was even gold in his ear. The other was half-clad, with ungroomed hair and long, dirty nails. But each provoked a similar reaction when, at their touch, miraculous cures of the body seemed to take place: an aging woman, twitching and frothing became calm, eyes rational. She got up, straightened her garments, and bowed her thanks. A youth with a crooked hand, its flesh withering, now pulled his fingers open and shut, to his great astonishment. Some in the crowd threw coins, but others muttered of demons and Baal-Zebub.

'What do you think?' I whispered to Stephen, who looked a little pale.

'Too scared to think,' he hiccupped. Santer turned his head. His eyes were wide, focused on his inner thoughts. Then he glanced at me, his gaze sharpened, eyebrows lifted.

'Mmm?,' he asks.

'Do they scare you?' I want to know. 'The magus?'

'No,' he says, his tone reflective. 'They make me think.'

We also went to a newly accessible library for the public, which held over 300,000 scrolls. Among them were Vergil's original manuscripts, the Eclogues and the four Georgics, which extolled the art of farming, and the Aeneid, which held many puzzles for me. The library awoke new yearnings in me: to go north, to Lesbos and Ilium; to Hierapolis, to the temple of Artemis, and Olympus, the great mountain of the gods which lay between Thessaly and Macedonia. But we could not, and I contented myself with buying maps and poems, beautifully scribed on the personal library scrolls. We returned to the same vessel for the southward journey, to Rhodes, then across to Cyprus, and soon, distressingly soon, down to our own coastline, past the ports of Sidon and Tyre. The day before we landed at Caesarea, Santer handed me a gift: a dozen little scrolls, all held in an ornately embroidered pouch, and scribed with my own poetry.

'Lamia said you would like this, Poet,' he says lightly.

I am so surprised I cannot speak. They are so beautiful and my words look so different, somehow, scribed by a hand that was not my own. It is as if they have an added lustre or have received through some medium of the scrivener that mysterious illuminatory power that to me, the words of all the other Poets had. It is as if they named me Poet at last. I hold the scrolls delicately, as I had those in the Cleopatra library, and though I cannot speak my pleasure, it must have been explicit on my face. Santer nods once, a pleased, definite nod that says he understands.

Together, we examine the scrolls one by one. The words are attractively placed within the space around them, the scrivener's hand flowing and sure. Santer points out phrases that he particularly likes and others that have woken his curiosity. We are absorbed in my words for nearly an hour, when from above, the stamp of sailors' feet and the bellowing cries of the captain signal something untoward. The vessel begins to rock violently. Stephen shouts our names and burst into the cabin as we get to our feet.

'Storm!' he says breathlessly. 'Captain says a bad one, we're in for a shaking, prepare for everything to get tossed about!'

I look around the cabin, strewn with our belongings. The boat rocks again, sitting me down hard. 'Come on,' I order, grabbing the nearest objects and putting them in a pile. They pitch in; the rocking of the ship kept us losing our balance, so much so that a wild hilarity comes over us, shrieking with laughter and insulting each other as we push everything into three mounds and stretch towels and robes over each of them. In my private mind, I'd been registering the ship's movements, a sort of sliding motion, followed by a huge impact that was like a blow.

'I've got to see!' I say when everything is done, and push myself to my feet.

'Where's Hiram?'

'Helping the sailors, but it's not a good idea for you to go up,' warns Stephen. 'The best thing we can do is to stay out of their way.'

But I have to see the storm. 'Just for a minute,' I tell

them. 'I want to see how it looks.'

The wood of the ladder is flecked and sticky with salt spray. I take one step up and look into a wet sky, several shades of scudding grey cloud racing across unripe olive green. There is huge noise, that I have never heard before; my ears stretch to the puzzle of it. I climb three more rungs. Then I realise: it is the wind. Wind, roaring. Another step, and I see the wind's force, rushing high above the wavetops and parallel to them, pulling whole waves upwards as if to swallow them. All the colour of swords and metal are in their bulk, iron and silver and a dull coppery green. Some waves were pulled into quivering pillars that shine in the low grey light. The ship stumbles and slides down the long slope of a wave and great spouts of water come smashing over the side. Water is flung across the deck directly onto my body and face. I fall back into the cabin, drenched and shouting of Homer's seas. Stephen grins sardonically. 'So. How does it look?'

'"Many a swollen wave rolls onward, and on high the spray is scattered beneath the blast of the wandering wind."' I exulted in Homer's own words, shaking water from me. 'You mean wet,' grins Stephen. Santer thrusts an arm into one of the piles and brings out a towel. I sit down very quickly as the vessel skitters down a slip-wave, and shudders from a resounding blow. That's water breaking, I think.

There is hardly any light left in the cabin. I laugh, squeeze water from my robe, and rub my hair.

'The bread is in the pile you're sitting on, Joshua,' remarks Stephen pointedly.

'Yes,' grunts Santer, forages briefly, finds it, and hands it around. The shriek of the wind makes it hard for us to talk. Presently, Hiram comes in. We sit in the dark, chewing bread, saying nothing. The ship creaks and groans, the storm roars around us, and I am completely happy.

But the following morning, looking toward the coastline where Caesarea is becoming more distinct, all my fears for the future swarm up again. I am filled with a sense of peril as the bright fast breeze brings us closer to the shore. 'I've got to talk with Joshua,' I say urgently to Hiram. He looks taken aback, but merely nods. Santer is further forward, talking with one of the other passage-buyers, who had come onto the ship at Rhodes and is going with it on the final leg of its return to Alexandria. They were deep in conversation, but Santer comes away when I ask him if we can talk alone.

'I was enjoying that,' he frowns. 'What's the matter?'

'I *cannot* go back and live in Joseph's house, Santer. I can't do it. It is like making myself voluntarily a slave, because there's no doubt at all that Joseph will immediately make marriage plans for me, if he hasn't already. He sees it as his duty — in Alexandria, he as good as told me my studies would make me marriageable. Santer, you know what the marriage rules are like — you know I can't do that. *I can't*. Even the thought of it makes me feel crazy.' Emotion runs through me, shudders of cold resolution. Santer's eyes are hidden from me as he frowns and studies his feet. 'I'll go back to the inn, that's the best. Perhaps Hannah will be glad of another woman in the house. Malachi will welcome me I know, and David won't object — .' I babble on, trying to convince myself.

'Stop it!' Santer commands me in a low voice. 'That's nonsense. How long do you think you could stand it now, bringing food to strangers and milking goats? You are no longer a child, to be satisfied with such things. Now listen to me. I've been thinking. I have thought this before, in fact, but you have such antipathy to it — but I think it is a sensible way. I think you ought to marry me.'

I gape at him.

'I understand why you hate the thought of marriage — you know I agree with you that the marriage rules make women like slaves. But if you could bear the thought of marriage to me, it's a workable solution for both of us.' He gives a humourless laugh and turns to look out at the sea. 'There's as much pressure for me to marry, maybe more. It's my duty — Joseph also spoke of it to me when he came to Alexandria. That's one of the main reasons that I have not sent word ahead that we are on our way home.'

We stand beside each other, watching the ship's forward progress in the curling waves. He put his hand around my shoulder, his touch light and warm. 'Could you do it, do you think, be betrothed to me and married, if it was to me? I wouldn't force you to live as the rules say, wash me or prepare my bed and my cup, all that.' He laughs. 'I could never see you doing it, though, even if I asked!' He gives my shoulder a squeeze and takes his hand away. 'Do you think you could? Bear it, I mean. If you could, we both would be free.'

'Yes,' I blurt out, not realising until then that I have been holding my breath.

'We do have to go to Joseph's house though — you can see we must. My mother. And all the things we've brought. But it will be different, if we are betrothed.'

'Yes,' I repeat, much more calmly. 'It's such a good idea, Santer! I hadn't thought of you having to marry but, of course, it's just as bad for you. It's so good a plan, it worries me! Could Joseph — would Joseph stop us? What will your mother say, do you think? Shall we be betrothed for the usual year?'

'Joseph couldn't really stop us, we're too old,' he says thoughtfully, 'but it's probably easiest for us if we follow the form and have a marriage contract, which he'll look to. My mother? I don't know. She's not predictable, as you know.'

The waters are getting paler, the statues in the harbour now distinct. I feel elated and like crying. I push my hair off my forehead and put a hand on his arm. 'I can't tell you how much better I feel, I was in such a panic!'

He narrows his eyes against the sun, and clasps his hands, watching the shore. 'The play that we saw in Athens — Hecuba — had two brilliant lines — .'

'Only two?' I interjected.

'No — but these two stuck with me. Both were said by Hecuba. The first was, "No man upon this earth is entirely free"; and the other, "There is strength in numbers, and we have surprise."' He takes my hand from his arm and tucks it under his elbow. 'That's what we've got, goatgirl. If we stand together, no one can touch us. We will give each other our chances.'

Though the robes were bulky, I could feel a pad of muscle, and underneath, a rib. I looked shoreward again, where the light lay hot on the long pale hills. 'I still don't know what you intend to do,' I remind him.

He glances at me briefly. 'No. I'm sorry. I can't speak of it. I don't really know myself. It's still more or less just an idea.'

'So it's not working with Joseph, travelling to get his artefacts, or scribing for him, or anything like that?'

'No.' He takes a deep breath. 'I — I —.' He let his breath out in an explosive puff. 'I really *have* to talk with my mother first. And to find out how things in Judaea really are. It's hard to judge from so far away. There are other things I have to find out as well, though that's a little later. You could help with that, but only if you want to.'

'Such mystery,' I say mockingly. 'You know how curious I am. I'll be delighted to help — I'll find out more that way.'

179

His eyes are amused. 'You might,' is all he would say. He presses my hand against his side with his arm, then releases it. 'There's Hiram with the first of our things. We'd better help.'

As we pick our way back to the cabin, I feel a surge of excitement about our future.

I could see us working on whatever project Santer was mulling over, and together, bringing it to great success. Words began to tumble in my mind, to do with chosen labour growth, and intensive birth. I thought of huge-bellied cattle, of olives ripening from hard green nubs, of smooth-shelled eggs and crowing cocks, of the gleaming skins of newborn goats. These would lead to the creations of humans, I would talk of poems swelling, and the hidden musical note, then of carvings and offerings, like the red obelisks at Alexandria, and bring in the Pyramids, which we had still not seen. Yes, that would work, I thought happily, for it will link perfectly with Olympus, home of the Titan gods.

In Caesarea we realised that in addition to horses, we would have to buy a little cart to carry the two sea-chests we'd brought, which were too awkward and heavy for donkey or horseback. We could choose camels, Hiram pointed out, but they were slower and would make us a prime target for the brigands of the hills. I was surprised how small Caesarea was now to my eyes, how narrow and rutted its streets were compared to the Canopic Way. The statues were undiminished in their grace, the temple too, but to my eyes these now seemed out of place, as if set down amid the brawl of the port by a passing godly hand, who had not yet returned to scoop them up again. The faces in the streets seemed narrow and closed. I began to carry my knife again.

As we wound our way through the Galilean hills, I saw the cruel face of poverty. It was drawn in the hard barren earth around the mean homes, in the defensive dark faces of the sun-scarred men and the weary-limbed movements of their pregnant wives. For the first time I saw how easily I could be a child of this country, how easily I might have wandered away from a gaping door. There were scraps of villages, yelping dogs, a few chickens a-scratch. Each well had a rutted circle round it, the biggest ones patronised by the water sellers, men who staggered under the weight of huge jars, carried on the back, but held steady by the straps which crossed and cut deeply into their foreheads.

'Were people here always so poor?' I asked Hiram, who was taking his turn at riding in the cart with me. 'Or has something drastic happened while we've been away?'

'Nothing new about any of this,' he said briefly.

'What a terrible life,' I muttered, staring and yet aware of the intrusiveness of my eyes to old, shawl-wrapped women who squatted in the black shade of doorways, their tattered cloths spread out to dry.

'Perhaps,' returned Hiram. 'Not many Romans here.'

'Meagre fare, if that's their only blessing,' I retorted.

Hiram only shrugged.

The face of poverty awoke a feeling in me which at first I couldn't define. I felt uneasy, almost furtive, yet indignant too, and helpless. But on the third day, as we sighted Jericho's tower and smelt the first stink of the tanneries, I realised that I felt guilty, guilty that I wore a robe spun of fine white cloth and under it, a delicate cotton tunic. Guilty that I rode while others, much older and in more need, walked. Guilty at the thought of the costly scrolls, ointments and artefacts we carried. Guilty about the food in our packs, even about the future we faced. I had raged against slavery almost all my life, but only now did I see that the slavery of poverty, which had so pitiless a face, was the most inexcusable of all. I thought of the Temple that Herod had ordered rebuilt forty years ago, with its marble floors and doors of gold; and of the building of five elaborate porticoes spanning Bethesda's twin pools, also Herod's gift to God. And wondered in the silence of my private mind if I was the only one who saw this as reflecting Herod's fear and greed, rather than extolling the glory of God.

'Have you been bitten or something?' Stephen grinned. 'You're snorting like a horse!' 'I am not,' I retorted immediately, realising that I was. 'Mind your business!'

'It is my business, especially if you've got fleas.'

We traded insults amiably as we climbed up into Jerusalem's tree-clad hill, going through the new city of Bezata, the outskirts of which now almost reached the inn that was my childhood home. We came to the most northerly of the city's walls, where the best of the garden lands were, one of which belonged to Joseph and was tended by Boaz. All around us were flourishing, tall grey-green chickpeas, lettuces, purple aubergines and the lilac-tipped spears of the white-bellied garlic. Almond and orange trees fringed the eastern groves of the garden, and olive trees, and figs. Gardeners, naked except for loincloths, worked between the vegetable rows, indifferent to the traffic on the road.

The shadows showed the sun well past its zenith as we went into Jerusalem under Genath, the Garden Gate, perhaps three hours of daylight left. We made slow progress down the clamouring market street but soon turned right, into the first of the side streets that led us eventually to Joseph's door.

The world thinks it knows what happened next, but what the world knows is mainly lies told through that wretched book that men insist contains the gospel truth.

Why were believed the mouths of men who thought the new blood of lambs and doves would turn God's eyes beneficent, yet damned the blood that bore their blessed sons? Such men saw that the truth Santer offered was too powerful, would sweep them all away. It's true he studied the prophecies, but that was because of his mother, and her plans for him. Later, even when our plans were in the early stage, they were our plans. I say 'our' because it was both of us, a truth which uncovers the greatest lie of all, that it was only him. It was together that we saw the people's increasing need, and together sought for ways to break the hammers of those hand-clasped powers: for, as Santer said, if the priests promulgate a God who blesses only those who can pay, they have made God a merchant, no higher than other merchants; and if the observances of respecting such a God, in a time of no kings, are open only to those who can pay, why should the priests be active against the Roman power? And he agreed with me that it was obscene to pervert the power of birth, to deny its ultimate holiness, and to make sacred instead only the sons of the race; obscene also to deny the succour and comfort of the feast days of God to those proscribed by the Old Words — 'women, children, slaves, blind or lame men, those of doubtful sex, those of double sex, sick or old men, and those who can not walk.' None of these could come to a feast day, which then became a celebration only by vigorous free men.

His mother, and Joseph, were with us at the core of it — and Lazarus, Martha, and the scatty impassioned Mary too. Stephen stayed with us and James, Santer's brother, was never very far.

That was all later. After our arrival from Alexandria, there were the long, long days with his mother, they conversing for hours, always apart. She was not troubled that we were betrothed, merely nodding, as if she'd

expected it, or already knew it. In those days with Santer, a deep serenity came about her, displacing, as I had
seen it do before, her usual veil of anxiety.

I did not plague Santer to tell me what he spoke of
with his mother, partly because a new calm had come to
me because of the betrothal, and partly because I was
frequently away. Though Mary did not mind that Santer
and I were betrothed, Joseph was incensed: he had
already spoken — obliquely but clearly — with the head
of a powerful family who had an unbetrothed daughter
of thirteen. On this future contract, it was clear he had
already erected several plans. I heard their argument,
Joseph's words spattering out like a spray of thorns,
Santer cold and firm: 'What contract, she has nothing,
you might as well marry a slave for all she brings you.
Have done with it.'

'What she brings is priceless, and she is a woman, not
a formless child. If you will not draw up the marriage
contract, I shall seek it elsewhere.'

So it was no surprise that Joseph's face darkened when
he saw me, and his manner was curt. So I went to stay
in Bethany, where Martha now completely managed the
house and, with Lazarus, the vines and groves as well.
Their father had died two years before, quickly, and in
the fields that he so loved.

Santer and I went to live in Capernaum after Passover
the following year, and Stephen came with us. I think if
it had been possible, Mary would have left Joseph and
James at that time, and come with us too. Her desire
fought with her duties as wife, but apart from stains of
anguish in her eyes when we left, she gave no indication
that she wished to came. Again she gave us money, and
begged me to make sure that the house we came to live
in was clean.

By the time we left, Joseph was reconciled to our
betrothal. Santer had also talked with him apart, as he

had done with his mother, and whatever he had said, it had brought Joseph's respect, as well as an allowance. He commanded us to send letters frequently, and gave us a wide shallow bowl of precious glass, blue with a gold rim and with a single star shape incised on it. I knew that it was from Persia, and had long been part of his collection, for I had been part of the household when it arrived, and it was an artefact that Joseph knew I admired.

Zeralia too came with us. James was well past the need for a nurse and though he doted on her, it was plain that she had no real place in the household any longer. Her broad face was the only one which shone with pleasure at my return and, when I was not at Bethany, she was my closest friend. Neither Joseph or Mary put up any resistance to her coming with me, but her heart was in pain as she said goodbye to James, and his face was solemn as he watched her go. On our journey, I told her that she was no longer a slave and gave her the papers that made her free. The happiness that this gave me, which I felt deeply, blinded me at first to the apprehension on her face.

'Does this mean I must go away?' she asked in a low voice, her head bent over the paper.

'It means you can go anywhere you wish,' I told her happily. She raised her face and I was shocked by the fear on it. 'What's wrong?' I involuntarily cried.

She put the paper down and rubbed her hands over her face, then folded them in her lap. She looked at me steadily. 'I thank you for my freedom, but what am I to do? I have known only this family since I was a young girl. Who would know my face on my father's lands, and as for my sisters, where should I begin to look?'

My cheeks went hot with embarrassment for my insensitivity. I put a hand on her knee. 'We are sisters,' I said, 'and you may live with me until you want to live

185

elsewhere. And we are friends. I hope we are friends?'
Comprehension came swiftly into her black, oval eyes.
She nodded, and gripped my hand very tightly.

In Capernaum, the betrothal allowed Santer and I to
share the same dwelling; also legally, Santer could call
me his wife, but we had set no date for a wedding. We
resumed our Alexandrian custom of sharing our supper
with other people but now it was done differently. The
guests were not students, or even teachers, though they
would not have been exempt. But one or two nights of
the week people with whom Santer had spoken during
the day shared our food, wood-sellers from the hills, tax
collectors, builders and dressers of stone, walnut har-
vesters, weavers, and the makers of public bread.

It was in Capernaum that Santer at last opened his
mind to me about the full extent of his plans. It was the
end of a Sabbath day. The candles still burned but the
prayers were ended, and we were relaxing after a small
meal. I had guessed that his plans were far-reaching, but
thought that they lay in the law, that he was preparing
to become an advocate for the people, that this reason
underlaid the invitations to our supper guests. But he
talked passionately of the merciless shape of religion, of
people who were discounted, and the increasing aloof-
ness and power of the priests.

Zeralia came in, with pomegranates and walnuts, put
them down and went out again, saying she'd bring the
wine jar.

'Then what is it you're going to do?' I take a pomegranate and break it open, its little red globes cool and
tart against my teeth.

He hesitates a little before saying, almost helplessly,
'I'm beginning it. It hasn't got a name. It's a — hearing
what people say, a listening. Then a sharing of the knowledge our studies have given us. It seems so simple, but
Mary — it feels right to be doing it.'

'Do they pay you?'

'They try to,' he admits, and runs a hand up into his hair. 'I tell them I do not want money, but they often bring me food.' He sighs a little and rubbed the back of his neck. 'It's such a delicate thing, a person's pride.'

'Wine for us all?' asks Zeralia happily as she returned. She tilts the wine jar and fills the cups.

Through the following months, he also continued studying, spending two or three days at this pursuit each week. He was re-studying, he said, the history of Israel, the times of its domination, the failures and successes of its wars, and the documented promises of God. Of these last, he now became exceedingly doubtful, a doubt which scourged him and at first nearly drove him mad.

'They sound too much like human desires,' he cries to me, 'all concerned with domination, and winning. Everything I look at, the warrings of the ancients, the actions of the Caesars — every one of them looks the same, and fits the same promises — "Join with me, kill our enemies, and you and your people will become great."' A heavy sound comes from his throat, a sound of disgust. 'The past well shows that to be a lie! What does that say then of the promises of God?'

He gives me a burning glance, his face twisted as if all his teeth were hurting, then whispers 'Do you believe there is God?'

The moment in the night of Bast's festival returned to me, when my senses had been enlarged and I listened to the breath of the aware world. I went to his side and put my arms round him. 'I believe in the Mystery,' I say, my voice very low. 'What do you believe?'

And he replies: 'I do not know.'

We talk until long into the night, his arm around my shoulder, my arm around his waist. He talks of the things we'd studied, how he'd searched for hints of the answers in the sheets of a thousand scrolls. For a time, in Alexandria, he thought that Philo was close to the answer, when he affirmed that the rites of our religion were merely symbols, not unchangeable rules. 'But he still felt it mandatory to observe all of them,' Santer remembers with annoyed bewilderment. 'When I challenged him, he said that nothing he could think would change God, and as I well knew, continuous observance of God was central to the practice of our beliefs.'

His philosophical studies had taught him how to ask questions that would clear a way to truths, and Truth. 'Then, in our debates, I tried to look at duty — do you remember, I used to talk about — ?'

'Absolute duty, yes I remember! You were almost boringly insistent about it for quite some time.'

'Mmm, I suppose I must have been. It was bothering me quite a lot.'

I lean against his shoulder. 'Santer. Where is this all going? Tell me what you think.' He is silent for a long time. I heard Stephen laughing in the kitchen, teasing Zeralia, who answers with a pleased, indignant voice. She had lit some cinnamon incense, its fragrance drifting into our candlelit room. His reply astounds me with its utter unexpectedness: 'I think I must see my mother again. I'll have to go to Jerusalem.'

In his absence, I concentrated on the work I was doing, with Zeralia's help, which was to go daily to the outskirts of the city and seek out the children who were hungry or sick. Zeralia knew how to help children become well again, which I was learning from her, and we always took with us a pouch of bread, olives, and fruit. In the evenings, I wrote of the realities the children faced, and their hunger themed my poems.

Santer sent me two letters, the first to tell me he was going to be away much longer than he had at first thought and the second, a few scrawling words, said he would be even further delayed. He was away altogether for several weeks, and on his return I could see in one glance that he was unutterably changed. He was well, but it was as if his body, which had been all health and strong flesh, had been reshaped somehow. His eyes seemed full of distance, as if he had looked on immeasurable dimensions and taken them in. His mother travelled with him, for he had told her the time had come for us to be married. I made her welcome, hurrying to cleanse properly a private room for her, Zeralia bringing her water, and a little food. My actions were automatic, as were the words I exchanged with Mary, for I couldn't get over the change to him, which occupied all of my mind. Eventually, spontaneously, I said to Mary, 'What has happened to him?'

Her face which carried that serenity she always had when he was with her, now seemed to reflect a triumphant happiness. She answered, to my enormous astonishment, 'He has been baptised.'

That drove all thought of respectful observances from me: I positively ran to Santer. He heard me coming and was waiting at the door. He slid his arm around my shoulder and we went outside, walking down the long-shadowed street and out into the uncut fields. There were small white meadow-flowers in the coarse drying grass, and the nesting holes of snakes. His arm around my shoulder felt like a bar of sunlight. I was conscious of its energy, like a radiating vibrancy which seemed to be entering me somehow, making my very bones ring. I was silent, waiting for him to speak, but I kept stealing covert glances at him. What I could only interpret as ecstasy, palpable as the sheen of oil, shone from him face.

'All the time I wondered,' he begins as we near the centre of the field, 'what was this feeling I have always had, like a hollow in the very centre of me, which seemed to pull at everything I did. That was one of the first things that made me like you, how positive you were — remember? You were in no doubt that you owned that riverbank!' I smile at the memory of my childself. We sit down, our backs to the city, the hills and field before us enamelled with a rich, mellowing light. The sky was cloud-free, aquamarine, and very deep. 'From that first meeting, you seemed to give coherence to my life,' he continued, 'and open new doors to me — would I have studied other cultures if it were not for you? Gone to Alexandria, to Athens — even to Crete? I don't think so.' He takes my hand, tracing the sinews on its back, the lines on its palm. Then he holds it lightly in his own. I am astonished by his words, by this view of myself and how he thinks of me. 'What you do not know of me,' he resumes, 'what I have not been able to say to anyone, even to you, is that my mother has told me, ever since I was very, very small, that I was a god-born child. That my father was not really my father, but that I was quickened in her womb by the holy Spirit.'

He presses my hand lightly and releases it, then lies down flat, looking up at me and into the dome of the sky. If I had been astonished before, I am now stunned, receptive but without a reaction to his words. 'It is not an easy thing to live with. When I was a child, her words made me squirm, made me feel different, and not in a good way. I thought that if my father was not really my father, then I was only half-balanced, only half-formed in some part of me. My mother's odd words, and the hollowness I felt, made all that worse.' He turns on his side, put up an arm to prop his head, his other hand idly separating strands of browning grass. 'When we went to live in Jerusalem, with Joseph, I thought that I would become properly balanced, and was determined to be a proper son to him. I wore clothes like the ones he wore, and was interested in what interested him.' He laughs. 'It worked for a little while — until you came! Then your why, why, whys, and your anger about slaves smashed right through that carefully built wall!'

The folds of the hills are filling with purple shadows. Nearby, a cricket gives a tentative croak. 'I had decided that I wanted to look for answers elsewhere some time before that evening when you raged at me about your life and said you were off to Greece! Your thoughts were again so complementary to mine — and gave me courage, I must admit. There didn't seem to be anything you weren't prepared to do. But I always knew I would have to come back here, that somehow, this was the only place that I could reach the heart-truth of my mother's words.'

He pushes himself up and looks at me; the clarity of his eyes were like a feathered blow. 'I apologise for almost forcing you to leave Alexandria. I would have agreed with your staying, if you had said you were staying, but it had to be your decision. I knew what I had to do.' He sits up, putting his arms around his knees. 'I went down to Jerusalem this time because there was still this hollow — much smaller now, but still there — at my centre. I hoped if I talked with my mother one more time, I could make the pieces of the puzzle fit at last. On the way, I heard of yet another prophet— you know how these hills have endlessly been home to that kind of man. This one was a little different, he was baptising people, in the name of a new and coming Messiah — though there have been many hopefuls make that claim here too!'

Again that flashing glance, as if his eyes are overlaid with a light like that from the moon. 'Talking with my mother helped, as it always did, but I still had that same feeling of uncertainty, of hollowness. I sent you that first note, knowing I could not return until *something* was clarified. Anything. Just as long as I wholly knew. I can't remember actually deciding to go to see this baptising prophet, whose name is John, but I must have asked directions and crossed the bridge, because next morning I had done so, and was on the east bank of the Jordan.' He is silent for a moment, watching the final flow of colour streaming from the sky. Then he gives a little chuckle and a single shake of his head. 'He's a wild one, John the Baptist. I think I made him nervous — I certainly wasn't like the other people who'd come to hear him and be baptised.' He chuckles again at the memory. 'He even asked me why I'd come! I said that I had heard he was baptising people, and also that he was a new Messiah.' 'I'm not that,' he told me straight away, 'but one is coming who is.' 'There's always one coming, isn't there?' I said to him. 'It's a favourite subject of poems in more than one place. I don't think he'd read Vergil, and he didn't like my tone of voice. He became very stern and told me that he'd seen the signs, that a genuine Messiah was at hand. What signs, I asked him and he said letters of flame in the heavens and, where arid rock had always stood, prayer for a sign had opened a bubbling spring. It was a bit awkward. I could think of nothing else except to ask him to baptise me, offering him money to do so. He struck the coins from my hand.' Again that low chuckle. 'I hope he found the coins later, he looked as if he needed a good meal!' Then he was silent, for a very long time.

Twilight deepened, thickened into blue night. The eastern star glowed just above a distant ridge. The cricket was chirruping steadily, others echoing its notes further away. 'I don't know what I expected the baptism to do,' he resumes reflectively. 'Perhaps douse me into clarity, end my so onerous uncertainty. But it didn't do anything of course, except get me very wet. I hadn't brought a change of clothing, either. When I left the Baptist, I was so fed up with everything, not in a rage, but a despair, a flat annihilating despair. I remember feeling that I wanted to run away, to get clean away, to be utterly gone. So I just — began to walk. I seemed blank in myself, if that makes any sense. I had gone quite a distance, when I remembered you. I didn't know where I was going, or how long I would be, but I knew I had to let you know. Yet I couldn't stand the thought of going back. But when I turned my steps, there was Hiram, walking a hundred yards behind me, leading my horse. I'd completely forgotten him — and the horse, but it was the forgetting of Hiram that shook me, and showed me the enormity of my despair. But as I walked back to him, I realised that I now had a certainty, and it was overwhelmingly clear. The certainty was that I must get away, must be alone.' He shook his head a little and a brief smile shows me his teeth, white in the blue dark. 'I can't tell you how that felt. I wanted to cry, and also to shout it out! Anyway. I told Hiram to go back to Jerusalem, to tell my mother and Joseph that I would be away for a time, and to send a letter to you, saying the same thing. Then I walked away.' His low chuckle, infectious, brings my lips up in a smile. 'It's a good thing it was Hiram — Stephen would have plagued me with questions! But Hiram, after one fairly shrewd look at me, just gave his usual nod, mounted the horse and rode off.'

He is silent again and the night voices fill our ears. The air is now like the elixir of the purest water. The eastern star has swung higher and on the rare dark air I hear the cries of goatherders mingled with the lead goat's bell. When his voice comes again, it was very quiet. I have to strain to hear: 'Then I was naked and there was nothing, nothing, no before or after, nothing. I cracked open, and it filled me up. Light like a shaft slicing into my skull, down my spine to my genitals, pouring into me. Then I was aware of —'. His voice completely dies away. Then: 'I saw it,' he breathes, 'and there was no doubt. It filled me. I was of it, and it was of me. The living Spirit.' He is quiet.

Minutes later, he reached for me, holding me to him, and I discover my cheeks are wet. His whole body, where it touches me, radiates the vibrancy I had noticed earlier, which now is transmitted to me, spreading through me with an indescribable sensation. I thought of Olympus, and ichor.

We stay in the field, talking and touching, becoming closer than I had ever dreamed it was possible for two people to be. The eastern star arched and sank to the further Sea. We heard the sound of wolves baying on the nightwind and listened to the world turn to its rest. Through those hours I knew the full meaning of union.

He was lighter in his being than I had ever known him. His whole demeanour had changed. He delighted in every moment, was aware of everything, both the near and far aspects of it, the quiet scent of the white meadow-flowers and the stellar scent of a small dawn moon. He could hear the slide of the worms through the closed earth and see through the folds of distance and time. The beautiful night stretched and diluted to grey. He turns to look behind us and says: 'Zeralia has woken and put on a robe trimmed with blue. She is heating orange juice for my mother.' Then he looks surprised and said, 'There is a child with her.'

My mind is wholly taken with the proofs he was declaring. I knew him soundly and deeply, that he was full of truth, and not mad. So I could have no doubt, not outwardly or in my private mind. And I realise I feel none. I knew his truth with my heart and my mind, my emotions and my body. I knew it as he knew it, with complete certainty.

How could he not speak of it? It was the centre of him, the miracle in his life. To me, to Lazarus, to Martha — and finally even to Joseph, he described what he had seen there, what had touched and filled him: shimmering limpidity, irrefutable Spirit. Of us and through us and around us — containing everyone, and holding all. The whole, plain and mountain, rock and bubbling spring, the warmth of beasts, the cool firmness of fish, the scent of a little child.

Events ran so quickly, when I look back: his own discovery of how the Spirit empowered him, and what that meant he could do for others. The word spreading about him, the people coming. The first healing, a spontaneous reaching out of his hand, and the fever leaving the child. More and more people coming, as he struggled with his empowerment, what it meant for him. He had no barriers to the Spirit, but the routine of days would gradually begin to close his continuity, and to renew it, he would go apart, to be by himself and fully open himself again.

The crowds, the gathering, believing crowds. They called him teacher and then, so quickly Messiah. His comprehension getting wider and wider until he could see his fate. We tried so hard to stop it, Joseph pleading in the Sanhedrin, and later devising the plan, giving orders to Boaz to take four stone-breakers to the northern garden to hollow out a tomb.

When she began to know they would kill him, Mary became utterly beside herself, wild in her mind. He took her apart with him one day, and when they returned, she was exalted with the Spirit as I had been exalted, and happy. After the sentencing, but only for a short time, Mary utterly collapsed, and I was filled with a terrible fear. Zeralia was our mainstay, calming us by a reiteration of the plans. 'We will save him,' she told us over and over again.

Joseph's money oiled the way to Pilate, and to the soldiers in the death-field. When Santer knew what was going to happen, saw that he could not avoid it, he came to me, shivering. I held him as fully as I could, my arms across him, the energy and emotion of my body wholly open to him. I pleaded with him to leave Jerusalem, to stay out of their trap. He leaned back and looked into my face. 'They want my life, one way or another,' he said, and I knew it was true. 'They would agree to me leaving Judaea and not returning, and they have repeatedly said I would be unharrassed if I vowed to stop speaking in public. But both those things are not for me to do.'

I did not try again, but spoke urgently with everyone.

Santer was unconscious when Joseph's money allowed us to take him down. We took him into the garden tomb, where Martha and Zeralia waited, with jars of balm and ointments for his wounds. We made bandages from the white cloth we had brought from Alexandria. Nicodemus, a physician Joseph brought to the tomb from the city, thought that he might live. We smuggled him out of the city to Szuzanna's inn, where Malachi and David guarded him. I went to the tomb early the next morning in case any of his followers arrived. Many did, and I told them that the tomb was empty, that his body had gone. Our plan was to get him right away, to make certain everyone thought he was dead and his body beneath the tomb's arch. We used our subtlest strategies.

Mary was right, there was room in the boat for me, as well as for herself, Martha and Zeralia, Hiram and Stephen too. Lazarus was always too frail to travel, and his sister Mary also did not join us, having married the year before and now being close to birthing her first child.

Santer regained consciousness and was aware of all of us, but was irreparably weak. He could not raise his voice above a whisper, and being in the airless cabin during the voyage sapped his strength further but we had no way to cradle him on deck. Two weeks after we arrived in the new land, he died, Mary and I each holding one of his hands. With the quietest of ceremonies, we buried him and centuries later I heard that on that spot there is now a tomb. By the next night, Mary had disappeared. We hunted the villages and hills for her, Joseph bewildered, then obsessive, then finally accepting she too was gone and would not come back. After a time, he too left the quiet place where we had come and went back to Jerusalem.

Martha, Zeralia and I stayed together and it was with them that it became clear I was eluding the blades of age. I thought and thought about how and why this should be, and came eventually to know that it happened that night in the meadow-flowered field. After their dyings, I was free to go where I would, to live across and with the world. And, like Santer, I sought long and sorrowfully for the task that I was to do. I watched the distortions taking place, the slow eradication of the truth, even to the changing of his birth time to that of Mithra's, with whose cult Santer's proselytisers stormily battled. Eventually, I became aware of a story, repeating and repeating, first in this country and then across the world, of a woman who seemed not of this world, who appeared on isolated hills, who clearly came to speak with children, with girls and young boys. From the words they said she told them, and the way they said she looked, I became convinced she was Mary. And so my search began.

RUMOURS OF DREAMS:

NOW

In the evenings, after Venus has risen, I use the telephone once, to call Sabe. She tells me of town inquiries into my whereabouts, from money officials looking for further exchanges, not aware that my contracts with them have ended, as Sabe has turned my silver into this country's erratic currency. Sabe asks about Rose, whose arrival in the garden of this watchtower house surprised her mightily. Until then, Sabe had helped me because of her love for Grace, whose life she had shared while she lived in England. When I spoke of Rose, I saw a tiny seed of doubt suspended in her eyes, dark like a mustard seed in an acrylic grasp. So I delighted in her reaction when Rose, who has her own secret ways of eluding the temporal embrace, strolled into the kitchen as I was making Sabe breakfast, chirruped a greeting to me then looked at Sabe inquiringly. I introduced them, then reached for Rose's bowl. Sabe, her mouth wide with astonishment, stared at Rose, and up to me. Rose sat down, waiting for her bowl to be filled.

'She's exactly as you said — exactly.' Her head shook in minute motions of disbelief turned to belief, and from that moment, I could feel that she had left the sidelines, had joined us. Her energy was healthy, clean and strong and eager, just the kind we need.

She asks about my health, and I tell her that I am well rested, and eating, and that I would like her to come again to the watchtower house by the sea. Perhaps it is because of my alignment with the earth's magnetic impulses that travelling by 'plane is so exhausting to me. Travel of any kind other than walking, horse-riding, or by a small boat dizzies me, though I have acclimatised fairly well to the car. But airplane journeys of any kind, even minor ones, leave me with a feeling of being ripped apart, and this one, the longest 'plane journey one can make across the world, left me cold, shaking, and feeling as I imagine it feels when the sundering of the spirit from the flesh is near.

Each day I walk somewhere by this beguiling southern ocean, getting myself ready for what is to come. Sometimes I get as far as the long pink sands of Pakari, a few kilometres away, where green waves prise up palm-sized shellfish and present them to my searching toes. The shellfish have creamy shells striped with old green, black, and the palest mauve. Inside, their bodies are slick, delicious, and of a yellow-toned grey, sweet and salty at the same time to my searching tongue.

If my day is busy, I forgo this sort of treat and content myself with bathing in the shallow hollows of the tiny bay below my house; but if I am triumphant, feeling nearer my goal, I reward myself with a visit to my salt-spray favourite, Goat Island, a broad curve of rocks and sand where the waters are deep and utterly clear. My body is pale among its cool kelp-strewn waters and exquisite summer-blue fish circle inquisitively around my waist and knees. The rocks are punctured with small holes from which the glassy black eyes of coral-bodied crabs peer. Under the surging water, I see starfish inch into the old dark sand and little fish swim silver among the olive vines of kelp. White-breasted gulls scream at my approach and a swift, unnamed bird flies low over the swelling waves.

Few people live hereabout, a handful of thick-bodied fishermen, some milk-and-butter farmers, and a weaver at a loom. From the former I barter sustenance for my table, but from the last, sharp-eyed Marjory whose fingers whisper among her threads, I have gathered stories of the region, tales of people I shall never meet, some who still live here, others who have long been gone.

None of her tales ring of Mary.

Marjory is curious about me, curious and cunning. She does not ask questions, rather seeks to draw facts from me during the sun-warmed contentment of afternoon tea, when her cheese- covered scones, hot from the oven and spread with fresh yellow butter, should make me lower my guard and spin my life's tale into her expectant ear.

'I went to Istanbul once,' she tells me. 'A beautiful and dirty place, smelling of the Bosphorus, and thick with cats. It's a noble river, don't you think, and the people quite foreign, like yourself.' Her old white eyes flicker over me as her hands nudge the butter and honey pots closer to my plate.

'Who is not a foreigner among strangers, Marjory?' I laugh, and cup my hands around a mug of her strong dark tea. 'In the right place, you are quite as foreign as I am.' She pulls at the throw around her wool-covered shoulders. 'I've lived here all my life,' she demurs, nettled at my evasion. 'You're the recent arrival, Stella Mante.'

'True,' I agree cheerfully, and stand up. I leave the custard and stewed apples I have brought her on the table. 'Thank you for that sumptuous tea.'

'Sumptuous — now that's the thing right there,' she says, screwing her neck around to look up at me. 'Who else round here would use a word like that? Most you could expect would be "terrific", or maybe "super".' She mimics the delivery perfectly and I laugh. She stays in her chair. In her eyes is a small pleading fury, enough to rouse a pang of compunction in me and the realisation that I must build this bridge carefully so that she is willing for me to cross.

'I want to tell you and will tell you, but not right now, Marjory. It's too soon,' I say quickly and give her a brief hug. Unspoken is the thought that I am recovering in some way, from an illness perhaps, or even a death. 'But soon,' I promise her. 'You will be the first to hear my story. Now I must go. I'll come again in a couple of days. If I may?'

She gives a short nod, but I can tell that she is pleased. She settles herself squarely to her loom again, as if to dismiss me, to show that I have interrupted her and that she puts up with my visits because she is known to be kind.

'I'll put the kettle on if I am here,' she says airily, in denial of her swollen, arthritic knees and her lack of a car. Though if she was not here when I next came, I would not be surprised. Marjory is also someone who moves to other rhythms in time, I suspect, who of a summer's eve has known the sweet dew of night on her breasts and the transcendent perfume of Asherah in her once thick hair.

That she is my next key to Mary, I am sure. There have been weavers before, their patternings bright in my dreams and my totems bright in theirs. With Marjory, something new was added: when I met her, I immediately felt well. I was aware too of a bigness about her, as if she was surrounded by a wrap of the negative ions that hold on the shoreline the vigour of the sea.

The other signs are here too: there is something restless and unusual in the air, precursive to alarm. The fishermen and farmers mutter and shake their heads. There is slippage and shifting alliances, they say, not seen here in the farmlands for many decades back. They are used to the violence of the cities, but rarely does it touch their lives out here.

It's the money, they say, and my heart hurts. They tell me how the powerholders of this shining land are issuing edicts of increased taxation, saying even the poorest folk have now to pay more tax. They tell me the news from the towns and cities is of people being forced from their homes by debt and that daily, more and more are found lying dead in the streets, especially the elderly and the very young.

Anguish filled me at the thought of their dyings, and the certainty that had I quickened my search and found Mary, revealing the truth that lies with her, their lives would not have been demanded by the entropic balancing force that holds money in one of its measuring hands.

I walk over the hills, home to my peach-coloured Rose, and watch tiny fluffs of cloud flame in the westering light. A red hawk hangs over a froth of bracken, its tail fanned out in balance, its head tick-ticking from side to side as it tracks the mouse or rabbit hiding there. I could take this as a sign, if I wished to, and sometimes I have read nature's actions this way. But am I the hawk or the hidden? Though sometimes I seem to pursue Mary, perhaps it is she who lays the pathway, who lures me to a future I cannot see.

A few days later, Sabe comes, arriving in a small silvery automobile, slick and complete as a japanned ornament, a badger perhaps with its long-pawed rump, or the scarabaeid beetles of departing spring. Once out of the vehicle, it seems improbable that her tall sienna beauty could be connected to it in any way. Her hair is short, the shape of her skull clear. Above her shoulder blades, tendons as graceful as Doric columns support her beautiful neck. A collarless cream shirt becomes her, tucked into deep green shorts. Her knees are the exact colour of strong tea. On her legs, specks smaller and blacker than pepper speak of razor blades and lustrous hair. In her ears are shards of the worshipped green stone, paunamu. I am pleased to see her, to know she is a friend. She looks up at the cloudless blue and draws a deep breath.

'My lungs want to know why I breathe any other air,' she drawls as she comes to the gate. I open it and take a satchel from her hand. It is leather and string, like the carrier vine-baskets of old Crete. In it are the shape of books, the corner of a shawl. Next to a chardonnay wine is a cardboard tube, capped with bright tin. 'The papers,' she says, intercepting my glance.

The house is too hot for sitting. I lead the way through the tall, green-flowered daphne whose scent will only spread at night and across the springy goosegrass to the bower, with its moss-patched floor and wisteria-shadowed walls. On a tray I have put two goblets of a shape first fashioned in Anatolia, and a wide brown bowl filled with macadamia nuts. We drink wine and eat the nuts, talking of Sabe's statistical work, of the pusillanimity of politicians, and lazily, of where we will swim at the end of the day. A plane stripes the blue with a white, momentarily perfect arc. Rose, eyes alien and objective, stands at the entrance of the bower. There is a wild tilt to her shoulders and the tip of her tail is atwitch. Her ears flick forward then back and, before Sabe has seen her, she slinks into the undergrowth where she glares at me from under a thatch of leaves, belly pressed to the cool earth. She does not like visitors and will not be wooed.

The papers swear me as Stella Mante and give me access to Sabe's bank, where she has opened an account for me in which she has deposited the large amount of money that I gave her. The papers also swear my existence in terms that the laws demand, a date and place of birth, and relatives, some of whom are deceased. Now I shall be able to move about fearlessly, go where I will, presenting to any forceful inquirers these authenticities. On one small oblong card, which licences me to drive, there is a photograph, not very sharp and not of me, but obviously female. I study it closely. 'According to instructions,' Sabe reminds me, and I nod.

'It's very good,' I tell her. Later, in the long dark, I will hold the card between my hands and think clearly of the soft-edged face. If my skills haven't left me, that face will soon look like my own.

At four o'clock we go in Sabe's car to Goat Island beach. There are one or two other bathers, just leaving the shelter of the boulders under the clifftop, their towels vivid against the tawny grey skin of the rocks. The buildings of the marine research centre can just be seen behind pohutukawas that lean lovingly toward the sea. I try not to think of the killing cities which are also folded into this perfect day.

The tide is at that long moment of absolute fullness, breathing and swaying, completely at rest with itself. The only waves are at the shore, tiny frills of white, bubbles turned to foam. We have to walk among them, the dark sand too hot for our naked feet. Far from the other bathers, we come to The Pool, a huge rectangle made by slabs of underwater rock which frame a space several arm lengths wide and twice as long. The rocks are bisected and split into narrow channels through which the tug of the tide is constantly swept.

The water is cold, marvellously refreshing. Sabe surfaces, dives, surfaces again. Her head, silhouetted against the melt-glare, is round and compact as a seal's. After crawling across The Pool several times to shake out my limbs, I dive. Down, down to the coarse-sanded bottom, the mutter of the sea pressing on my ears. Kelp sways from the rockface, investigated by placid, pink-sided fish.

The dead I have known crowd before my eyes as if to see my pleasure, to have again a testimony to the ordinary miracle of life. In the sand on the bottom, I see stones, round and oval, smooth as eggs. One is purply-green, the other white with a thin line of red. As I reach down for them, the sand shifts and my fingers just touch the tightly muscled body of a racing black eel. I watch it rush into one of the channels, which is lit in patches, where the sunlight has been broken into wavery bars by the sea. With wonder and disbelief, I see that there is a word carved into the left hand wall of the channel, incised deeply into the rock.

My ears begin to ring, my body now aware of the water's chill, but I pay no heed. I go closer to the channel, staring hard at the intaglio. There are four definite letters there, and possibly a fifth. They are letters in a language I do not know, which surprises me as I have assiduously studied most of the world's poets in their own languages down through my long years.

The letters are halfway down the channel. Try as I will, I cannot make sense of them, nor even touch them to make sense of them with my fingers. The force of a seventh wave rolls up sand and there are now definite black spots in front of my eyes. My feet push against the rock's solidity and I swoosh up, gasping as I break the surface, temples pounding.

'There you are,' calls Sabe. 'I was beginning to wonder.' She is standing, the water just above her knees, on top of the beach-side rock. 'I might have had enough. Are you coming out?'

'Yes,' I call back, my breath uneven.

As we lie in the late afternoon heat, not talking about death or money, I think about the letters, which Sabe once remembers seeing. There is a local legend about them, she tells me, of a time when people ran against the proper order of things in these hills and had to be saved by the intervention of Papatuanuku, earth mother, and the benign taniwha of the local sea. 'They say she carved the word on the rocks to remind people of that time, but when the taniwha turned back to the deep water, the rocks broke and the word fell into the sea.'

By seven, the light is extraordinary, so pellucid it has achieved a telescopic quality that makes even tiny details on the off-shore Goat Island clear: individual needles on the limb of a dark pine, the teal wingtips of a small home-flying dove. My body is heavy with relaxation, powdered with black sand fine as ground poppyseed. I am calm, empty. My mind is thinking only of surface things: the fish we shall eat in the arbour at twilight, the citronella candles to ward off mosquitoes. I remind myself to give Sabe unscented body lotion to use after her shower, so as not to entice them to her.

Sabe moves her legs and speaks of Grace, who has rung to hear news of me. I think of the rippled walls of her home and how its painted Syrens would be perfectly in place here. Backward from Grace is a looping chain of people I have come from, stretching back to Santer. All of their lives have been extended and increased: who could remain the same after being filled by that invisible radiance, that crackling heady glow?

Though many delight in the deification of Santer, we are appalled. As Santer would be, for he never claimed to be anything other than human, and a man. It's true he challenged the Old Words, and the ill-mannered authority of the priests, but he did so because they had come to exclude more people than they served. The priests frankly angered him, with their increasing insistence on blood money and sacrifice.

The Pharisees chanted more loudly than ever as they passed Absalom's Tomb and their phylacteries grew longer, as did their curls of hair. But they gave solace and ease to so few, caring mainly for pious show. Not so the Sadducees, whose garments spoke of rank and power and their obeisances to the mingled courts of Rome. He would be annoyed with Mark and Luke, and probably severe with Matthew, but he would excuse the bumbling inaccuracies in their geriatric, James-goaded accounts. John he would laugh with and be angry with at the same time, for he revelled in John's vigour and surety. Though he would hate the intent, he would admire John's suave rhetoric and persuasive scholarship, and see the cleverness in his revelatory codes. John knew what people wanted to hear — that the prophecies had been filled, that the eschatological winds were blowing. Few of us can face that we each must do the task.

It is Paul he would condemn, condemn as destroyer and calumniator, Paul who never knew him and who stole him as precious things are stolen by a thief. Paul, claiming his right hand was divinely held, laying his unwomanly plans, his nostrils aflare with repugnance at the scent of Venus. Paul, who wished he could have sprung into existence full-grown, without any writhings or blood, and whose mind was enfuried by the laughter of not-men. It was he who wished to be godlike, and he who made god in his image and he who ever and ever denied the power of mortal love.

In the cool night, with Sabe sleeping deeply in the room below, I listen to the boom of the far returning tide and hold the photograph between my hands, grateful to the woman who faced, as I may not, the camera's searching eye. When its conversion is achieved, I compose myself for sleep. Rose is already curled at the end of the bed, wishing I too would settle. But with my focus released, I am open to the world. I feel balances trembling, rifts widening. On the apple- scented breeze lifting through my window comes a trace of the tired smell of despair. I grit my teeth, force myself to narrow my thoughts and begin to make some plans. First Marjory, and then, if she is my weaver, probably a car. And though she will hate it, a temporary attendant for Rose. She catches my drift and raises her head. Though I don't sit up, I know she's regarding me with an exasperated look. A moment later she leaves me, thumping heavily off the bed.

The day I choose to go to Marjory, a few days later, is full of the austere light of dropless rain and near mist. Wavy topped mushrooms, large as plates, hold little pools in their dells. The air is invigorating, the tiny pebbles of the gravelled paths wet and showing their best colours, tawny browns, bright rust, and shades of cream. It is also full of chirruping, clear whistles, melodious warblings. From the fold of a tree-clad chasm comes a chorale of song. In the grass outside Marjory's home, white daisies star the thick green, with yellow buttercups and love-in-the-mist with its frothing flowers of blue.

Marjory is not in a good humour, barely pleased to see me. 'The damp grits my bones girl,' she says tartly. 'I can't move, only creep.' Two logs burn in the fireplace, more embers than flame. I tell her I will attend to everything, settling her by the warmth and elicit her approval for my offering of a leek and potato pie. I put small twigs and sticks on the embers, which quickly catch fire, then I make a pot of tea. While it brews, I kneel by her and take her knobbled hands in mine, and tell her to close her eyes. Edgy, grumbling and suspicious, she nonetheless does what I ask. She gives a little grunt when she feels the warmth stealing into her hands and spreading up her arms, then a little sigh, as if she has been relieved of an unwelcome bundle she has had to carry far too long.

'Nice to have visitors, isn't it,' she says casually when she has a cup of tea in her hands. I think she means my visit to her, and this is her roundabout way of saying thanks for making her feel stronger. But I am wrong. 'Friends with the natives already,' she prods, and I realise she means Sabe. I laugh, mostly at the gossip network this comment makes visible. But this is as good an opening as any, and I take it.

'She's a friend of a friend,' I say, 'and our mutual friend is in Britain. Her name is Sabe and she's helping me settle in. My friend in Britain — whose name is Grace — is an anthropologist, and has studied archaeology too.' What I choose to tell Marjory is halfway fiction, halfway truth: that I am looking for a certain woman, that I have followed her through many countries of the world. And that my reasons are spiritual and political, and integral to my art, which is poetry, as hers is weaving. She listens avidly, intent and quiet even when I pause to slice the pie.

I finish my story and say lightly, ' — and what a tapestry all that would make. Don't you think?'

'If it was to be as long as the Bayeux,' she concedes. 'An embarrassment of riches for poor old hands like mine.'

'Mmm,' I murmur. 'But nice to muse on, for all that. What background theme would you use, if you did, what repeating motif? If you were to set it here, say.' My voice is warm, casual, inviting dreams.

'Here?' she snorts. 'In this village? Don't be daft.'

'I meant this country,' I clarify and smile with my heart at her.

'Right,' she retorts. 'Best to be precise.' She nods meaningfully, her eyes very bright. Her cheeks are flushed as if she had been dancing, and the air around her is as vibrant as a teenage girl's. She stares at me and then through me. 'A motif is it you want, then,' she says in a singsong voice. 'What she wants is a motif.' Her voice has lengthened to the stride of a chant. She turns and looks into the fire. With a leap of hope, I realise she is away. Her hands begin to move against her knees. The silence deepens. I hear the knitting voice of the kitchen clock and the fire's tranquil hiss. Somewhere a hen announces that she has yet again performed her duty to the world.

'Up hill and down again, down hill and up.' Marjory begins to croon, eyes fixed on the glowing wood. 'A hill all alone, wide like a gypsies' tower, ashes among its trees. Up hill and down hill, down hill and up.' Her voice dies away, but her eyes are still seeing other things. Her whispering lips are just a little darker than her downy old face which is criss-crossed with a thousand minuscule lines. An image of a strangely formed dark shape fleetingly appears in my private mind. The fire snaps. Seconds later, a motor-cycle goes whining by. Marjory glares at me and demands another cup of tea.

Later in the week, I ask the children from a nearby house whether they would like to earn some money by feeding Rose for me. Their mother, a handsome woman named Sarah, is proud of them, and reminds them of the questions they should ask: how many times each day, and when will I be home. This last I cannot answer. But there is plenty of food, I tell them, and I will telephone.

The bus service to the village is twice a week, Tuesdays and Fridays. The Friday bus proves to be old, stains of rust dribbling from each rivet, the grey and white paint dulled with a scummy bloom. Inside, black vinyl seats are hard and cracked, their corners split open. Remnants of pride are still visible — deep-lidded ashtrays of polished chrome, and round lampglasses for reading, their glasses sparkling. I am the first passenger of this day, which had the colourless dawn that presages intense heat. The driver greets me, putting my bag in the luggage compartment as he tells me his name is Wheeler. He is cheerful, gap-toothed, talkative. I have his full repertoire down twelve winding roads at the end of which is the next village, where three more passengers get on.

These are patently Wheeler's regulars, who glance at me inquisitively.

'Going to the city,' Wheeler tells them. 'Research library.'

They looked shocked, the two men frowning deeply, the woman's eyes alarmed. 'I don't think you want to do that dear,' she says doubtfully. 'Not the city, not just now.'

'I have friends there,' I offer, hoping this will quell their philanthropic fear. All of them could have grand-children in their ropes of life. One of the men pokes my shoulder. 'Best thing is, postpone it. Or do it on the Net. Or even the telephone.'

'You don't want to go down there now,' reiterates the woman, whose glasses make her anxious bluegrey eyes huge.

'Guns, bang you're dead, that's what you're going into,' says the second man. Behind his words is a faint trace of glee.

'Now then,' interjects Wheeler, who has been eyeing us all through his mirror. 'Perhaps it can't be helped.'

'Can it?' asks the woman, as if I were her daughter.

'No,' I return positively, and they all subside.

We crank along for a few more kilometres, the road taking the crest of the hills. The sea, ultramarine at this distance, is lipstick smooth, a mere filler of gaps to the hills scalloped together under the high pale sky.

Only one other passenger joins us before Wheeler arrives in the town of Warkworth, and swings the bus into a long, dark garage smelling pleasantly of earth and grease. He parks beside two other buses which lean together in its gloom, scarlet jacks under different parts of their bellies. The falsely bright voice of a radio announcer assures us it is nine forty-three, then introduces a lover's tune. Warkworth is still fifty-odd kilometres from Auckland, but this is as far as Wheeler goes.

The other passengers go off together, talking desultorily of the weather, and the prospects for hay. Seeing them, and hearing the comfortable play of their voices, for a moment I feel in exile, a stranger ever at the gates. Then Grace comes to my mind, and Jenna, and Tilsit, and all the others who, like Sabe, befriend me and enrich me, and I chide myself for forgetting who I am.

'The car rental place is up there, on Te Teke Street,' says Wheeler, pointing across the road with a tattooed arm. 'You'll see it once you get round that corner.' It is the nature of his face to be cheery but as he hands me my bag his eyes are sober, reflecting the other passenger's concern. 'Mind how you go,' he allows himself. 'Be quick.' 'Thank you,' I say, and wish there were more adequate words to tell him that I appreciate his ordinary humanity.

There are no cars available, but the manager offers me a van at a cheaper rate. The steering wheel seems thin and slippery, the engine almost too powerful for the plastic body and smallish, ribbed tyres. On its side, the van advertises the rental agency in red, drop-shadow lettering, with a flourish curving under the address.

'You don't mind, do you?' the manager asks quickly, seeing my look.

'Well — ,' I demur, and he instantly drops the price. 'Cash, though — we don't do credit cards anymore, since they've got so unreliable. Cash in advance for two days, plus the insurance deposit.' Then, worriedly, 'Can you do cash?'

I tell him I can, but that I must go to the bank first. He nods, relieved, saying he'll reserve the vehicle for me. I know this means that if I change my mind, there will be a fee. The bank is halfway up a small hill, with a post office on the corner and a small supermarket facing it. Though it is mid-morning, there are not many people about. The bank is a graceful little building with classic lines, and even a pediment. It is built of stone, washed a warm cream. Tall, double-paned windows let in the sun, which gleams on brass appointments and mahogany surrounds. The grey hoods of computers crouch beneath the bars of the teller's cage. My transaction is accomplished smoothly; silently I thank Sabe's efficiency.

Because the road continues to run along the seaward crest of the hills, I can see the city long before I reach it. The gauzy look all far places have is crowned by trails of smoke which rise from several points in its chunked mass. The smoke is wreathed about the waisted length of the telecommunications tower, Sky City, and I wonder if the tower has been under attack. Closer, I see that one of the bridge turrets seems crumpled. It is now nearly noon and the light seems to press downward, squashing all colour from the landscape except, at the very edges, a haze of gunpowder blue. At the bridge which links the North Shore to the centre of Auckland city, there is a police barrier where once there were toll-gates, all the traffic — mainly vehicles of commerce — channelled into one lane.

'Driver's licence please,' the officer says tersely. I hand her the little oblong card. She looks at me, then at the photo, then hands it back.

'What is your business in the city?' she asks briskly, as if she has a right.

'I beg your pardon?' I say, tolerant but not amused.

'If it could be done at another time, that would be a great help,' she tells me. There is worry and strain in her face, but, when she sees me looking at her, she slides officialdom over it.

I am firm. 'It cannot wait,' I say, and put in the clutch.

'One moment please,' she orders loudly. 'I'd like to search your van.'

'Certainly.' I pull on the brake, get out and hand her

the keys. 'I heard things were difficult. I don't want to obstruct.'

My apology reassures her though she takes a quick look in the van, where my satchel makes a point of its emptiness. 'The fewer people we have to worry about, the easier it is for us,' she confides, and waves me on.

Less than a mile further on, I see two bodies lying, quite orderly, on the grass verge. They are clearly dead, both young and dressed similarly, black jeans, white T-shirts, blood and bullet holes. Their shoulders touch as they lie there, the woman on the right of the man. They look as if someone has arranged them for collection, lying so tidily under the suburban oleander trees. I swerve back into the traffic, my hands slick on the wheel and slightly trembling. It is a long time since I have voluntarily gone into violence and death. Automatically my hand goes to my breasts, but I no longer carry my little knife. I think of Rose, of her hunter mode, feel my survival senses come alert. Fear drops from me. I settle my shoulders, fill my lungs with air. No doubting, I instruct myself, and take a firmer grip on the wheel.

The library is open, watchful guards at the door. I wonder why, and what is happening to cause guards to be put on the books. The reference sections are on the ground floor, all but two of the six viewers in use. There seems to be a rumpled feeling in the air, not its usual severe calm. 'What about something on Merriweather?' a young man demands of a librarian, whose face is surrounded by several escaping tendrils of hair. 'What do you have on her?' His tone is peremptory.

'There's not much in the file, but we've done our best,' she said unapologetically. 'Do you want it for cb or tv?'

'No, the bank,' he snaps. 'Where would be a better place to go?'

She is now affronted, which she tries to conceal. 'I'm

not sure,' she says as if really considering the problem. 'Let's see. Perhaps — the university?' She permits herself a slight relaxation of her lips and eyes. 'Yes — Humanities would be the faculty, or economics, of course. They'd probably be able to help you when they get back in six weeks.'

He shouldered past me, muttering a rift of damns. The librarian meets my eyes, her own warm with satisfaction, and I smile briefly as I move past her desk to the Natural History section.

I came here shortly after I arrived, and sought out the books covering the area where I now live. The whole village was encompassed in one aerial shot, the little watchtower house like a salt cellar on the point. Today, I am interested only in geography, looking for a hill shaped wide like a gypsies' tower — though I am not sure what Marjory meant by that — perhaps where battles were fought, so that there would be ashes among its trees.

There are quite a number of books devoted specifically to mountains, and the long smooth ranges of hills. The mountains buttress the east of this island and, after a wide sea-threaded estuary, angle across to the South Island. The photographs give many interpretations of the word mountain, all the nuances from grandeur to friendly. There is no dearth of mountains that stand alone — Taranaki and Ngarahoe, Rangitoto and Maunganui, among others, all with names which the tongue savours and loves to repeat. But none, by even the longest stretch of the imagination, look like that dark, odd shape that appeared on the mirror of my private mind when Marjory was entranced.

My head seems woolly, unable to think. Perhaps it is the heat, I tell myself, though the library is air-conditioned and cool. Sabe meets me in the library foyer when she finishes work, and is not happy when she sees the van with its hire message from Warkworth. She worries that it might draw attention to us from people whose eyes we would rather not catch.

'Why would they want us?' I ask. 'We're nobody.'

She doesn't react to this ungrammatical trope. 'Hostages,' she says briefly. 'They usually choose visitors for hostages.' She takes a circuitous route to her home, her hands expert on the wheel. She checks the rear view mirror frequently. The traffic is heavy, fast moving, and we are driving west, towards the Waitakere Hills, and into the sun.

'Between who, precisely,' I want to know. The windows of the van are now open, admitting the scent of the afternoon: hot asphalt and summer dust, the astringency of ti-tree and once, the foetid smell of something very dead. I thought of the bodies on the verge.

'Merriweather's lot, I suppose, and the fringers, with the police,' she replies.

'I heard Merriweather's name in the library this morning,' I remark.

'Did you? Not surprising, it's on practically everyone's tongue.'

'Who is she?' I take off my sunglasses.

She throws me a look of near incredulity. 'You really don't know?'

'No.'

'She's a professor at the university. Economics. Twenty years ago, her thesis created quite an international stir — Fundamental Flaws in Free Enterprise Economics, I think was its title. It was on the best seller list for weeks.'

'Sorry, I don't recall it.' I thought back twenty years. Argentina, remote valleys, uncomplicated children, the flaming letters in the sky. A time when I was close to finding Mary, but the children were chastised by the church, and the signs of her presence faded too quickly for me to follow. 'At that time, I wasn't in the West.'

'Ah,' understands Sabe and guides the van round a

sharp corner. I recognise her street. She lives on the side of a steep ravine, thickly wooded. Two concrete strips, like the trails of twin giant slugs, run up the southern flank of the ravine to her house. As we breast the rise, an intruder alarm gives tongue. She scrabbles in her bag for the control, turns off the ignition and hands me the keys. 'Welcome to my humble, again. I've put you in the corner room.' Her dogs whine and yelp at the van's door.

'Isn't Taren home?'

She shakes her head. 'No — diving somewhere off the coast of Reykjavek, for one of the big eco companies.' She greets the dogs, one a heavy-shouldered rottweiler, the other an old collie.

'Cold work,' I comment, taking my satchel from the van.

'Gold work too, the money's that good,' she says happily. 'She went off just after I came back from visiting you.'

The dogs romp round her and she speaks to them as we go to the door. As we reach the step, the rottweiler turns and thrusts its nose between my legs, sniffing rapidly. Satisfied, it sneezes and shakes its jowls. The collie, stiff but still daintily stepping, gives me a collusive glance from the corner of its eye.

'What if Sunder didn't like my smell?' I asked, dropping the satchel on a chair.

'That's not what it's about,' laughs Sabe, slapping the dog affectionately. Her hands are strong and beautiful on its glossy black. 'He's recognising you as a pack member, aren't you, sookie?' The dog reaches a wide pink tongue to her fingers. 'It would only be different if you smelled of fear.'

'Of course,' I return, thinking how different are the ways of cats.

'Drink?' she asks. 'Whisky? Absinthe? Wine? Beer?'

'Red wine, please,' I request, and suddenly long for

Santer.

She throws open the doors to the terrace, built of wood as her house is, going out from it like a massive diving board and offering a heady view of the city with a shine of water at its feet. The chairs are slings of navy canvas, deep and comfortable. I sip my wine, looking out into the trees. Sabe talks with the dogs, promising them a walk later as she opens and shuts cupboard doors, fills their bowls, and checks her answering machine. An economics professor. There is something odd here. Sabe joins me, bringing the bottle of red, and one of whisky, which is her drink.

'Why is an economics professor named Merriweather in the public eye?' Sunder comes padding in from the kitchen and flops to the floor at Sabe's feet with a heavy sigh. Sabe looks down at her and laughs. 'Exactly how I feel, boy, exactly!' She leans back in the chair and runs a hand through her hair. 'Why? Well, I suppose recommending that insurance companies be disbanded, and that money be converted into something she calls "a more sensible" unit of measurement are starters. You can imagine how the power brokers interpreted that. She was interviewed extensively when her book was published, because it attracted such a lot of attention overseas.'

She took a mouthful of the whisky, savouring it on her tongue before she swallowed. She thought for a minute, then smiled. 'She was a bit of a dagg with the interviews, actually. Wouldn't go on Holmes who's the top tv mouth, or even Kim Hill on National Radio. Said she wanted to be interviewed by someone with frontline experience, and her preference was for Ngahuia Te Awekotuku who's a professor at the university in Wellington, but if she wasn't a starter, then Marilyn Waring, who's an ex-MP, or Charmaine Poutney, who used to head up Auckland Girls. None of them are interviewers, really, but the interviews were extraordinary. Maybe because

of that. Both Ngahuia and Charmaine talked with her.'
She drank some more whisky, then shook her head.
'When I listened to them, I really agreed with her. I
think she's a bit idealistic, though. You can't just stop
having money, can you?'

'I don't know — I suppose you could, but it would
need a good deal of planning first. That'd be the hardest
thing. Is the situation affecting you at work?'

'Not really. Nothing much upsets the Stats Pack.' This
is her appellation for her colleagues in Statistics, whom
she thinks a boring and phlegmatic lot. 'Except for getting there and back, of course. That can be hellish.
Sometimes half the inner roads to the city are blocked.'

'What, by the police?'

'No — oh, sometimes, yes. But mostly by the fire
department. Sometimes ambulances, and the mortuary
van.' She brings the glass to her lips, finishing her drink.
I see again the dead young couple under the oleanders.

We put a meal together and eat on the deck. Salmon
salad, cherry tomatoes, ciabatta warmed slightly, and
ending with quince jelly garnishing strong blue cheese.
With the dark come the mosquitoes. Sabe changes into a
long loose robe patterned with the bold strokes of
African fabric art. As she lights the two mosquito coils,
one on either side of us, she looks as ancient and wise as
an icon.

'I'm looking for a hill,' I say later, with a wodge of
moon now glittering through the trees.

'Of course you are,' she says, now mildly drunk.
'They get lost so easily.'

'No, listen,' I command. 'It's a particular one and I
have to go to it. It is shaped like a gypsies' tower and I
think there were battles among its trees. Where would
that be?' I was not wholly sober myself.

'There are no gypsies here,' is her rejoinder. 'And
what does a gypsies' tower look like, anyway?'

The red wine has furred my head as well as my teeth. I yawn fiercely, considering the image that had appeared briefly in my private mind. 'Tall, but not wide, is the closest I can say.' I hesitated, aware that the image had a rounded bulge to one side that I couldn't explain. 'And it stands alone.'

'That really nails it down, doesn't it,' she says with light sarcasm, then follows my yawn. 'Plenty that stand alone, but you already know that,' she says through it. I go to bed wondering if I'd been completely wrong about Marjory, feeling doleful at the thought of starting all over again. The strands I follow are so subtle, and I have so often been wrong. Yet Marjory's weaving seemed so positive. I lie on the bed, not quite tired enough to crawl under the covers. The room, which I like very much, is small but juts out over the ravine on the opposite corner of the house to the deck. The screened windows are open to the night air, freshened here by the faint trickle of water that runs at the bottom of the ravine. Concentrating on its murmur, rather than my failure, I drift into sleep.

A muffled explosion and a scatter of gunshots jerks me awake after only two hours. My heart thumps extravagantly and it takes me several moments to identify where I am. I get off the bed and go upstairs in the darkness, and out onto the deck. The skyline of the city shows a large fire near its centre. Even from here I can see lights flashing neon blue and scarlet, and more gunfire rattles a staccato accompaniment. Below me, a rectangle of light from Sabe's bedroom illuminates the trees. In a moment she appears, her head bent to a murmuring radio.

'I wondered if it would wake you,' she greets me.

'What's happening?'

'Merriweather has blown up the bank, and two insurance company buildings.'

'The bank?'

'She's been threatening to for days.'

She turns up the volume and the breathless voices pour in. The bank has been completely demolished and its surrounding buildings threatened by the fire. There has been no loss of life, but two security guards have been knocked out and each could possibly have concussion.

'And possibly not,' comments Sabe sardonically.

The bank's manager makes a brief statement, saying the damage could run to billions. 'And possibly not,' we say together, and grin.

The interviewer asks for an estimate of the loss of funds and securities, but the manager easily evades this by saying he can't make any further comment at this time. Both the insurance company buildings are severely damaged, but not to the same extent. Neither company manager is available for comment, but an enterprising reporter succeeds in getting a senior executive to come to the blaze. He was frankly hysterical.

'They should be shot for this,' he kept repeating, 'they should be bloody shot.'

'The Fire Chief has promised us a word in just a few minutes now that the fires are under control,' says the reporter in a high, rapid voice. 'Uh — that looks like — yes, it is, it's the mayor — Mayor Kyoto? Excuse me, Mr Mayor?' I wonder what the mayor can offer, having just arrived, but he, astute politician, gives the reporter a few words, promising increased security in the city, and saying he 'will put the city on full alert as of this moment, even bringing in the military if we have to.'

'That'll make someone snap to order,' remarks Sabe as she turns down the radio.

'Do you think the library will be open tomorrow?' I ask.

'Possibly.' A small frown brings tiny wrinkles across

the bridge of her nose. She has wrapped a kitenge cloth around her, her shoulders bare above its primal patterns. 'Most probably, because they've been trying to keep the usual services open. It helps keep people calm. But I'm glad it's the mid-term break. I wouldn't trust a child of mine to the streets just now.'

'Child hostages?' She nods. Of course. Despicable and effective. 'I don't think I like Ms Merriweather.'

'It's not Merriweather who's taking hostages, Stella. No — no, she said categorically that her group would not and will not attack any of the "decencies of life", as she put it. The killings and lootings and hostages are — just fallout, I suppose.' Shadows fall across the long planes of her cheek as she turns to the window. Her shoulders hunch upward in a shudder and she gives a dry, brittle laugh. 'No prizes for guessing who the fall-out is. Or are, I should say, since it's always more than one fucked-over group.'

I suddenly feel enormously separated from Sabe. This is her country, these struggles, however disparate, are part of its lifeblood, its vitality. To me, they are sickeningly similar to a thousand others I have seen. I feel again that terrible urgency, to find Mary wherever she is in my country, which is the world. Between us, I am certain we can bring alive a promise, one that most of the world's people would work to see fulfilled.

There are no words to connect Sabe's current reality with my present truth. But I go to her, put my arm around her waist and stand with her, looking across to the city where the flashing lights circle the fire.

An hour or so later, Sabe returns to bed, but I know it's pointless for me as I will not sleep again. I take paper and pen from my satchel, push a chair to the window and turn off all the lights. I have started a poem, haunted by that word in the sea. I think of *The Carpathians*, a book I have read written by a woman of this country,

Janet Frame, which tells of a time when vowels and consonants and punctuation marks leave their 'rightful' places, come out of mouths and off pages, and float through the sky. This leaves everybody dumb, but makes them live their truth. I think of that other book, written by men for men, mostly ad-libbed mendacity, and wish its words could float out of its billions of minds and pages. A lie at the heart of the matter births conflict, like the conflict here written so vividly on the night sky. On my paper, I have scrawled a thought: Truth is immortal, but can be buried for eternity. I slide my fingers along my pen and begin:

> Where is my water mallet, my pearling wedge?
> The tousled tide roars out the letters of a name ...

By four-thirty, the night is lifting, the trees and houses discernible by five. At seven, I make a pot of coffee and take Sabe a cup. She growls when she sees me and waves me away. Back in the kitchen, I eat an orange and listen to the radio. Merriweather's group claim responsibility for only three of the night's many explosions. Food stores and jewellery shops have been blown, and recreational electronics, clothing and shoe stores. There have also been street riots and much gunfire. The reporter, whose voice now shows his exhaustion, says almost tearfully that 'at least one hundred and fifty of us are dead.' Startled, I at first interpret this to mean reporters, then realise he means people of the city. A rush of warmth rises in me that he should so instinctively identify with the story he is reporting, though no doubt later he will receive an editorial reprimand.

Someone from Sabe's workplace phones shortly after eight, to construct a carpool and devise a route into the city from the constant police reports. 'Do you want to come with us?' she asks, holding the telephone with her shoulder, pen and paper in her hands. 'There is room.'

'I think I might like to have transport,' I say. 'I'll go in the van.'

She makes a face, then says: 'I could arrange a car to take you and bring you back.'

'That makes me feel like a parcel,' I say, amused.

'I'm thinking of your safety,' she says seriously.

'I'm not afraid,' I tell her. 'I think the worst times are at night. I'll go in the van.' She stares at me for a moment, then speaks into the phone. 'No, it seems not. Right, in half an hour? Great. 'Bye, Zan.'

We arrange that she will come to the library as she did yesterday, and that if I finish early, or change my plans, I will phone. When Zan arrives, they discuss the least obstructive roads into the city, and quickly sketch me their map. When they've gone, I telephone the van hire office in Warkworth. The manager assures me there will be no problem with my keeping the van a little longer. Pleasure makes his voice unctuous. I also phone Sarah and ask about Rose.

'She's eating, but not everything they put out. I suppose she doesn't like it when you are away.'

'I'm afraid I won't be able to get back for a day or two; can the children cope?'

'They love it. They've drawn up a chart, so they each get exact turns in taking the dish to her. How are things there? By the news, dreadful. Oh, and old Marjory rang yesterday, when the kids were over feeding Rose. She didn't leave a message, though.'

'Thank you Sarah, and thank the children for me. I'll see you in a couple of days, or I'll phone again.' I ring Marjory, wondering if she has more to tell me, but she just wants to chat.

By noon, in the Natural History section of the library, I face the fact that in all of the material on geographic formations here, none even come close to fitting the less-than-exact description Marjory gave, nor the image that came to my mind. After thinking hard, I go to the Local History section to inquire about architecture. Buildings now no longer keep to the rectangular shape that has dominated them for so long; many cities have buildings that soar and swoop. I ask the junior librarian who is assisting me about new architecture in the city.

'If you are interested in avant-grade architecture, you ought to go out to Hopelands,' he tells me. I raise an eyebrow in question. 'It's that new development south of Manukau City,' he says. 'It's a few kilometres out, but only about thirty minutes at this time of day, if you hop on the motorway.'

'Is the architecture of Hopelands anything like this?' I ask, putting my finger on a photograph of a London building that is like a ziggurat on one side, but sheerly vertical on the other. He gives it a critical glance. 'Uh-huh, there's plenty like that.'

'Have you any photographs of them?'

'Quite a few. There's been lots in the papers about them.' He shows me where to access those files. The coverage was excellent, but for my purposes, tantalisingly inconclusive. The photographs were taken from different locations in Homelands, and featured several unusual buildings. Amid massive circles and soaring wings, I could glimpse other buildings, taller and narrow, pointed at their tips. By the time I finish, it is nearly one o'clock. I go down to the cafeteria for a sandwich and some fruit. I decide to go to Homelands, determined to follow every lead, no matter how slender, before I throw in this trail and start again. It seems unlikely to me that a drive to the southern suburb will be dangerous. And perhaps my longevity gives me a feeling of safety that others haven't got. I ring Sabe.

'I'm going to Hopelands, to look at some buildings.'

'Damn it all, Stella, it's not a brilliant idea. Are they like hills?'

'Maybe.'

She sighs audibly. 'You haven't even got a mobile phone. But ring me. If I don't hear from you every hour, I'll come out there. What building are you headed for?' I tell her of the tipped building that appears behind the others in the photo. She muffles the phone after telling me to hold on. Her voice, its tones tenor within her ribs, booms gently down the line.

'Zan says he knows that building, but that it's commercial, not residential. Does that matter?'

'I don't know,' I tell her. 'I'm fumbling in the dark.'

'Be careful,' she admonishes loudly. 'Phone me back at two o'clock.'

'Two-thirty,' I counter. 'It's already twenty past one.'

'Two-thirty,' she confirms, then, inspired, 'Maybe I should come with you.'

'Sabe. Don't worry. I'll call you at half-past-two or before. All right?' I can almost hear her grit her teeth, but she agrees. Her support of me is comforting.

The entrance to the southern motorway is less than half a mile away, funnelling me onto a wide, separated motorway which runs straight between massive, structured grassy slopes. Huge signs, easy to read even at high speed, soon arrow me into Hopelands. I have already discovered that the camber of any road seems to upset the equilibrium of the van drastically, but the steepness of this exit curve gives me the sensation that the van is in imminent danger of toppling sideways, and shudders under my hands. Off the ramp, the road narrows. I see an unusual skyline ahead, suggesting pyramids, obelisks, ovals. A sign says: *Welcome to Hopelands*. Underneath, small lettering flanked by a stylised Saturn on either side assures me that Hopelands is *The City of The Future*.

A long row of poplars lines the suburb's entrance street. Once among the extraordinary buildings, each set on a generous plot of land on either side of a broad avenue, I feel a sense of delight and familiarity. With a little frisson, I realise it reminds me of Alexandria in its sense of unhurried order and its majesty of buildings, which also grace the eye. Perhaps, I dare to think, perhaps.

As I drive, constantly ducking my head to get a longer view, the buildings seem to slide and change places, and I decide to get out and walk. Away from the avenue, the suburb proves to be still in mid-development. The buildings which face the avenue are complete, as is a supermarket mall; but the others are mostly at the frame stage, their bodies just being fleshed out on their structural bones. The tall, tipped building, when I reach it, is empty: through numerous windows I can see right through it to the mounds of yellow clay on the other side, no desks or partitions to obstruct the view. Wiring hangs down from the ceiling like the pallid skin of snakes. There are bollards in front of the building. I lean against one, imbued with a bitter sense of anti-climax. There is nothing here, not even an intangible hint of anything. 'Chasing the underside of shadows,' I scoff at myself as Rhiaon once did, and wonder for the thousandth time, what is to be next.

I decide I have exhausted this trail I thought set by Marjory, and feel despair at the thought of starting again. So many starts, all winding through my battles against slavery, giving dreams and courage to the battlers, sometimes being able to arrange the screens of coincidence, sometimes only able to give hope.

I walk back to the supermarket, find a telephone and tell Sabe it has been a wasted trip. 'Will you return to the library?' she wants to know.

'No. I can't seem to think clearly at the moment. I might set off for home.'

'No, Stella, wait 'til morning.' Her voice is authoritative, brooking no arguments. 'Get yourself back to my place, cool off, have a G and T. I'll see you just after six, and we'll talk about it. OK?'

It feels good to have someone take charge for a moment, almost restful. I feel her concern for me hum down the line. Driving back, I feel close to tears. Hopelessness, which I have vanquished many times, seeps into my muscles and my body feels sore. I admit to myself I have been on a wild goose chase, as the language says, though few who use it will ever have genuinely taken part in that madcap, half-crazed hunt, with its fell intent. Tears begin to blur my eyes, and I know I must give way and cry. I steer the van to the verge, pull on the brake, and give way to my despair.

A few minutes later, a light tap on my window startles me very much. Looking in at me is an attractive woman, not more than twenty-five. I am conscious of my bleary nose, my swollen eyes.

'Can I help?' she asks solicitously.

'Did you stop because you saw me crying?' I ask, incredulous.

Her eyelids, soft with a natural sheen, momentarily shutter her large brown eyes. 'No,' she says demurely. 'I stopped because I'd like some help myself. But when I got to your van — well,' she gestures expressively.

'What help do you need?'

'My car,' she says, putting a hand up to shade her eyes and looking behind us. The afternoon zephyr ripples her long, silken skirt. A wide belt with an intricate buckle admirably displays her slender waist, and a very fine neckband of amber lays over her silk singlet and is wound around her throat. I open the door and look back. An older model car stands ten or so metres away. 'Flat tyre,' she explain, adding, 'and I have no jack.'

'There must be a jack in here,' I say, slewing round to look down the van. 'It's a rental van, so there must be one, mustn't there.'

'I'd say so,' she agrees. 'Would you like me to look in the back?'

The van's back doors are locked. 'I'll bring the keys,' I say, taking them from the ignition. We walk to the back of the van together and I fit the key in the lock. With astonishment, I feel her fingers on my neck and my senses begin to swim. Then unconsciousness.

When I come round, I am slumped in a broad-armed, tweedy armchair that is comfortable but very worn. My lips are painfully dry. When I run my tongue over them, they are sticky, and taste sweet. My head seems stuffy, but otherwise I realise I am unhurt. I straighten and find myself looking directly into the keenly assessing blue eyes of a woman in her middle years. She has thick, wavy, well-cut, short, mainly grey hair, a slim nose; wrinkled jowl skin does not conceal a strong jawline and she has a wide, unlipsticked mouth. She sits, relaxed but radiating authority, in a wheelchair. 'I very much apologise for this inconvenience to you, Miss Mante, but we rather needed your vehicle.' She wheels herself closer to me and holds out her hand. 'Alice Merriweather,' she says. 'I imagine you will have heard of me.'

I nod and put my hand in hers. Her grasp is firm and warm and does not linger. She holds out a glass of water. 'I'm sure you will want this,' she says briskly. 'The anaesthetic will have made your mouth rather dry.'

'Yes,' I say, taking the water. 'I am very thirsty.'

'I do very much regret having to adopt such intrusive strictures, Miss Mante,' she continues, 'and in ordinary circumstances, I know you will believe me when I assure you I would not. But certain people are behaving very irresponsibly, rather forcing my hand.'

'How do you know my name?'

'From the rental contract,' she says. 'It was in the glove box.'

'Of course,' I nod. Then, 'Anaesthetic?' I drink the last of the water.

'Yes — again, my apologies, but the Out touch does-n't keep a person unconscious for very long and we had to move a good distance rather quickly. You can see my position.' Her eyes are considerate, her mouth firm. Her elbows rest on each arm of the wheelchair, her hands in her lap. 'Would you like some more water?'

'No thank you.' I feel grubby and cramped and very much want to wash my face, to get the stickiness off my mouth. 'What is the situation, please? I am your prison-er, that is obvious. A hostage, is that it?'

'No — no, indeed not. You are free to leave whenever you choose — or when your van returns, I should say. I am exceedingly grateful to you for its use. It has been a godsend. Perhaps you might like to know where the bathroom and toilet are?'

'I would, yes.' Through the resentment I feel at having been treated so summarily, I feel an admiration dawning for her.

'Let me show you. Have a bath if you wish, there's plenty of hot water, and you have time for a long soak because I don't expect Atawhai to return with your van for at least another two hours. It's this way.'

She turns the wheelchair precisely, and leads me down a corridor, past two closed doors, then into a second cor-ridor off which is a spacious bathroom, white fixtures surrounded by pleasant wood, and a stack of thick pale yellow towels. 'Help yourself to anything, please do. There's some rather nice bath salts, and shampoo — .'

I break in on this, having just remembered Sabe, and look at my watch. It is quarter-past-six. 'Excuse me — do you have a telephone?'

She immediately becomes alert. 'Why do you ask, Miss Mante?'

I tell her that if Sabe doesn't hear from me she will

undoubtedly call the police. Merriweather listens intently, then say, 'Very well. This way.'

We go back down the corridor and she opens one of the doors. The room is a bedroom, but also an office of sorts, with a dozen or more street maps on the walls, a crowded desk piled with tools: wire cutters, hammers, wrenches, and coils of electrical wire. And a telephone.

Merriweather indicates this, saying, 'Once again, I must apologise for being intrusive, but I am certain you can understand how necessary it is for me to assure myself that you are indeed calling your friend.' She wheels noiselessly to the desk, opens a drawer and takes out a remote listener. I nod, and pick up the receiver.

'The code for the city is 09,' she says quietly. 'We are a little outside the perimeter here.'

I feel very odd. Merriweather is acting like the perfect hostess, which nullifies the validity of my natural responses. I feel blank, a little disoriented. I dial Sabe's number, hearing her telephone ring twice then cut off and the reeling sound which presages the answering machine. I cannot restrain a groan, and think that I must leave a message, for Sabe is a worrier, and given to action. The message is halfway through when Sabe's voice shouts over her own words: 'I'm here, hang on while I shut this off!'

'Sabe, it's Stella.'

'Where the hell are you? Dammit — I was just about to drive out to Hopelands, or call the police.'

'I'm all right. I got sidetracked a little, and didn't realise the time. I'll be home later, don't worry.'

'Where are you?'

'It's a long story, Sabe. I'll tell you when I see you.'

'When will that be?'

'Just a minute.' I put the receiver behind my back and press it into my buttock. 'How long will it take me to get back to the city?' I ask Merriweather.

'Approximately three hours,' she says, 'but Atawhai is not likely to return for another two hours, at the very least. You are welcome to stay with us and return in the morning, if you prefer driving in the daylight.' She turns off the remote.

I put the receiver back to my ear. 'Either very late tonight, or tomorrow morning.'

'So where are you?' she asks, all curiosity.

'Somewhere in the country, I don't know where exactly. If I decide to stay overnight, I'll phone again. All right?'

'Is it mountainous, Stella?'

'In a way,' I tell her sadly.

Merriweather thanks me as I hang up, then suggests I put my clothes in her washing machine and have a bath, saying she's certain my nervous system needs soothing after its shock. This makes me smile.

'The world would be a happier place if all criminals were like you,' I tell her.

'But I am only a criminal in the legal sense,' she says briskly. 'The law itself is criminal you know, especially when it comes to money. We write the damn laws and forget that we have done so, we invent money and in doing so, invent a rod for our backs.' She brakes her chair for a moment to take up a light cotton bathrobe from the next room as we return to the bathroom. I hand her my clothing through the door, then run a deep bath and soak in it, and even wash my hair.

In the bath, I decide that I like Merriweather and that while I don't wholly understand her fight, it is clearly against economic chicanery, and therefore a fight against poverty, which means that I am on her side. I feel very much better when I have reached this decision, and hum a little as I towel-dry my hair. My long curls were clipped in my thirty-fifth year, and since then I have worn my hair no longer than my earlobes. I walk back through the house, following voices to the kitchen. Three young people and Merriweather sit at a large wooden table. At the stove, a fourth person, this one a little older, is stirring something that smells very pleasant. Merriweather's companions are all men.

'Miss Mante! I trust you are quite recovered?' She looks at me with a hint of a smile. I return the smile and nod. 'Yes. Thank you. The bath was perfect.'

'Excellent!' she approves. 'Would you care for some fruit juice, or beer? Or perhaps a glass of iced tea?'

'I would like some juice, thank you.'

'Excellent!' she says again, and I can tell she is pleased. 'Jeref, apple juice for Miss Mante, and a beer for me, please. We shall be outside. I think you'll find our back yard pleasant, Miss Mante.'

I follow her chair out through French doors onto a patio, with grapevines hanging above and throwing their dappled shade. There are wicker chairs, cracked and old but still sturdy, and a little wicker coffee table, thick with newspapers and scores of scribbled-on sheets. Merriweather bundles these into a tidy pile and drops them behind her chair as Jeref comes out with apple juice in a pitcher, glasses, some biscuits on a plate, and a can of beer.

'Thank you, Jeref. Help yourself, Miss Mante,' she says as Jeref goes. I pour a glass of apple juice, and take a biscuit. She opens a beer. The low mumble of the men's voices come from the kitchen, interspersed now and then with gusts of laughter. Bees hum over a lemon tree at the side of the patio. Though it is after seven, the day is still bright, the air warm. Merriweather looks thoughtful, but is silent.

Two minutes pass, then five. I am feeling more and more relaxed.

Finally, Merriweather says: 'You are a most remarkable person, Miss Mante. I expected you to be angry, perhaps even afraid, and definitely full of questions. Yet, apart from the to-be-expected questions as you returned to consciousness, you have not been any of these. I thought you would want to know why I am doing what I am doing, that you would be eager to question me. But it seems not. Remarkable. I salute you for upsetting all my expectations.' She raised her beer can to me.

'You told me I was not a hostage,' I reply. 'That was the most important question answered. And when you offered me a bath, I thought the least I could do was to be a well-mannered guest. Besides, while I was in your bath, I thought about what I know of what you are doing, and I think I am on your side.'

'Excellent!' she cried, and raised the can to me again.

She too was unusual, I thought, in not asking me any personal questions, which is the most common approach of strangers. A sound like laughter comes from out left. 'Pukekoes,' she smiles. 'Have you seen them?' I shake my head. 'You must,' she says and motions me to follow her. Her chair goes readily across flattened grass, to a little knoll, and she points. At first I can see nothing but then, amazingly, a large blue bird with a scarlet beak leaps upward out of the grass in a field twenty metres away, swiftly followed by another, and a third and a fourth. 'Pukekoes dancing,' she says softly, and again comes the call that sounds like laughter. We watch the leaping birds for many minutes and the magic of the natural world comes stealing over me, lingering long after we return to the patio.

We talk lightly of several things, among them architecture and vehicles, and I feel that of all the people I have known, this Merriweather is someone who would believe my life without having to be touched by the energy, connected in that way. And she is a woman of the mind as well as resourceful in action. Our conversation turns to more serious things: refugees and food, the rise of the old diseases coupled to the creep of AIDS, and the still-tenacious grip of the patriarchy. 'You realise AIDS is almost a godsend to them,' she declares without waiting for a reply. 'Cooked up in a laboratory, as seems obvious to me — how could there be no connection between the development of a serum which stops the immune system from rejecting a transplanted heart, and the rise of a disease which attacks the immune system? Huh! Just as there is no connection between money and starvation, or money and war. As for insurance companies — .' She breaks off to look at Jeref, who says that a meal will be ready in a few minutes. Merriweather looks at her watch. 'Atawhai should be back with your van soon, Miss Mante. If you'll excuse me, I'll just wash my hands before we eat.'

Left alone, I get up and stroll down the rough lawn to the grove of trees that screen the view at the lawn's further end. Not far away, sheep protest at some evening upset and a dog argues back. The grass is coarsely cropped and springy underfoot. I am curious, thinking I can see water behind the trees. I pick my way through the grove, which is shadowed, and smells of humus and dry leaves. Just beyond it, the land falls away quite sharply, its slope covered by low, scrubby bush. I'm delighted to see there is a lake, its shoreline a scrabble of yellowish dirt giving way to shallow water thick with reeds. Cooler air comes from the lake, which is streaked grey and gold by the leaving light.

The lake seems to be circular and in its centre, casting a shadow of deep amethyst in front of it is a small island — the living shape of the image I saw in my private mind, even to the protuberance on its left side. 'A hill all alone, wide like a gypsies' tower,' Marjory said, and there it is, tall and narrow for the volcanic cone that it almost certainly is, shaped roughly like the lookout towers the people of the road used in the long summers in the Persian hills.

I stare at it as if it is an apparition, the rest of Marjory's words now sliding into my mind and making sense, for as a volcanic cone, there are bound to be 'ashes among its trees'. As I stare as the island, I am flooded with the certainty that Mary is there. Excitement surges; my heart begins a heavy thump.

I feel like plunging into the water, swimming to the island. I look wildly around for a boat. There are the reeds, a ripped tyre half-submerged in the yellow mud, and nothing else. I pick up the skirt of the bathrobe and run back to the house.

'Excellent timing!' Merriweather says, then looks more carefully at my face. 'What has happened?'

'I'd like my clothes, please, and a boat. I must get to the island.'

The murmurs of the kitchen still, the chink of cutlery, the low-voiced conversation of the young men. The cook turns slowly, as if not to interrupt, and carefully places in the centre of the table a large platter of steaming corn.

'Your clothes may not be wholly dry, but that will not matter because you can borrow some of mine,' say Merriweather briskly. 'As for a boat — Yinmur, please take a look and see whether the dinghy in the shed is sound, and if there are two oars. Now, Miss Mante, could you eat something?'

Food, in this floodtide? 'I don't think so.'

'Then assess whether your clothes are wearable. They are on a clothesline outside the bathroom. By the time you have changed, Yinmur will know whether you can use the boat. If not, we shall think of something else.'

Her instructions clarify my eagerness, and her immediate, unquestioning acceptance of my needs settles me in my purpose. I thank her and go to the clothesline, discover my clothes are dry enough to wear. After I'm dressed, I return to the kitchen, where Merriweather and the others are cheerfully munching corn.

'Oh good, dry enough, I see. I'm having Jeref make you a sandwich to take. That seems the best idea.' Jeref grins at me as he butters some bread. I feel a spread of affection for Merriweather, with her supportive and courteous pragmatism.

I touch her hand. 'Thank you, very much,' I say rather breathlessly, excitement and conviction squashing my lungs against my ribs.

She waves a hand and chuckles. 'Next time, I won't need anaesthetic,' she says.

Yinmur is standing by the cupboards, eating a cob of corn. Butter runs along his fingers and down the back of his hand. I look at him with my eyebrows raised. Mouth full, he nods.

'Yes to the boat, Miss Mante,' says Merriweather, wiping her mouth, 'But no to the oars. However, there is a small motor there: five horsepower, very small. Do you mind the sound of a motor?'

'Not at all,' I say, delighted. I've never been very skilled at rowing. 'I don't mind if they hear me coming.' Jeref hands me a cup, which proves to be full of onion soup. I sip it, scarcely aware of its taste.

'Very well.' She turns to Yinmur. 'Please would you assess how much fuel the motor has in it, Yinmur, so Miss Mante can make firm plans.' He nods and glances over at one of the other men. They leave together, Yinmur still busy with his corn.

'There is no additional fuel, I am afraid, only what's in the engine's tank now. I hope it will be enough.' She gives me a humour-filled look. 'You are obviously ready to leap into action. Is there anything further I can do? Yinmur and Kor will take the dinghy to the shore, and Jeref has made you a little food.' She indicates a brown paper bag sitting on the end of the table.

'Cheese and pickle sandwiches, a couple of little tomatoes, a banana and an apple,' Jeref enumerates. 'Anything in that lot you don't like?'

'No, I like all of those,' I assure him. 'I appreciate it, thank you.' My pulses are pounding, hurry, hurry, hurry.

'What about your friend?' asks Merriweather.

For a second I think she means Mary and give her a bemused glance.

'Do you want to telephone her again?' she continues, and I realise she means Sabe.

'Sabe! Yes — yes, I must ring here. Thank you. I seem to have forgotten how to think.' As I dial, I wonder what to tell Sabe. If I tell her I think I have found the mountain, she will want to know all about it, and there is nothing to tell, nothing but the urgency in my mind. Her answering machine is on, and there is a message for me on it, saying she has taken the dogs for their walk and to call back later if I can. I merely tell her that I will travel tomorrow, or else will phone again.

Yinmur and Kor return, saying the dinghy is ready, the engine not quite a quarter full of fuel. 'It's certainly enough to get you to the island and probably back,' says Merriweather, and holds out her hand. 'Good luck in your endeavour, whatever it is. I hope I will see you again, but if we are not here on your return, I shall leave the keys on the rear left-hand wheel of the van.'

'I am very grateful to you,' I tell her. 'Someday I will tell you why.' I shake her hand. Her eyes burn very blue. 'I shall look forward to it,' she assures me. I turn from her and follow Yinmur out into the day's last light.

To the left of the house stands an outbuilding, some farm machinery, and other small sheds. A path swerves between these, going into a large vegetable garden, tomatoes glowing like altar lamps on their vines. We skirt the garden and go into a hillocky pasture. I give a little grunt of pleasure to see a pair of black goats. One lifts its head and watches us, grass hanging from its active mouth, alert interest in its eyes and hairy ears. Yinmur unclips a bolt-lock that holds the five-barred gate in place, and we go through.

Now the grass is high, untamed. Whitened frond-heads brush my hips. The path leads through it, well defined and narrow. The grass thins. Sticky shore mud begins to squelch beneath our feet. Ahead, there is the island, and the boat. I touch Yinmur's arm. 'It's too muddy for my shoes,' I tell him. 'I'm going to take mine off.'

'I should have found you boots,' he says, waiting as I slip off my sandals.

A haze of midges dances above the shallows around the dinghy. Yinmur explains the simple workings of the engine, and pushes me off. Very soon I am well beyond the midges, in the deeper water of the lake. The light is now breaking up, everything not close at hand indistinct. The little engine chonkers along. The island grows larger, lights pricking the dark at its water edge.

I feel completely alert, the blood urgent at my wrists. I put first one foot, and then the other over the side to rinse the mud from them, then slide my sandals on again. I wonder what my first words to her will be, and suddenly wonder if I will know her, will recognise her on sight? Anything could have changed her down all these long years. I wonder what she is doing on this island, and why I have no doubt that she is here. I have felt certain of being close to her before, but never like this, never with such clarity, without any doubt. How will I ask for her? I do not even know her living name. I shake my head, hold the tiller more firmly, and think how fruitless these worryings are. When has my path ever been pre-planned? Of course I will know her. A line from Yu Hsuan-chi comes to me: '*Though the bird has flown, your mirror stayed behind.*'

Now the last of the light is gone and I can see much

better. A line of lamps marks the shore, a few more stretch into the lake to mark a jetty. I wonder for the first time if there are any public buildings, a cafe or hotel. I am now only a hundred or so metres from the jetty and become aware that the hurrying urgency I was feeling has lessened, but my inner certainty has not. I feel young, full of energy.

Less than twenty metres from the jetty, I am suddenly blinded by a glaring light. I shield my eyes with an arm and turn my face half away.

'Who are you?' a man's voice shouts. 'What do you want?'

'It's a woman,' someone exclaims, and the light is turned from my face to throw a path. In its whiteness, the water is rocking and slapping, black as squid ink. Someone shouts to come to the other side of the jetty, to follow the light.

On the jetty's other side, several dinghies lie belly-up in an orderly row. A concrete apron comes into the water. Beyond, a low-roofed building, its front a wall mainly of glass. I can see several people in silhouette. I can even read the sign on the wall of the building: *Istadevata Boat Club*. Underneath it says, in flowing writing, *Welcomes All*. I shut off the ignition and lift the engine up. Hands grip the boat and pull it onto the apron. The man closest to me straightens, holds out his hand: 'Brian Seppen,' he says. 'Welcome to Istadevata. Are you lost?'

'No,' I say, looking eagerly around. 'I have come deliberately.'

'Come into the club room,' he says, and we all troupe into the brightly lit room. There is a bar, some tables, a scatter of chairs. I see now that there are two women as part of my eight-member welcoming committee. One is short and plump, with light grey eyes and silvery hair. The other is taller, gracefully young, her amber skin lustrous, her belly rounding in pregnancy.

The people move slowly, waiting for me to speak. I take a deep breath, conscious now of my crumpled shirt, the rolled up trousers and my sandals. My hair suddenly feels wild. 'My name is Stella Mante,' I tell them. 'I know it's an odd time to arrive but I had a sudden urge to be here, away from all that.' This is so the right thing to say, though I don't know why I said it. 'I should have decided earlier, perhaps telephoned, but I just got hold of a boat a little earlier this evening, is there anywhere I can stay — perhaps sleep here on the floor?'

There is a momentary silence. I am aware of the older woman's eyes, and glance at her. 'There is a bit of a daybed here,' says Brian Seppen doubtfully. 'There isn't a hotel. Were you expecting to stay with friends?'

'I don't know what I was expecting,' I say truthfully. 'I'm not sure I know anyone here.'

'That cot is barely adequate,' declares the older woman who was looking at me. She steps forward, holding out her hand. 'I've an extra room at home. Flora Hakanoa. You won't have to worry about bullets on Istadevata. You're safe here.'

I walk behind her up the long slope, her friends calling goodnights to one another below. The shoulder of the island is black against a violet sky in which are some tiny, faraway stars. The air is still and warm. There is a scent of unknown flowers on it, a little like stephanotis, and a crunching underfoot.

'You know you're walking on a volcano,' Flora says over her shoulder.

'I guessed, from the shape of the island, that it was a volcanic cone. It's a rather steep one.' My breath was getting shorter. 'It's not active, though, is it?'

'Not so's we've noticed, but you never really know, do you? Personally, I pay my respects to Mahuika, our goddess of fire, when I'm up near the cone. Can't hurt, can it? It definitely can't hurt. It's left here, careful.'

244

We turn away from the shoulder and are climbing. A downward glance shows me the light on the cement apron far below. It is much darker. I follow Flora more by her body heat than by actually seeing her. My breath is very short by the time Flora says:

'This is it. Wait here, I'll get the light.'

A few moments later, light springs out of an open doorway and Flora calls for me to come in. I walk into one long curving room, its further reaches full of shadows and pillars and low furniture. It follows the shape of the mountain and, like the boathouse, its facing wall is all glass. The kitchen is extremely modern, metallic surfaces and clean lines. Beyond, two small sofas sit at right angles to each other, between them a low table on which a sizeable chunk of nephite sits at the feet of a Makondi bond-carving in black wood, with two little animal skulls nearby. Flora points down the room.

'Toilet is second door, spare room the first. Help yourself. I'm having a gin — join me?'

'Yes, please.' I feel light-bodied as it is, but not so much that I'd get silly on a drink. The bedroom is wedge-shaped, painted yellow, narrower on the facing wall. There is a chest of drawers, on which I put the paper bag with Jeref's sandwich in it. I look at it, registering with amusement that it's my only luggage.

Above the chest of drawers is a little calligraphic sketch, all lovely curls in shades of silver, bright yellow, navy and poppy red. After a moment, my eye begins to sort the letters out, and suddenly I see the words: *An eye for an eye makes the whole world blind. — Gandhi.*

When I return to Flora, she conducts me to two armchairs in the shadowy room, placed so as to look out through the sweep of windows. She has turned all the lights off except one small lamp over the sink. I sit down, and she hands me a clinking glass. 'Moon be up soon. Like to watch it. Cheers,' she says.

I settle back in the couch as my eyes adjust, and soon the lovely nightscape becomes visible, the violet sky and stars, the smooth velvet dark which is the water and beyond that, yellow points of light that must be Merriweather's. I feel almost weightless, that if I give a little bounce, I shall spring into the air, cross the mountain in a stride. Though the pulsing hurry is gone, the sharp alertness is still with me. I see everything as though it has been rinsed by crystal rain.

'You a teacher?' she asks, voice casual.

'I have taught,' I say cautiously.

'Thought so,' she says with great satisfaction. 'I can always tell. Taught for forty years myself so I should be able to. Mostly eleven- and twelve-year-olds. Bloody good age, brains at their best, I think. Chemistry was my subject. Yours?'

'Literature. Poetry.'

'Ah! They love to mix things, that's the secret of teaching them chemistry. Give them the ingredients, let them do it themselves. Can't miss; they really love the stinks. Good-oh! Up she comes!'

The horizon beyond Merriweather's farm has gradually become tinged with a buttery-yellow haze. Now a long arc of the same colour, but pure and solid, appears. I wonder, as I have done many times, what the speed of the world would feel like, and have again the image that flashes with this thought, of the weight and glory of this rolling planet, celestial ballerina in her dew-drenched tutu spinning an eternal solo for her sister spheres.

'Puts us in our places,' remarks Flora. 'Another gin?'

I nod and, feeling stifled in here, say: 'I would quite like to go outside.'

'Damn good idea, but there'll be mozzies, and I'm out of coils.'

'I don't mind.'

'Right you are, then. I'll fill our glasses on the way.'

Everything is changed by the rise of the moon. The lake waters sparkle a broad gold path and quick ripples of gold come and go, almost too rapidly for the eye to see. I glance toward the cone-tip, feeling she is up there. The air has cooled a little, is delectably fresh. There are rustles in the shrubs. The moon splashes its light all along the window glass and darkens the roof shadows to soot.

'Here,' grunts Flora, and we come to a bench, high-backed and with arms, made from the boles of slender trees. We sit there, night-enchanted, for a long while, hardly speaking, then go in to bed.

I cannot sleep, but am very glad to be alone, because I am getting an increasingly strong sense of Szuzanna and Santer. I take off my trousers and sit cross-legged on the bed, wondering what will happen next. I have imagined this meeting so many times, but never with me wearing soiled clothing and without a single resource. Yet it is right, the rightness of it runs through me. She is so close that I can almost hear her breathing in the dark.

I eventually doze, but the first bird calls, throstling whistles and long calls, herald me into a clear green dawn. I splash water on my face, dry it on the guest towel Flora has given me, and run one of her combs through my hair. I pick up the paper bag and go out into the curved room.

Flora's bedroom door is firmly closed, but the kitchen door stands open; I can't remember whether she shut it when we came in last night. Outside, the birdsong is a flung chorus, so riotous it makes me laugh. I am filled with a kind of exhilarated suspense. I eat the sandwich as I survey the ground.

My sense of Mary comes from above me, at the cone-tip. I follow the path that leads back to the main path, thinking that it will intersect with another, leading up. The trees are scarcely trees, more like tall shrubs, and there are swinging yellow flowers and the long white bells of the plant I know as datura. Thick and obvious on the ground between the shrubs are chunks and smatters of pitted rock, all of them the reddish grey that is the mark of the fire's maw.

Flora's path meets the main path which, as I expected, continues upward, though not directly so: it angles upward easily, loping over the shoulder of the mountain, round which it disappears long before it reaches the top. I set off, and soon sweat sticks my hair to my forehead and runs into the hollow of my throat. As if filled with a magnetic force, I climb and climb and climb.

I turn a corner and she is there. How could I have thought I would not know her, even down all these long years? I recognise her instantly, the small angular body, the quick big eyes, and the mouth, her mouth: the way the musculature runs along her cheek to lie under the skin and shape her mouth full of promise, as if behind her lips she holds a morsel of the most delectable fruit, grown in a garden planted at the dawn of time, when all the seeds were fresh and new, and the earth itself rich, fecund, and without stain.

She is standing in front of a small house, an apple half-eaten in her hand. She is wearing a knee-length, seashell and flower strewn lava-lava and her feet are bare. Her hair is around her shoulders and I recognise even its curling, lustreless length. 'There you are,' she says, as if it was she who had been looking for me.

'Yes,' I say, blowing out my breath and putting my arm up to wipe the sweat from my forehead.

'I was just going to bathe,' she says. 'It's this way.'

I walk behind her, unable to speak. Her skin is very brown, the swell of her calves graceful, her toes wide and authoritative on the crackly dust. My mind is a blank, my body redolent with sweat. The force that fuelled my climb has left me. I feel hollow as a gourd, as an emptied water jar. There is no Santer, no Szuzanna, only the eggshell sky, the birdsong and the woman walking before me finishing her apple, eating even the pips.

She leads me to a little promontory, the 'bump' on the tower shape I saw in my mind. This has a natural hot pool steaming three metres from its lip. The water in the pool is bright turquoise, the sides of the pool a flagrant orange. Little bubbles stream up, as if the water is champagne. There are steps down into the pool and, under the water along the hill side of it, a bench. A short curve of wall and projecting canopy protect an open cupboard with towels in it. Beside it, several hooks, some of which hold bathrobes and bodycloths. Just beyond the wall is a water tap, with a bucket underneath.

'Hang up your clothes and I'll sluice you,' she says, going to the tap. She turns it on and water thuds into the bucket. I go to the hooks, unbuttoning my shirt, hanging it and the rest of my clothes from a hook. When I turn back, she has taken off her cloth, is as naked as me. She shuts off the tap and looks at me. 'It's not too cold,' she tells me. 'Ready?'

I nod and turn to stand with my back to her, then she throws a sweep of water over me. Though I have been expecting it, I gasp as it crashes along my back, is parted by my neck and streams over my breasts and down my belly. I laugh with the pleasure of it.

'Now me,' she says, and hands me the bucket. She jumps a little as the water hits her, shakes her hands, then goes to the pool. Her spine is very slightly curved between her shoulder blades, making them prominent triangles of brown. Her hair is wet at the ends and has become thick small curls. She slides down into the water and vees her hands forward, going across the pool, making her hair float out from her shoulders like delicate black seaweed. I follow her in, my motions sending the exuberant bubbles to break the surface and releasing hints of salt and sulphur into the air.

'It's very powerful water,' she says. 'We can only stay in it for a few minutes at a time.' In the pool, it seems as if we are held at a midpoint of the sky. The only ground that I can see is the few feet of earth that leads to the promontory's edge, then nothing but immensities of cloudless summer blue. If I stand on the steps, I can look down on the circle of the lake with the spreading fields beyond. But here in the water, there is only this cupped turquoise pool, and the sky. There is so much to say that I cannot think where to begin. My thoughts seemed to have stopped just by coming to her.

But after several moments in the pool, holding the edge and letting my feet rise, the fact of our surroundings brings a question out of me almost by itself: 'Why here?' I look at her and she meets my eyes steadily.

Though she is the same, I now see that she is also different, different in her inner self. There is no anxiety in her — her eyes are open and free of pain. She is calm.

She looks around then lifts her hands up, drops of water sparkling from her fingers. 'I didn't know it would be here, either, tucked away under the bottom of the world. But there is an unusual feeling in this country, have you noticed? Like something is moving, a sense of change in the air. Do you feel it?'

I think of the explosion that broke my sleep at Sabe's, and Merriweather's determined face. 'And see it,' I return dryly. I think of all the places we have nearly met, all the days and years since France. 'Why now, after so long?'

She lifts her shoulders in a delicate shrug. 'It did not happen, that's enough to know. As for why — .' She pauses, and her mouth moves as she thinks. 'Clearly, we were not ready — or something was not ready,' she says, forestalling my protest.

There is sense in that for me, for the general world is

only just beginning to accept what the women of Crete knew thousands of years ago. Other women have touched on it, and one, Barbara McClintock, put it in words in her book *A Feeling for the Organism* — that we can connect with our natural world at the deepest cellular level without the need for machine or fuel. And further, that genetic material can change of its own volition, transforming itself in response to the environment.

The feeling between us is getting more and more comfortable, and we begin to talk easily, as if we have all the time in the world. Which we have. Questions rise naturally like the water's bubbles, and I ask them lazily as the water's heat seeps into my bones.

'Why did you go away like that? Without a word?'

She turns to face the sky, her profile sharp in the bright morning light. 'I wanted no one, after my son died.' Her eyes wander the sky, her hands stroke the water. I realise, with a shock, this is not a woman that I really know. All through the centuries of my search for her, what has been vivid in my mind is a woman who lived anxiously in her days and was fragile as a candle flame, who seldom left the sheltering walls of her home. This woman has calm poise and is naturally at her ease, naked in this aqua pool on the flank of a dormant volcano. Her eyes come back to me. 'I thought the pain would kill me. I didn't want to live. I could not eat, or sleep. I longed to die.'

'Yes,' I say, remembering.

She takes a deep breath then sinks below the water, rising almost immediately and stroking the hair back over her head with both hands. 'Can you believe we're still alive?' she says. She gestures, and we climb out of the pool, my body flushing tawny and heavy with the heat, and go to the tap.

'I've wanted to talk with you about that for — '

'— hundreds of years,' she says simultaneously, and

251

we both smile.

'Yes. Because the energy began with you, didn't it? It didn't begin with Santer,' I say. This is the question I have wanted to ask, the truth I needed confirmed, which I first suspected when I went to Crete, at a time when slavery and slaughter were only too current there. It was there, gazing at the secrets of the seals, that I finally saw the truth about the power of women.

She gives me a swift glance, then lifts the bucket and pours water across her body. 'Elisabeth had it too,' she says obliquely. 'Then Sarah found out how to use hers, but it took her a long time.'

'Did you go to Crete — of course you went to Crete — what do you think?' I turn on the tap over the bucket as she goes for the towels, droplets on her glittering like some gossamer garment over her warm brown skin.

'Yes — it's clear they knew it too. Six hundred years they managed, and it's not ever been beaten, that record.'

She thought a second, and added: 'Pity.'

My bucket is half full; I turn off the tap and sluice myself. Mary puts my towel on a seat. I want to ask her how she came to be as she is now, so changed and so free, to ask her all the million things you ask a friend you've had no contact with for many years. But the realisation that I don't really know her is making me awkward; I don't know how to begin.

With towels wrapped around us, we sit down and she brings two bottles of apple juice from a cache under the bench, handing one to me. I realise what the main difference between us now is: I no longer feel protective of her. Through the hour we have been together, the connection between us has shifted into one of balance. I feel I can ask her anything now.

'So how did you first find out about the energy? When you got pregnant?'

She nods. I look at her wonderingly, trying to imagine

her living with that knowledge.

'What happened?' The question came from my depths, woman to woman.

After a long moment, she sighs. 'Well, I killed him. He came towards me, and I knew he was going to hurt me. I was so young. I didn't know I had any power, and he scared me so much. Then he was on top of me, inside me, and with all my being, I wished him dead. And then he was.' She sighs again, the puff of sorrow alien in the bright morning.

'Who was he?' I ask, wanting the whole event clear in my mind.

'The bully of the village — Ezra, he was named.' A little pause, and then she delicately shrugs: 'When the others came, I couldn't speak, but my state was clear enough. I know that the fear affected my mind, when you first knew me. If it hadn't been for Joshua then, I probably would have lost my tether on reality completely.'

She draws a deep breath, and straightens her back. 'I was thirteen. I didn't realise that I was pregnant for a long time, but the other older women could tell quite soon. I've never been very big anyway. They kept me safe, really, arranging for me to marry an older family friend so that I wouldn't be judged immoral, and forced out of the village.'

She shakes her bottle of apple juice, but it is empty. She bends to put it under the bench. Her hair falls forward, baring an amber nape. She sits up and shakes her hair back, looking at me. 'Why have you come here?' she asks, her voice indescribably gentle.

I drain my bottle, and put it under the bench by hers. 'I've come to this country because of you, as I have gone almost everywhere since you left. Not that you were always the primary reason, you weren't: mostly it has been my battle against slavery — I've never stopped fighting that.' A baby zephyr fingers the steam rising from the pond. 'Slavery has changed, though — there's more of it, horrifically. More people than ever are skewered to lives they can hardly bear.' Out of the corner of my eye, the ghost of Zeralia smiles.

I stand up and go closer to the edge of the hill. The trees are thick below, then arc upward several hundred metres away, like a giant hammock. I realise we are on the rim of the volcanic cone itself. I turn back to her, my voice cracking now as I speak thoughts that have rolled in me for so long. 'I've seen what you've done in various places you've been. And I know what I can do, alone.' She gets up and moves to me, comes to stand by me, putting her arm around my waist.

'I thought — together — with all that we know, and the others who are waiting — we could probably make it change.' Words pour out of me, strategies and whole plans that I had first begun to make in Alexandria so long ago, examples of what I've been able to achieve, visions of what is possible together. I talk until I have no more words left. I am empty, a wrung-out glove. The perfect day glows around us, lake water gleaming, flowers a-bumble in the dark leaves, a high bird carolling. Mary reaches for my hand, holds it, looks fully at me. Her eyes are vivid with life, and eager. 'We will do it,' she says.

AUTHOR'S NOTE

There are stories so famous they become the servants of history, which in turn transmutes them into fact. Their secrets are kept because they come down the years largely unquestioned.

I have, for many years, been deeply interested in what daily realities may lie behind one such story which began in a Mediterranean culture 2000 years ago, and is now inextricably woven into the fabric of Western life.

The story our age knows tells of a few brief years in a boy's life — his birth, and a handful of childhood years, even fewer years of his manhood, and his early, cruel death.

My interest lay in trying to glimpse more clearly three major characters in that story: a woman who was pregnant without social sanction, a boy who is told from birth that his life has been deliberately planned by The Divine, and an orphaned girl who becomes his trusted confidante.

Before I began my research, I knew that life for a 13 year-old girl is perilous enough today, and even more so if she is beautiful. Nothing in that research indicated that it was less so two millennia ago.

It is axiomatic to say (but I am!) that as a woman whose education, thought, and writing has been formed by Western culture, my story reflects these foci.

My research for this book spanned five years, and I am indebted to the libraries and staff of the Universities of Berkeley, (California), Vancouver and Simon Fraser, (Canada); the British Museum; and the public libraries of Leicester, and Ealing, (England) and Auckland (New Zealand).

I would also particularly like to acknowledge insights from Elaine Pagels in *The Gnostic Gospels*; Marina

Warner in *Alone of All Her Sex: the Myth and Cult of the Virgin Mary*; J. J. Bachofen in *Myth, Religion, and Mother Right*; Robert Graves and Raphael Patai in *Herbrew Myths*; Erich Neumann in *The Great Mother*; Constantine Cavafy in *Alexandria*; and the pantheon of published works of both Mary Daly, and Merlin Stone.

I am indebted to many scholars and writers who have followed similar paths of research, and most particularly to Marina Warner for the insight into the etymology of the word virgin: 'The most plausible argument derives *virgin* from the Greek ὀpyń (orge), 'impulse' or 'passion, and from the verb ὀpyá-w (orga-o) 'to swell, to be puffed up'. This is the same root as that for orgy, and both are related to the Sanskrit ūrǵ, ūrgá, ūrgás — meaning 'fullness of power, sap, energy.' This possible root gives both virga, (a rod or stem), and virgo (a young girl). (Marina Warner, *Joan of Arc, the Image of Female Heroism*, Weidenfeld & Nicolson, London, 1981, p.179.)

The translation of Sappho's poetry that appears on pages 122–23 is by Mary Barnard, (*Sappho*, Shambhala Publications, Boston, 1994.)